WIDDERSHINS

WIDDERSHINS

Helen Steadman

First Published 2017
by Impress Books Ltd
Innovation Centre, Rennes Drive, University of Exeter Campus,
Exeter EX4 4RN

Typeset in Garamond by Swales & Willis Ltd, Exeter, Devon

Printed and bound in England by Short Run Press Ltd, Exeter, Devon, UK

British Library Cataloguing in Publication Data

A catalogue record for this book is available from the British Library

ISBN: 978-1-911293-04-0 (pbk)
ISBN: 978-1-911293-05-7 (ebk)

For Oliver and Leon

"Teeth hadst thou in thy head when thou wast born,
To signify thou camest to bite the world:"
History of Henry VI, William Shakespeare

CONTENTS

Part Three

Acknowledgements

Thank you to the experts who generously shared their knowledge with me: Ross Menzies, BSc, DBTH, MIRCH Registered Medical Herbalist, for teaching me to make medicine from trees at Dilston Physic Garden, which is an amazing source of information about the healing power of plants, curated by Emeritus Professor Elaine Perry; Mark Constable, FWCB, master blacksmith, for helping me to forge a fire steel and teaching me how to make fire; Arthur Harkness from Consett and District Heritage Initiative for information on local witches; the staff from the Tyne & Wear Archives for helpful assistance with old documents and microfiche; the staff from Newcastle Castle for information on where the prisoners were kept; and John North, City Guide, for talking to me about Newcastle's quayside and bridges. Thanks must also go to: Florence Welch who made me want to write about witches when 'Rabbit Heart (Raise It Up)' jumped into my head one day; to Ralph Gardiner, without whose grievances I might not have been inspired to write this particular story; and to William Brockie whose report of a woman possessed inspired the chapter, 'The Devil Himself'. I am grateful to everyone from the Manchester Writing School who offered gentle criticism: tutors Sherry Ashworth, Helen Marshall, Livi Michael and Nicholas Royle; classmates, Susana Aikin, Cynnamon Conway, Anj Karakus, Eleanor Moore, Marita Karin Over, Julie Taylor, Chris Thomas and Cate West; and the DIY group, Jodie Baptie, Dot Devey Smith, Zöe Feeney, Fin Gray, Nicola Ní Leannáin,

Bee Lewis, Jane Masumy and Sue Smith for hand-holding and much-needed not-so-gentle criticism. I am also very grateful to Laura Christopher and Julian Webb from Impress Books for their painstaking efforts and care in editing and publishing *Widdershins*. Finally, special thanks to: Neil, Oliver and Leon Steadman for suffering neglect and the herbal remedies that took over the house, garden and medicine cabinet while I wrote this book; and to the late, great Archie Scottie Dog for accompanying me on woodland walks where I did most of the 'freethinking' that became this book. Any errors and omissions are my own, and I apologise sincerely for them in advance.

Part One

1

John

The Afflicted Messenger

Dora Shaw was my midwife, and I'd lived with her since the day I was born. I never tired of hearing the tale of my birth, and I'd often make Dora repeat it to me. Her story never altered once and it was always fresh in my mind. Now I was old enough to labour on the farm, my father wanted me back. So, before returning to the father I'd rarely met, I made Dora tell the story to me one more time, so that I might keep the story in my mind in case I never saw her again.

For the three days before I was born, Dora had watched Mercury chase Mars across the sky, when he suddenly turned tail and began to move backward. My midwife worried what missive the afflicted messenger might bring. By dint of her monstrous scrying, she concluded that the omens were unhappy ones, and she hoped I'd bide my time for a few more days. This celestial reversal didn't bode well. Not for my mother at the time. And not for me in the future. By the time Dora gained entry to our dwelling, my mother was running with sweat. Her shift was stretched across her swollen belly and her greying locks clung to her face. Dora looked at my father and then she glanced at my suffering mother.

'Shame on you, Sharpe, fancy getting a bairn on the lass at her age.'

'Mind your tongue, hag. It's God's work.'

Ignoring him, Dora touched my mother's upper arm. 'Bertha, you're very wet. How long have you been this way?'

My mother's voice was no more than a whisper. 'Morning before last. Dora, please, save my child.'

'I'll do everything I can, Bertha. You can be sure of that.' Dora inhaled near my mother's face and shook her head at my father. 'Listen, Sharpe, you should have had the physic here long since.'

'Aye, but physics cost coin I don't have.'

Dora turned her back on him. 'Set water to boil and fetch clean rags. Bertha will have set some aside.' She waited a heartbeat. 'Do it now, Sharpe, for there's none other to do it.' She examined my mother to see how near I was to birthing. 'The bairn's crowning, Bertha, but you're very narrow-hipped. And bless you, but your advanced years are against us. Sharpe, bring that water and mop your wife's brow to bring out the fever. Quickly, the boiling water.'

Dora untied a bundle of silver-green fronds and added them to the water, where they wilted and gave off their bitter aroma. Then she opened a pouch at her belt, took out some red berries crowned with five-pointed stars and added these too.

My father glared at her. 'What's that? I won't pay for any witch nonsense.'

'Just mugwort leaves and hawthorn berries. Bertha needs to keep strength in her heart for the heaving. They'll calm her boiling blood.' She held a bottle to my mother's lips. 'Take a sip, Bertha. This tincture will cool your blood.'

'You're giving her berries from the bread-and-butter tree and a few sticks of muggins? Aye, well, plenty of both growing hereabouts, so you won't have the neck to expect any coin. Bertha's had no bother with her heart before.'

'Carrying a bairn at her age can weaken the strongest of hearts, especially when the blood heats up like this. Just mop her brow, Sharpe, and speak in a soothing voice. She looks set for birthing convulsions and may not be sensible enough to take your words in, but a soft tone may bring her comfort.'

It was beyond my father to utter soft words, and so Dora could hardly be taken aback when he uttered none at all. But he did try to mop my mother's brow, all the while keeping a sharp eye on Dora, who was crouched between my mother's knees. My mother began a high keening, purple in the face, and then she screamed. With a nimble turn of her arm, Dora eased me into the world on a gush of blood, followed by a rattling breath from my mother.

Dora looked at my mother and closed her eyes for a second. 'You have a laddie, Sharpe, see.' She nipped the cord and scrubbed me until I lost my waxen coating, then passed me, wailing, to my father.

A look of outrage crossed his face. 'Why give him to me? He's after his mother's tit.'

Dora shook her head and pressed me to him. 'Bertha's beyond giving milk, God rest her. Take the laddie while I bless Bertha and see to her.'

My father's eyes bulged, and I began to bawl.

'You've saved the wrong one, you stupid hag. What use is a babe with no tit to suckle him?' My father was shouting. All the bones in his face were apparent through the tautening skin.

'See, witch, what you've done to her? It was washing her down with that devil's muck. Well, I'll pay no coin for this, and by God, you'll burn for it. My woman dying unshriven at your hand. Her brother will have something to say about this.'

Dora began to wash and bind my mother. 'Never mind her brother. You'll need a wet nurse for the bairn. I know of one nearby. Once I've seen to Bertha, I'll give your laddie a quick feed myself and then I'll fetch the nurse.'

She rinsed her hands in the herb water, reached for me, and in one practised movement, she swaddled my squalling self within her clothes. When I latched on, she cringed as my tiny teeth caught her teat. My father stared, mouthing air until his words found him again.

'And what demonic capering is this? A crone with no issue from her belly in decades. You were born for the fire, woman, make no mistake.'

Dora rocked me as I suckled, and she spoke to my father in a low voice. 'It's no trick, Sharpe, many midwives keep their milk flowing to help out a little, when …' she nodded at my mother, who'd taken on a waxen sheen.

5

My father scowled. 'Well, you can bide here and feed the babe till he's weaned. I'll pay for no wet nurse. You killed Bertha, so you can take her place.'

Replete, I unlatched and yawned, revealing my milk teeth. Dora raised me to her shoulder to relieve my wind.

'An easy lad you have there, Sharpe. He'll sleep while I go for the wet nurse and a woman to tend Bertha.' She placed me into my dry-eyed father's arms.

'My wife dead and an infant born with teeth? Oh, what imps have been at work here this night?'

Dora eyed him and took me back. She reckoned it was better if the man cried. When he didn't, it was better to take the baby.

* * *

So that was how I came to be raised at the teat of my midwife, who was the only woman who ever cared for me. But she was often busy gathering herbs, pinching other children's cheeks, or giving advice to women in the family way. I rarely saw my father, apart from his yearly visit to size me up, when he would tell me that Dora Shaw's wickedness had caused me to grow up motherless. That's when he wasn't blaming me for killing my own mother.

It struck me as odd that Father would leave me with a woman he knew to be wicked, and I worried for my soul. Uncle James – my mother's brother – was a pastor, and he would also warn me about Dora. But it was hard to believe badly of Dora when she was nothing but kind to me. Her greatest sin was looking for signs in the sky, which was an abomination against God, according to Uncle James. But the moving celestial bodies were pushed by angels, so how wicked could her sky-watching really be? When asked why I could not live with him or my father, Uncle James told me small boys were too much trouble, and best minded by women, even wicked ones.

Still, he let me visit him now and then. His kirk was filled with families, complete with mothers, who were always clucking over wee ones, picking them up and kissing away their tears. I envied these children. Their mothers fascinated me, but they were not warm and soft with me. Instead, they were silent, and wouldn't even drop a kind word in my ear. Sometimes, though, when the wind was right, their singing carried to my ears from the kirk. I'd hide in the bole of the old oak tree, hug my little dog, Jinny, and rock myself, imagining my own mother singing to me.

But now, Father had deemed me big enough to earn my keep and he'd taken me and Jinny under his roof. I'd not been home a week when Dora found me one morning, weeping and rocking in the bole of my old oak, with Jinny tucked under my arm.

'John Sharpe? What on earth is the matter? Come out of that old tree, and when you've told me what the matter is, you can have this apple.'

Once I'd been lured from the tree with the promise of the rosy apple, we sat at the foot of the oak, leaning against its rough trunk.

'Come on, laddie, tell me what's wrong.'

Through hiccups and tears, I confessed my dreadful secret. 'Last night, Father was on the drink.'

'How did you know he'd been on the drink, John?'

'Well, his eyes were glassy, and he smelt sour.'

Dora clicked her tongue. 'Shouting, was he?'

'Aye. I kept me and Jinny out of his way, because Father thinks dogs and lads are just for kicking—'

Dora patted my knee. 'Go on, son, get it all out of you.'

'When he woke up, Father was sore-headed, and started to curse me. I put the dog under the table, crawled after her and covered my head.'

'Was he on about you killing your mother again?'

I nodded and my chin quivered as I repeated his words to myself. 'It's your fault she's dead. You were too greedy by half. Eating away at your own mother from the inside. Not content with listening to her heartbeat – being so greedy, you had to have a bite of her soft heart. You weakened her heart and made yourself even bigger. The blessed woman was too slight to pass such a big, greedy boy. You killed your mother with your greed and your demon teeth.'

At the memory of my father's speech, I collapsed into Dora's arms. 'I swear not to be greedy again, Dora, if it would bring back my mother. Every night, I say sorry to Father and to God for that bite I took from my mother's heart.'

'Oh, John, lad, that's not how your mother's passing came about. Your father ... well, he's still grief-stricken and he's not been able to accept that sometimes God just calls His own back to Him. But you mustn't go without food. No amount of going without can bring her back, you know.'

'But Father swears I ate my mother's heart from the inside with my demon teeth and killed her.'

Dora shook her head. 'That's simply not true. Plenty of babies are born with teeth and their mothers live. Your mother was very sick and she already had fever in her blood when I arrived. Birthing fits are what carried her away. Listen, lad, your mother was well past the bairning age, and she'd been sick for days before I ever got there. God wanted her for His own, and it was nothing to do with you. Nothing on this earth could have spared her.' She took my hands between hers. 'As soon as I set eyes on your mother, I knew her past saving. But your mother held on till your father fetched me. She wanted you to be born.'

This worried me. 'Could you have chosen to save my mother and not me?'

Dora shook her head. 'No, there was no choosing. Your mother was more than halfway to heaven and so I spared you. That's what she wanted. She wanted you saved. Those were her last words on this earth.'

I swallowed. 'Father wishes I'd died as well.'

'That's grief talking, John. He's still mourning your mother, even after all these years. You're a fine boy. Your mother would be proud of you and she'd want you to eat so that you grow big and strong. So, do you want this apple?'

I nodded and took the apple. 'I'll keep it to share with Father.'

* * *

Even after all these years, Father was convinced that I'd killed my mother in childbirth. Time upon time, he'd threatened to avenge her death and kick the demon teeth out of my head. On this day, it finally happened. The old man returned from the fields with me in tow and Jinny skulking at my heels. Darkness was falling and sweat ran cold down my back. When we reached our shack, the fire was out.

'Is it too much for a man to warm his arse by the fire after a day's work? There'll be no broth and I'll freeze before the night's out.'

I bowed my head, knowing that an apology was the same as a confession.

'So, John, what have you to say for yourself?' Father grabbed me by my jerkin so tightly that his knuckles dug into my collarbone. He back-handed me with his free hand and blood ran freely from my nose. 'Get yourself back to the farm and fetch a light. Go on, away, you big snot.'

It was cold, my back ached and my nose was gushing blood. More than anything, I wanted to sleep. The thought of the cold walk made my thin shoulders sag and I began to snivel. At once, Father was all fists, feet and sharp bones. He pounced on me and flung me to the floor.

'You snivelling wretch. What are you greeting for? If you hadn't killed your mother with your greedy, sharp teeth, she'd be here now, keeping the fire burning and the broth warming.'

'Please, Father, it wasn't me—'

Father sneered, my words spilling from his twisted mouth. 'It wasn't me, it wasn't me. It wasn't me that spilt the milk. It wasn't me that let the fire go out. It wasn't me that lamed the horse. It wasn't me that killed my mother.'

I lost control of myself. Moisture seeped out of me and chilled in a wet patch.

But still he kept going. 'It wasn't me that pissed my breeks. Look at you lying there in your own mess, worse than yon bitch.'

Jinny cowered in the corner, her dark eyes pleading. I prayed she'd not defend me again. The last time, Father kicked her in the belly, and she lost her pups and nearly bled to death. I bit my lip.

'I'm sorry Father, it won't happen again.'

'What won't happen again?' Father's voice was soft. 'Tell me, what won't happen again, John?'

With breath coming out in shudders, I tried to keep my voice level. 'The fire, Father. I won't let the fire go out again.'

9

'So you were the one who let the fire go out!' At this, he kicked me in the guts.

I doubled up and vomited. Jinny shot out from the table and attached herself to Father's calf, sinking her teeth into the skin. But even this didn't stop him.

'You were the one that lamed the horse.' He kicked away my little dog, who smashed head first against the far wall, before sliding to the ground.

'Jinny, Jinny! What was that for, Father?' I crawled over to my dog.

Father minced about. 'Oh, Jinny, Jinny. What was that for, Father? To teach you, laddie, that you must face the consequences of your actions. You were the one that killed your mother!' His face was a purple, spitting snarl as he buried his clogged foot in my face.

* * *

When I came round, it felt like I was drowning in my own blood. My gums were a red mush of flesh and floating teeth. I began to choke on the combination of snot, tears and blood, and I curled into a ball, begging God's mercy.

Jinny lay broken-necked and still-eyed. It pained me that she'd had no scraps and went to her reward on an empty belly. Even poisoners died better deaths than that. Father had gone, no doubt in search of drink and comfort. I rocked myself to calmness, wiped my nose, spat my milk teeth into one hand and put them in my pouch. When my nose stopped gushing, I limped outside to dig a hole for Jinny. Once it was deep enough to keep the foxes off, I placed her in the earth.

'I'm heart sorry, Jinny, that you never had a kinder home, or a meal inside your shrunken belly before you were killed. I can't spare anything to keep you warm in your grave, but I'll give you some of my teeth. For these teeth couldn't withstand Father's clog, so they can't possibly have bitten through Mother's heart. Goodbye, sweet Jinny, I promise to find out who killed my mother and turned Father against us both. And when I do, you can be sure they'll pay for it.'

Tears blinded me as I placed some teeth in Jinny's grave. I covered her broken body with cold earth, mounded it above her and tamped it down with my feet.

'I'll find some rocks to build a cairn. But for the time being, goodnight, sweet Jinny, and God bless you. So be it.'

With that, I wiped my hands across my face and went back inside to curl up in my corner. Jinny had been my one comfort in life. She was always pleased to see me, kept me warm at night and stopped me being afraid of the dark. I was truly alone. Crying hot tears, and nearly toothless, I fell to my sleep.

* * *

On my way to the farm, Dora leaned out of her door as I passed through the woods.

'John? Where's old Jinny? And your father? And what happened to you?'

At Jinny's name, my face crumpled and tears welled in my swollen eyes.

'Just look at you. What's that raging man gone and done this time? Come and let me put some sage on your nose. You could do with the barber-surgeon taking a crack at that beak. May the saints preserve us, laddie, where are your teeth?'

I withdrew the bloody pearls from my pouch and held them out for inspection.

She took a sharp breath. 'Let me take a look at those wounds. You're not fit for work like this.'

I didn't want her to minister to my wounds. Uncle James had warned me often enough not to allow her to meddle with God's will. But when I tried to speak, my mouth wouldn't open properly.

'I know, John, I know, you have to work or that man will take it out of your hide. Just bide here while I sort out the worst and then you can get to your bit job.'

Dora wiped my face with muslin soaked in brown tea, which made me cringe. I closed my eyes and prayed to God, begging Him to forgive me for being weak and putting myself in Dora's hands.

'Aye, aye, it's a sage tincture and colder than the pastor's heart, but it'll take the swelling down.'

I winced and my hand went to my gut.

Dora's eyes followed. 'Lift that jerkin, lad, or must I lift it for you?' She raised my bloodied garment. 'Born to hang, that man, born to hang.' She held up a hand. 'Aye, aye, I know you must honour your father, but there is naught on God's earth to make me say a kind word about him.'

My skin was purple and black, and there was a bad swelling under my ribs.

'He's nigh on kicked the spleen out of you, lad. It's a miracle you're still breathing, let alone walking. Here, get this down you.'

She threw a handful of dry yellow sprigs into a bowl and poured hot water onto them. 'Yarrow. You'll know it as woundwort. It'll heal your innards if there's blood there. Sip it slowly while I see to your middle section.'

It was a sign of my weakness that I didn't even try to turn down the yarrow tea. But surely God would understand. He wouldn't wish children to suffer pain, would He? Dora lifted down a crock and spooned generous measures of dried leaves into her mortar, grinding them with the pestle. The sharp smell made me gag.

'Too strong to stand sometimes. But old comfrey knitbone will mend your ribs.'

She added hot water and dipped wide strips of muslin into the resulting paste. When I'd finished the forbidden drink, Dora wound me tightly in the hot cloths and, as the pain receded, I imagined the devil tightening his grip on me.

'This poultice will stiffen and you'll feel like an old wife in her stays, but keep it on, do you hear?'

I nodded. She pressed her lips together and then turned to her stores, smeared some bread with honey and held it out.

'Here, take this piece. I can hear your belly's been empty for days.'

I took the hunk of bread and nodded my thanks. It would be all right to eat as long as I said grace over it first.

'And once you've grieved for Jinny, come and see me. I'll get you a dog that your father won't dare lay a foot on – and he'll think twice before touching you again.'

I shook my head and sniffed, tasting blood again at the back of my throat. There would never be a time that I stopped grieving for Jinny, so I could never love another dog. And I could allow no more dogs within range of my father. I gulped to hold back tears at the thought of Jinny and then left Dora's shack, determined to get to the farm so I wasn't docked for tardiness – or worse, finished altogether. Father had warned me that I must start earlier, work harder and leave later than the others because I was a useless, skinny streak and the farm would as soon be rid of me for a burly lad worth his keep.

Each step made every bone in my body throb. It felt as though my insides wanted to escape, and that only Dora's poultice was holding my guts in place. The poultice was stiffening and it made it hard to get a proper deep breath in. How on earth would I manage to work like this? And what price would I pay for allowing Dora to tend my wounds?

2

Jane

Infernal Creature

I put down my sewing and opened the door on a wizened woman who was bowed under her burden. It was Meg Wetherby, the green woman in Mutton Clog.

'Afternoon, Jane. Mind, it's colder than charity out here!'

'Hello, Meg. Come on in out of the cold. What have you got for Mam this week?'

'Plenty, Jane Chandler, plenty. For this time of year, at least. The forage is never plentiful in the white months. Mind you, I've just made Tom Verger a happy lad.' Meg shuffled to the hearth where she put down her sack and settled on a cracket. 'Hello there, Annie. Busy the day?'

My mother paused at her work with the pestle.

'Hello, Meg. I never stop, as usual. Get yourself warm by the fire, and Jane will fetch you some pottage.'

I ladled pottage from the cauldron into a wooden platter and passed it to Meg.

'You're a kind lass. Thank you, hinny.' Meg smiled, revealing a vile stew of grey tongue and gums.

I had to look away. 'How have you made Tom Verger happy, Meg?'

'I've just taken my favourite lad a gift fresh from the smith. A bonny fire steel with the curved neck of a swan. Ask him to show it to you when you seem him next. Very quick he was to make it spark. A clever lad, Tom, a clever lad. Now, straighten your face and open yon sack, Jane. There's a pleasing notion in there for you as well.'

Tom would love his treasure. Not just because of its utility, but because it came from Meg, who had taken the place of his mother in his heart. But still I hesitated, hand poised above the damp sack, and glanced at Mam.

She nodded at me. 'Come on, Jane, don't be daft. Open it. Meg wouldn't wish any harm on you.'

But these winter sacks made me cautious. They seldom held anything welcome. When the earth was hard as iron and dressed in white, she turned hoarder and withdrew her bounty to her dark womb. The white months afforded very little that wasn't dried, or else preserved with salt or soured wine. It was a time of bittered barks and dried leaves. Strange packages sourced from strange places.

Meg waggled her head. 'Go on, Jane, open that sack, and be quick about it.'

My hand entered the sack, drawing out dried teasels, hardened berries and gnarled bark. At the bottom of the sack was a bundle of sticks sprouting yellow blooms. I held these queer stems at arm's length to show my mother.

'What are these, Mam? Their flowers look like caterpillars. And in the winter, too!'

Mam shrugged. 'I don't know, Jane; they're like nothing I've seen. Meg'll tell us, won't you, Meg?'

But the green woman was enjoying herself by the fire, gumming pottage and swilling it down with ale, then fidgeting about under her garments. When her mouth was clear, she finally turned and looked me in the eye.

'Hamamelis, it's called, Jane. Hamamelis. Or, witch hazel.'

My mouth formed a silent O and the stems clattered to the floor.

Mam glared at me. 'Jane! Get those picked up.'

The old woman just laughed, then her cackle turned to a hockle and she spat into the fire. The flare and hiss of steam carried the dreadful smell of the old woman's innards, and its putrid odour made me turn away, pressing a hand to my nose and mouth as I gathered the flowering sticks.

My mother took one from me. 'Meg, what on earth are these? What were you thinking? The name alone—'

Meg waved her away. 'Pay it no mind, Annie, it's just an old name for a bending tree. Plant these sticks, and in two years' time, they'll give black seeds, and then you can grow more than you'll ever need.'

Mam's eyes narrowed. 'Meg, where are these sticks from?'

Meg shrugged. 'Why, they came all the way from the New World, Annie.'

Even for Meg, this was unlikely. She was a magician when it came to finding goods from the east, and spices were relatively easy for her to obtain from the merchants on the Tyne, but she'd never brought plants from the New World before.

Reverend Foster entered the room and noticed the sticks. 'Meg, those stems wouldn't, by any chance, be from Sir Jack's botanical collection? I've heard that he employs a plant hunter in the New World.' He looked at Meg until she looked down. 'Do I have to remind you, Meg Wetherby, of the eighth commandment?'

But Meg grinned her toothless smile and slapped her knee. 'Reverend, you mistake me. There's no need to steal when a body has a tongue such as this.'

She stuck the horrible thing out and the Reverend closed his eyes.

'Barter, Reverend, barter. Fair exchange is no robbery. There's plants in these parts that Sir Jack's plant hunter knows naught of, and these stems come with his blessing.'

The Reverend turned to Mam. 'Even so, Annie, plant them outside the church boundary, if you please. Now, I'm off to my corner to prepare my sermon.'

'We'll try not to disturb you, Reverend.' Mam held a stem to her face and inhaled. 'Its fragrance is sharp, but pleasing, especially for the depths of winter. What are its properties, Meg?'

'Manyfold, hinny, manyfold.' Meg looked at her empty platter. 'Maybe a drop more pottage, if you can spare it?'

'Hmm. Jane, fetch Meg another helping. But only a small one, mind.'

I refilled the platter and set it in front of Meg, who stirred it with a finger to turn it to mush, and then she fumbled in her garments until she fished out a ball of reluctant black fur. She poked the ball with a sodden finger until tiny teeth appeared and the mouth began to suck. My eyes widened.

'A kitten! Mam, look, a black kitten!'

Mam frowned at it. 'Yes, I wondered what was moving about inside Meg's garments.'

'It's a lad, so you won't be overrun, Annie. Spurned by his mother and left to die in the cold. But old Meg, see, she keeps him warm and feeds him mush, and he thrives, mother cat or none.'

I stared at the kitten. 'I'll call him Gyb. Can I feed him, Meg?'

'Aye, hinny, but go canny, he has claws like needles and doesn't trust you yet.'

Mam's mouth tightened. 'Remember our last Gyb? There'll be no more cats here, Jane. And never a black one. There's enough whispering around here as it is.'

Meg passed the kitten to me and proceeded to drain the platter. The kitten mewed, and I caught Mam's eye.

'Oh, very well, Jane. Give him some more to eat, but only a little.'

Reverend Foster looked up from his sermon and scowled at Mam, but she wouldn't meet his gaze. Meg slurped at her platter and Mam turned back to the blooming sticks, bundled them and set them near the open mouth of the sack. The kitten's claws left a trail of red across the back of my wrist, causing me to gasp.

Meg cackled. 'Cats for you. Dogs are pathetically grateful. But never a cat.'

Mam grimaced at Meg. 'Well, perhaps you should have brought a pup then, Meg. Pups are useful. And not so prone to attracting mischief and gossip. Jane, suck that wrist until it mends. And give that kitten back to Meg.'

The kitten opened its green eyes and nudged me with its tiny paws, padding at my belly.

'Ah, Mam, it seeks milk, bless it.' I dipped a finger in some dripping and held it to the kitten. Gyb sucked my finger while I sucked my wrist.

Meg nodded towards the larder. 'You'll have no bother with mice, Annie.'

Mam clicked her tongue. 'I'm not troubled by mice, anyway. Mine is a clean house.'

The crone nodded. 'Still, there's always rats this near the river.'

'Rubbish, Meg, we're too high on the hill for rats. And Jane, you can't have that cat. They carry the plague.'

My eyes flew wide, partly at the mention of the plague, and partly at little Gyb nicking my finger with his teeth.

Meg raised her hand. 'Hadaway, hadaway, it's never the cats, it's the rats that carry the Great Mortality. The numbskulls killed all the cats they could lay their stupid hands on. A premium on black cats, and that's why they're so hard to come by these days. The rat king must have cheered once his enemy was no more. His subjects feasted and bred, running across the land, and taking their nasty scourge wherever they went.'

Mam looked at Gyb. 'Rats? Rats carry the plague? I've not heard that before.'

'Aye, mark my words, Annie, and mark them well. That's what they're whispering at the mart. It was a bad day when they purged the cats. Once word gets out that cats are blameless, there'll be no buying a cat for love nor money. Now, enough of cats. Have you heard any whispering about the carry-on over the moor?'

Mam's head turned at the mention of the troubled village. Meg often brought terrible tales from over the moor. When I was very small, and when Mam's back was turned, Meg filled my ready ears with tales from her own childhood, of how cunning women were burnt to death there. On Meg's last visit, she was full of news about a girl being whipped in public. Mam had shuddered, perhaps at the thought of a girl like me being flogged. It wouldn't do for Mam to show interest, though, as Meg could quickly detect whether something had value, and priced it accordingly. But Mam knew how to play the game and stayed silent, relying on food and warmth to draw the tale from old Meg.

'A Puritan turn of mind's come over the place. Since Carr's lass was whipped for not being properly covered, the women look like they're in mourning weeds. Covered neck to ankle, and not a speck of colour to be seen on woman or girl.'

'Oh, Meg, that doesn't bode well.' Mam's eyes flicked at me. 'And must the men dress this way as well?'

Meg shrugged. 'Men are as men are. But there's worse to tell than that. There's talk in Newcastle again.'

'Talk? In Newcastle?' As soon as she spoke, Mam closed her eyes.

It was too late though, and Meg grinned in triumph.

'Hah! I knew it! You've been drawn in. It's too late, Annie, so you'll have to pay the price.'

'And I suspect the price will no doubt include giving house-room to that wretched cat.'

Mam reached for her lemon-balm tea and began to drink slowly. But Meg watched and waited until she drained it before speaking again. I huddled near to the fire, tantalising Gyb with a scrap of yarn. The kit lay on his back and scrabbled at the yarn with all four paws, his claws unsheathed.

'Aye, there's talk, Annie, of witches.'

At this news, Mam almost choked and wiped her mouth on her pinny. 'Meg! Is this a subject fit for Jane's ears?'

I looked up, hoping Mam wouldn't be able to resist the pleading look in my eyes. This sounded too interesting to miss.

'Of course it is, Annie, of course it is. Better by far to be wise before the event than after.'

My mother looked at me and gave in. 'Very well, Meg, I suppose it's better for Jane to hear it as not.'

Meg settled back on her cracket. 'Aye, the Puritans are up in arms about sorcerers, shape-shifters, witches and all kinds of nonsense. Though old Meg thinks it more likely the physics are up in arms about cunning women and they've talked the Puritans up into a high fret.'

Reverend Foster turned from his books. 'And is there any substance to this high fret, Meg?'

'Aye. Mind, it's only hearsay, but there's talk of bringing down Scottish witch-finders.'

The Reverend shook his head. 'Scottish witch-finders? As if there's not plenty of locals willing to do the job. May God spare us from the Puritans.' He peered at Meg. 'No wonder you were so keen to palm off that furred beast, you old trout, for yours is a neck ready for the rope, if ever there was one.'

Meg affected a pained expression, but then rubbed her swollen hands together and wriggled her eyebrows. 'It's time Meg was on her way. So, shall we settle up, Annie? Take the puss, for … say … tuppence, and I'll give you the flowering sticks. Everything else, normal prices apply.'

Mam looked steadily at Meg and reached inside her shawl. She extracted a farthing and held it up. The firelight caught the coin and made it glint. Meg's eyes caught the glint and she reached for the farthing, but Mam made to return it to her shawl.

'A farthing the lot. And that's only because it's winter and I'm sorry for your old bones.'

'Pah!' Meg hockled into the fire and the green gobbet hissed. 'You're nothing but a knave, robbing an old woman of her meagre belongings.'

Mam moved the farthing nearer to her shawl. Meg's eyes followed it, but then flitted quickly to the cupboard where the wine and mead were kept. Since the old soul clearly knew where they rested, it might be wise to find a new keeping place.

Meg coughed and pulled her thin shawl about her bony shoulders. 'A pint of your sweet mead to seal the bargain. It's so cold, my chest aches.'

'Jane, fetch Meg a half-pint of mead. And leave that cat there.' Mam passed the farthing to Meg. 'There's only one knave around here. Now, tell me the properties of the flowering sticks.'

'Almost magical. A decoction is grand for bulging veins, whether in leg or backside; a poultice is a blessing for ulcers, and a tonic will stop all kinds of bleeding.'

I hefted the jar of mead onto the table. Carefully, I measured out half a pint of the sticky liquid, covered the jar and stopped a bottle. When I returned, Mam and Meg were huddled over the hearth and Meg passed a dark glass vial to Mam, which she tucked into her shawl. I stood in silence, not interrupting.

Eventually, the conversation broke and Meg tore her gaze from the fire, her eyes lighting on the bottle. And no wonder, since mead in the white months was a choice gift. But I was certain Mam's mead wouldn't be going to warm Meg's chest. Already, she'd be totting its value in her machine of a mind. I wondered whose belly it would finally lodge in and what tittle-tattle it would buy in return.

'Jane, guard that cat. Grease his paws, keep him close and you'll never have a rat across the threshold again.'

The bottle of mead vanished into the layers swaddling Meg and she reached for her sack with a gnarled hand. I saw her to the door, waving her off with one hand while trying to extricate Gyb from my hair with the other.

'Same time next week, Meg?'

'Aye, Jane, if God wills it. If God wills it.'

While seeing Meg out, I saw Bill Verger resting his spade against a gravestone.

'Reverend, Bill's out there with his spade. Shall I go and see him for you?'

The Reverend looked up. 'No, I'll go. You stay here with your infernal creature.'

But I put the kitten down, drew on my cloak and followed the Reverend outside. Without any snow, the earth was still harder than iron and it didn't give as I crossed it. Bill Verger tugged the brim of his hat.

'Afternoon, Reverend Foster. What brings you out in this cold?'

'I'm hoping to learn that the soil's fit for planting.'

The verger shook his head. 'No, Reverend. Me and our Tom tried again just before, but only the top soil could be budged, and that only with some effort.'

'And how is it beneath the surface, Bill?'

'Hard as the hobs of hell underneath, Reverend. Another moon needs to pass before we can plant.'

I huddled in the frigid air while the Reverend interrogated the verger. 'What's their condition, those unfortunate souls in the crypt, and how many are they?'

Bill rubbed his tatty beard. 'Nine big uns and seventeen little uns. They're still frozen solid, but the queer weather might change that at any time.'

Reverend Foster scuffed the hard earth with his toe. 'Will they soften and spoil before the earth yields, do you think?'

'Hard to say, Reverend. I'll keep watch. It's the little uns that spoil first. Best get them out of the way.' Bill picked up his spade and hacked at the ground. 'I'll keep on at it, and maybe get some of the river lads up to help.'

'Just do your best, Bill. But get yourself inside and out of this cold for the time being.'

I drew my cloak around me and watched Bill's retreating back.

'Come on, Jane, and stop your eavesdropping. It's the worst time of the year, this, for everyone. Provisions running short and no meat on the bones of man nor beast. The ground too hard to accept the departed. Families unable to grieve and suffering greatly at the thought of loved ones lying frozen solid, blue and hellish in the crypt.' He saw my face and grimaced. 'Sorry, Jane, my mouth's running away with me again.'

Even the Reverend couldn't bring himself to go in there; he could only bless the bodies before Bill and Tom took them in. Then he blessed and anointed the entrance to the crypt, sealing it with prayers. It was always a race to do the winter burials. A race between the hard earth thawing and the hard bodies spoiling. This was the coldest winter we'd known in these parts. Too cold even for proper snow. At this time, there should have been a thick blanket of white to seal the holes and burrows. Instead, there was only ice, and lots of it. And the earth remained too hard for digging.

A sudden flash of movement caught my eye and I saw Mam marching past, carrying the flowering sticks and Bill's spade. I stopped myself from calling out and watched as Mam stripped the yellow blooms away. Using the spade as a makeshift hammer, she hit a stick until one end was under the soil by about two inches. Then she withdrew the stick, scraped the soil off with her knife, chewed it, and then planted its newly frayed end into the waiting hole, stamping the soil down with her feet. She spat and repeated the process a few feet away, stripping, jabbing, chewing, stamping and spitting.

Reverend Foster sighed. 'If only Bill Verger's job were as easy.'

3

John

Stranger Beasts

After a particularly bad night of drinking, Father picked a fight with two sergeants who were trying to quiet his raging ways. They threw him into the street, where he crawled away on his hands and knees, cursing the moon for not providing enough light to see by. Those futile curses at the moon were the last words uttered by him, for his quiet form was found tangled at the dam near Dora Shaw's dwelling place. His head was caved in, but it was impossible to tell whether someone had taken a stone to his skull and tossed him into the river, or whether he'd fallen into the rushing water and dashed his head on the rocks. Dora pulled me tightly to her, and we watched the sergeants haul his dripping corpse from the water. One of them haled Dora and walked over to us.

'Cannot say there'll be many mourning this one's passing.'

Dora scowled. 'Maybe, but he was a father, and this laddie is an orphan.'

'Aye, Dora? And you not a hundred steps from the man's watery grave.'

Dora paled. 'You have no right to say that, sergeant. Why, I brought you and all your brothers safely into this world.'

The sergeant looked away, but did not apologise. 'Be that as it may. What of the lad?'

'John may bide with me, sergeant, or he may go to his uncle if he prefers.'

'His mother's brother?' The sergeant glanced at me and then took me to one side. 'That might be better for you, laddie. Your uncle is a man of the kirk. What are you? Fourteen? He'll get you out of the fields and teach you your letters. You'll be set on the right path in life. And if you're fortunate, he might be able to keep you out of the wars.'

I looked towards Dora. At her familiar face. 'But Dora has always been very kind to me … and my uncle has never wanted me before now.'

The sergeant turned his back to Dora. 'Listen, lad, I'm not convinced the old witch didn't have something to do with your father's passing. It may just take us time to prove it. The hag may seem kind, but whenever there's misery or death, Dora Shaw is never far away. Think about it. She took your mother. It looks to me as though she's taken your father. She could well be collecting souls and yours might be next. Take heed, lad, take heed. Save your soul. Your uncle will take you now you can earn your keep.'

I looked at Dora Shaw and wondered about her ungodly ways. Had she really killed my mother? It seemed hard to believe. And why would she kill my father? All the same, she had never liked him and often wished a bad end on him. It had always troubled me that a woman so seemingly kind on the surface bubbled beneath with darkness. My father had not long since plucked me from her clutches. And although my body had suffered mightily from his blows, I felt my soul was all the safer for it. It would not do to put myself back in her hands now, however kind she might appear to be.

* * *

So I took myself to my uncle's home, snot-nosed though I was, and still bloodied and broken from the blows received from my father's hands and feet. Hands and feet stilled forever by the hand of God. That was what my mother's brother said to me on my first night in his home.

'John, your father's hands and feet have been stilled forever by the hand of God. They can hurt you no more.'

I liked that. His words made me feel as though God's eye had finally found its way to me and now I was cared for by the Almighty. And by Uncle James.

'Uncle, I only wish God might have stilled my father's hands and feet before they killed old Jinny—'

He stopped me with an open hand. 'Who was Jinny?'

I turned my milk teeth over in my pouch. 'My old dog, you see …'

But at this, Uncle James' face darkened. 'You must never expect the Lord's intervention for a dumb animal, John, for they have no soul. So it is a sin, a blasphemy, do you see? But not so great a sin as wishing your own father dead. Though, in truth, few could blame you. For dishonouring your father, you will miss your supper tonight.'

Uncle James' hand quickly ran out to fondle the ears of a lumpen black dog at his side. This gave lie to his stern words, and I knew that Jinny had a soul just like mine. When I went to heaven, Jinny and her pups would be waiting for me, along with Mother. The devil would take Father, though, of that I was certain.

Uncle James' dog was not at all like Jinny. Its face was lopsided and it looked stupid. But worse than that, it was wall-eyed, which meant it was hexed. This made me afraid, so I kept my distance from it. When Uncle invited me to pet it, I shook my head and took a step back, certain that this dog had the evil eye. Perhaps Uncle didn't know the dog was hexed.

'Uncle James, do you know your dog has something the matter with it?'

Uncle smiled at the dog. 'Oh, certainly, Nosewise is a most unfortunate dog and he has plenty wrong with him. He was a runt and thrown to the fighting dogs as bait. Barely survived, and no better than blooded meat when I got him. But he's recovered well enough under my care, though granted, he's no beauty.'

The dog's hard life didn't convince me into liking its queer expression, its wall eye, or its curled lip.

'Come, John, there is hope for us all to heal here, no matter how desperate a case we might seem on arrival. Do you see?'

I shrugged, hoping Uncle James was not comparing me to the cursed dog.

'You will see, John, for there are many stranger beasts in the world than old Nosewise.'

* * *

One morning after kirk, Uncle James pulled on his cloak and beckoned me away from my Bible study.

'Come, lad, we'll go to visit the sick and the needy. It will improve your mood to see others worse off than yourself. The Slaters have no woman in the house and the father has fallen sick, with five mouths to feed. And the eldest girl, Kirstie, has fallen wrong, as if they didn't have woes enough to contend with. Kirstie has already bewitched one decent man out of his wits, and he swung for it, so fill your heart with prayer before we enter the dwelling, lest you go the way of the late Arthur Murray.'

I nodded and followed my uncle. My heart raced with excitement at the notion of a maid fallen wrong. And especially one who had bewitched a man out of his wits. It seemed strange that my uncle would want to visit such a household. But I knew he only wanted to take my mind off my troubles. In truth, I felt guilty for drawing his sympathy so. Yes, I'd lost my mother and my loving dog, and those twin sorrows would live in my heart always. But my final orphaning through the death of my father, well, in many ways, that was a blessing. It was wrong to have these thoughts and God would no doubt punish me for having them. But God, who saw all, would surely understand my relief at escaping my father's fists and clogs. I'd been kicked so many times that my ribs ached all the time, and I'd almost grown used to taking short, gasping breaths so that my bones moved as little as possible while they knitted themselves back together.

The poultices applied by Dora Shaw over the years had helped me, but it was against God to use magical herbs. God would heal me, or not, as He saw fit. Uncle taught me this, and I realised that Dora's interference in my birth had perhaps kept me on earth when God intended to take me straight to my reward in heaven with Mother. All those cruel years endured at the hands of Father were perhaps my just punishment for the ungodly tinkering of

Dora Shaw. I sighed. If only she hadn't meddled, I might have died with Mother, or lived with Mother. Either way, I'd have been safe from Father's rages.

After seeing Uncle James' more kindly approach to life, I vowed not to become a raging man like Father. If ever anger rose in my heart, it would be quelled through prayer or will. It would remain within and not be unleashed on innocents through my hands and feet. And I'd do something about these women who went around practising their dark arts on unsuspecting innocents like myself and my mother. Oh, they did it with cheerful countenance, but beneath lay disguised their ill intentions.

'You are somewhat silent today, John, is all well with you?'

'Yes, Uncle, only I'm thinking about my parents and about Dora Shaw.'

'Ah, the old witch. Push her from your thoughts, John. It was wrong of your father to expose your tender soul to her dark ways after the end she brought to your blessed mother.'

'But Dora always seemed so kind. It's hard for me to believe badly of her.'

'Well, lad, the Bible teaches us that if Satan can disguise himself as an angel of light, then his servants will almost certainly follow suit. People and things are not always what they seem. You must treat everyone and everything with suspicion. It's the only way to root out evil.' He rested a hand upon my shoulder. 'It's no surprise that you've grown fond of the hag, I suppose, but it will not serve you to dwell so much in your thoughts. You must push that woman from your mind and turn your heart cold against her if you are to live under my roof and become a true servant of righteousness. Come, once we've visited the local families and you've witnessed true suffering close at hand, you may take Nosewise out for his run.'

Uncle smiled, which obliged me to smile back. This run with Nosewise was offered as if it were a great blessing from heaven, when Nosewise was a vile beast, given to slobbering and lunging at sheep. And when he caught a certain scent on the air, his ears would move to the side, his tail would take on a kink and he'd bound off in search of whatever bitch was in season. Many times,

I returned minus the dog. Uncle James never blamed me, but I felt reproved even so.

'It's only a dog's way, John, and often man's as well. But dogs are creatures of nature and don't know better. We're men of God and must control our base desires by transmuting them into love for God.'

* * *

When we arrived at the village, we entered the Slaters' shack, which reeked of ailment. A man lay near the fire, with sweat glistening on his face. Beside him, a young girl with a curved belly mopped his brow with a dirty rag, and then mopped at her own tear-stained face.

'How does your father fare, Kirstie?'

'He's no better, Pastor, and I've no food for the wee ones, so they just howl with hunger.'

'John, give Kirstie the loaf and the cheese. It's not much, but it'll line your bellies for today.'

The girl curtsied. 'And what about after that, Pastor?'

Uncle James eyed the sick man. 'I expect God will have taken your father and you'll all be taken in by the kirk, where we will feed you.'

The girl's tears flowed more quickly then. 'So, we've already lost our mother, and now we must pray our father is taken from us so our bellies might be filled?'

Uncle scowled. 'I would not put it in quite such blunt terms, but your father would want you all to be cared for.'

The girl picked up a crying infant, kissed him and put him down again. 'If you could stay with Father and the wee ones awhile, I could walk to the rabbit woods to find Dora Shaw. It's said that she can lift the fever. Then our father would be saved–'

My breath grew shallow. Uncle crossed the room in two strides. He struck Kirstie across the face so hard that she fell to the ground. Then he picked her up.

'Forgive me, lassie, but someone needed to knock the devil from you. It is God who will decide whether your father lives or dies, not that witch in the woods. You must not entertain such foul thoughts. Do not invite the dark one into your home, or into your heart. John knows this lesson all too well, so perhaps you can learn from his example. Come, kneel, and we'll pray to God for His mercy.'

4

Jane

It Heals Most Ills

Mam had sent me on a message to Meg. On my way, I walked through the woods, watching the magpies fly back and forth to feed their young, who were tucked safely in a nest in the bare, upper branches of a poplar. The tree was just starting to green from the bottom up, so the nest was not fully screened. The ash trees were still naked and their black-tipped branches had yet to push any leaf buds out. So no birds made their nest there. The ash was not favoured by the magpies in any case. They had patrolled the poplar for some time before choosing the site for their nest. Perched on the uppermost twig, the magpies kept watch for predators. In the nest, the young would be bare, their beaks not yet hardened, still soft-lipped trumpets blaring for more food.

Further along, two swans were nesting. The huge nest sat proud, built up on a mound by the riverbank. The pen slept on her nest, her long neck gracefully coiled on top of her body. The cob slept downhill of her, never fully asleep, and alert to would-be egg stealers and cygnet hunters. It was possible to perch ten feet away on a tree stump and watch them. They trusted me, but a step too near would turn these elegant beauties into rampant attackers. Mostly, I liked to watch the swans walking to the river's edge. There was no hint of their waterborne grace when they ambled overland, their legs making clumsy circular movements.

Beyond the meadow, the herons made their shallow nests high in the trees. Their swooping, grey wings seemed to beat not quite fast enough to hold them in the air. They were more cautious than the swans, taking care not to reveal their nests by laying a false, looping trail in the air before returning home. But it was easy for me to find their nests. Like magpies, the heron would perch on the topmost twig of its chosen tree. But the heron was a heavy bird and the top twig would bend under its weight. By following the bent twigs, my eye could swiftly place the nest.

At this time of year, there were plenty of pretty shells to gather for my little garden. My favourites were the green robin eggs with their delicate hue. Birds were my favourite creatures, but I also liked to think of the life springing forth under my feet, small animals alive in the warm, dark womb of the earth, sunk into the hot, milky bellies of their mothers. Perhaps they heard the world above, smelling it on their returning mother's fur, her jaws red with her fresh kill, her flanks getting thinner every day. I wondered at the infant creatures' move from sweet mother's milk to pulverised flesh, cooked only in the juices of the mother's mouth. How quickly the taste for blood must develop in the young so that they could learn to feed themselves.

On these walks, I practised being quiet. A smooth, round pebble on my tongue filled my mouth and brought it some rest from the desire to talk incessantly. Its weight pressed my tongue into silence and the earthy taste weighted me down and soothed me, taking me out of the airy element somewhat and holding me fast to earth. With my tongue so stilled, my inner voice was also quieted and I could stay, silent and patient, watching for birds and animals. In this way, my true self was changed and disguised so that I merged with nature.

Due to my silent approach and being upwind of my quarry, I was able to watch a young doe giving birth. The doe lay on her side, her stomach writhing, and then she stood up. Finally, a leg began to emerge, gleaming from its birth sac. The doe nimbly ducked through her own legs and used her mouth to pull the fawn towards the light and air. It was tiny. A single fawn, and one so small and born so very early in the year, was a sign of a bad harvest coming.

The doe straightened up, lightened from the burden of the birthing. I held my breath as she licked her fawn from tip to toe. The fawn unfurled its gangly limbs and wobbled to its feet, then crept towards its mother's belly in search of milk. Though tiny, it already seemed much too big to have been inside its mother. As the fawn suckled and began to dry, its pelt became a pure white. Poor little soul. White deer were greatly prized by hunters and this fawn would have a price on its head once word spread. I'd tell no one about this, so no one would learn of the pale fawn. The longer she stayed hidden, the safer she'd be.

For a while longer, I sat in silence, watching the doe eat the afterbirth for nourishment and to remove any smell of blood. To pass the time, I pulled three blades of tall grass and braided them with flowers into a chain – buttercups for the golden mother and daisies for the silver fawn. This charm would protect them, and I tucked it underneath a rock near my hiding place. We were deep in the wood, and this part was not reachable on horseback because of the dense undergrowth. It could only be reached through the secret deer paths. If the fawn stayed deep in the wood and survived the week, she might become sturdy and properly learned in the nervous ways of deer. Most importantly, she would gain fear of man the predator.

* * *

When I finally reached Meg's dwelling, she was busy over her fire with a griddle, and a delicious smell filled the air, along with the sizzling sound of butter.

'Hello, Meg. Oh, Meg, you're making singing hinnies!'

'Yes, I am, hinny, I must have known you were coming to see me. Sit yourself down and they'll be ready soon enough. I've had some currants from the market doing nothing for months and I daren't keep them any longer.'

Meg flipped the hot scones over on the griddle and the smell of butter and currants filled the air once more.

'Just a short while, hinny, and then we can enjoy them with a fresh brew. You go and fetch me some mugwort and I'll get the pot boiling.'

I knew exactly where to find the mugwort and quickly found a clump of silver spears rustling in the breeze. The tender new shoots were best and it was only a minute's work to nip out a few handfuls before returning to Meg. I added the leaves to two bowls, and she lifted the cauldron from the fire and carefully ladled boiling water into them. Tendrils of steam rose up. It was lovely to hold my bowl and breathe in the astringent fragrance, blowing on the water's surface to make it ripple and send up steam into my face.

'Well, these hinnies have stopped singing now, so it's time to enjoy them while they're hot.'

Meg flipped six hot scones onto a wooden plate and quickly dabbed a knob of butter over them. My mouth watered at the smell.

'Here, Jane, get them down you quick, that's best butter, mind.'

The hinnies were a perfect mix of currants, sugar and salted butter. I closed my eyes on a heavenly mouthful, wishing there were more than three to look forward to.

'So, Jane, did you have a message, or have you just come to eat me out of house and home?'

I smiled and shook my head, still chewing. 'Mam sent me to see whether you'd had anything from the apothecary.'

Meg nodded. 'I was in Newcastle the week before last. Good-wife Keen gave me some glass vials for your mother. Maybe I should hang on to them till I'm next round your doors. Then again, maybe your mother's in a hurry for them. Can you get them home without breaking them?'

'Glass vials? Of course I can. They'll be quite safe in my hands. What's in them?'

'Never you mind, hinny, now get yourself away home as soon as you've finished your brew, else your mother will wonder where you've got to.'

'Meg, I watched a doe giving birth to a white fawn on my way here. Do you think she'll be safe? They were deep in the woods on the deer paths.'

Meg frowned and poked the fire, looking deeply into the flames. 'As much as any of us are ever safe. Oh, Jane, to see a white fawn at birth is a rare omen, but not a good one. It's a message from the other world, warning of danger and trespassers. So you must take great care.'

* * *

When I returned home, I put the vials away in Mam's pantry. The pantry was a constant delight to me, and I loved to work my way through the stores, learning their names by sight and smell. Everything Mam knew, I learnt. Watching Mam as she picked, plucked and planted, I helped to press, dry and turn bright-green leaves into soft, pale powders.

Mam found me as I left the pantry.

'Mam, what's in those glass vials that Meg sent from the apothecary?'

'Nothing for you to worry your head about, Jane. Now, come and help me gather the early marigolds.'

I loved to fill flat baskets with fragrant petals and leaves from the garden, and Mam checked my learning as we went.

'Now, let's test that memory of yours and see if you've been paying attention. What's the best time to pick the flowers?'

'Two or three hours after the sun wakes up, Mam.'

'And why is that, pet?'

I scrunched up my eyes and tried to remember. 'So that the dewdrops have gone.'

She tousled my hair. 'That's right. Today, we'll pick as many marigolds as we can, and we'll make calendula ointment to soften the skin.'

I raised some cheerful orange and yellow blooms to my face. 'They look so pretty, but I like the smell of roses better.'

'Of course, Jane, the rose is the most wondrous smell on God's earth. Marigold smells halfway beautiful and halfway ugly. But she's a lovely remedy for wounds – gentle enough for babies and kind to aged people.' She chucked me under the chin. 'And she makes a lovely cream to keep ladies' faces soft and pretty.'

I gave my mother a puzzled look. She still had brown hair and eyes like my own, but her skin was no longer soft or pretty.

She laughed. 'Jane, don't examine me with such an earnest expression. My face doesn't need to be soft and pretty, but my lotions are popular with the ladies who visit the apothecary. Come, let's get on.'

When we returned to the scullery, my mother arranged a huge crock in a cauldron of water and half-filled the crock with flowers. Next, she topped up the crock with beeswax.

'Keep back, Jane, while I light the fire beneath the cauldron. When the water bubbles, it'll melt the beeswax and the warm wax will take the goodness from the petals. Stop scowling; if the smell is so bad, go and sit near the window because the smell of the rendering marigolds will be quite overpowering in a little while.'

I shrugged, walked to the far side of the scullery and turned to the open window.

'Oh, you'll get used to it in time, believe me.' As Mam spoke, she took a metal hook and lifted the crock of hot beeswax from the fire. 'We'll let it cool awhile, but not too long, else it sets. Here, come and take out the petals.'

I took a slotted spoon and began lifting the wilted petals from the liquid wax.

'Now, we'll leave it to set until it's ready to mix into salves.'

I dipped a finger into the warm wax and then held it in the air. Once the wax was cool, I peeled it off my finger.

Mam smiled at me. 'Now, Jane, calendula salve. Take note of the method, and if you make nothing else in life, make this as it heals most ills.'

I rolled the wax around in my palm. 'I don't need to know how to make it, Mam, because I can always come and ask you.'

'But, Jane, I'll not always be here. And you'll not always be here, either.'

These words made me pause. 'Mam, I saw a white fawn born in the woods this morning and Meg said it was a bad omen.'

She looked at me sharply. 'Then you should heed Meg. And tell no one else of it.'

5

John

The Devil Himself

'Uncle James. It's me, John. Wake up. Please, please, you must come, Uncle.'

I watched the stupor of sleep leave his face.

'Steady on, John, and take a breath. What can be so bad that it warrants this much fuss?'

'Please, Uncle, the devil himself is unleashed at the Cummins' place. They've all seen him. Terrible he is, by all accounts. And he's entered Cummins' wife. Furry-bodied and flaming, and with the stink of hell on him.'

Uncle James sat up. 'Entered, you say?'

'Yes. Possessed, she is. Thrashing about on the floor like a dying trout, but with froth coming out of her mouth. Please, Uncle, you must come, for all our sakes. The barber-surgeon is there, but even he can't help her.'

'Very well, John. Light a lantern, or we'll never find our way there and back.'

I fetched the lantern and stood near the door, ready to leave.

'Uncle, is it really possible to be possessed by the devil?'

He wrapped himself in his cloak. 'Undoubtedly. But don't forget that there's plenty of evil about, although it mostly stems from men's love of strong drink, avarice for fertile land and desire for soft flesh. Come, I'm ready.'

I nodded and started walking. 'Yes, and I suppose that evil could be embodied in the form of a furred and stinking demon.'

Uncle panted, struggling to keep pace with me. 'But whether furred demon or mere fancy, whatever it is, I sincerely wish it wasn't situated at the top of the glen. My legs are trembling already. We should have brought Nosewise on a rope and he could have hauled me to the top.'

'Would you like to rest, Uncle?'

'No, no. We've only just set out, so keep going. I'd be too ashamed of putting my own comfort above the salvation of an innocent soul.'

When we reached the Cummins' farm, there came the anguished cries of women and children, cut through by shrieking.

Uncle paused to listen. 'No doubt that was the tortured soul of Margaret Cummins.'

Inside, the assembly included the barber-surgeon, MacBain. He was trying, with limited success, to keep the throng from crowding the convulsing woman. The froth issuing from her mouth had turned bloody. Uncle stood in silence, drawing in long breaths before raising his voice to a suitable register.

'Someone tell me what has happened here. I have John's account, of course. Cummins? If it does not distress you too much?'

The gaunt husband cast his eyes down. 'Well, Pastor, there was first a shadowy beast that threw my goodwife to the ground.'

'And did you see the beast?'

The man shook his head. 'No, more's the pity. I was outside attending to nature and missed the spectacle. When I came back in, the whole household were on their knees and praying. I never saw the beast, but my sister's lassie, she saw it. And everyone saw the state of my goodwife. Then there's the definite sulphury stench that might be straight from the mouth of hell. And my goodwife's sister says she saw the flames as the devil himself entered my wife.'

Uncle turned to MacBain, who looked keen to speak.

'Aye, Pastor, her own sister tried to get Goodwife Cummins to pray, but in vain. The distressed woman thrashed about on the floor like a dying ... that is to say, she's not a well woman, as you know. Though no woman can be well when Old Iniquity's been residing within her very soul, to say nothing of other places–'

'MacBain! That's enough. We must act quickly to save this woman's soul. Everyone, quickly form a circle around Goodwife Cummins. Face outwards so that your backs are turned on the demon.'

'But surely we need to keep our eyes fastened on him?' This from Cummins, who was pale and sweating.

'The reverse is true, Cummins. If we turn our eyes upon him, the demon knows he has our full attention, and he feeds upon it. Who knows what he might do if he reaches his full power? Is that a chance anyone here present wishes to take?'

The assembled relatives shook their heads and turned around, but not before I noticed a thrill run through them.

'Close your eyes! We'll commence with prayer and I'll bless this goodwife.' Uncle began to speak in resonant tones, 'Dear Lord, lay your peace on this dwelling and on the Cummins family.' He knelt before Goodwife Cummins. 'Please, Lord, forgive our past transgressions and those of our forebears, whose sins are ever with us. Cast out the demon lately come amongst us, redeem us and spare us your rage. Righteous Lord, forgive us and save us.'

The assembled began to intone, 'Our Father, which art in Heaven, hallowed be thy name ...'

Uncle held his hand out to place his blessing upon Goodwife Cummins' forehead. He looked at me and I saw his predicament. To hold her head long enough to bless her would be to break her neck, so he held his hand in the air above her head. It would be impossible to bless someone moving in such a vigorous and unpredictable fashion, so he also blessed the air around her.

'... thy kingdom come, thy will be done, in earth as it is in heaven ...'

The barber-surgeon wrangled something from his belt and held it as near to Goodwife Cummins' face as he could. Even from several feet away, I caught the stench of hartshorn, which brought water to my eyes and made me cough. Some of the congregation must have also breathed it – albeit more distantly – as they turned to face us and were rubbing at their eyes.

'… Give us this day our daily bread, and forgive us our trespasses as we forgive them that trespass against us. And lead us not into temptation, but deliver us from evil. For thine is the kingdom, power and glory, for ever and ever. So be it.'

'So be it. Uncle, the devil must be on the move, I can smell his stench.'

'Yes, he makes my eyes water, John.'

'Mother, I'm afeared.' A young girl coughed and pressed herself into her mother's side.

The woman on the floor was stilling and MacBain drew his cloak over her. Uncle blessed Goodwife Cummins' head and urgently drew the sign of the cross on her forehead. He kissed his cross and held it before him. Although blood still foamed from her mouth, she sat up, took the cross in her hands and kissed it.

Cummins wept and rushed forward to gather his wife in his arms. 'My suffering lassie, I thought you were taken to hell for certain.'

The onlookers joined their hands in prayer, the children were giddy and chattering, and some of the women looked fit for fainting. Goodwife Cummins' sister was on her knees, hands clasped before her, eyes shining.

'Oh, I can see the of an angel, a shining-faced cherub. Oh, it is a miracle.'

I looked around me, but could see no cherubim, shining-faced or otherwise. Perhaps I needed to look harder.

Uncle James stood up and raised his arms. 'Now that Goodwife Cummins is well, perhaps we may all depart and let her sleep.'

No one appeared in a hurry to depart though, since such entertainment was rare indeed, especially in the dead of night, so Uncle put some cold iron into his voice.

'Come, get back to your own beds, for I'll expect each and every one of you at kirk in the morning to give thanks to God.'

To say nothing of the collection plate. Uncle's words seemed to stir them. One by one, and casting regretful glances over their shoulders, they began to move towards the door.

MacBain retrieved his cloak. 'Pastor, I'll share your lantern on the walk back, if you don't mind?'

'Aye, as long as you don't mind travelling at a slow pace. I'm not cut out for running about the glen in the middle of the night.'

* * *

By the time we reached home, light was breaking in the east, and Uncle sighed. He looked down at the dew soaking the bottom of his cloak.

'Not much time for sleep, John, and no breakfast until after kirk.'

'Well, Uncle, you'd best ready yourself for a busy few moons.'

'Aye, knowing how men's minds work, furred demons will no doubt be appearing left and right for weeks to come.'

The barber-surgeon sniggered. 'There might be a grain of truth in it. And it's no wonder the devil has chosen to call on these parts.'

Uncle looked at MacBain. 'Why on earth would the dark saint bother himself in this corner of the world when there's whole continents lacking any Christian guidance?'

'Well, let me enlighten you, Pastor, but telling tales is thirsty work.'

'Very well, MacBain, come in and wet your whistle. I suppose there'll be no kirk for you, so it won't matter whether you're fasted or not.'

'Just right, Pastor, just right.'

When we went inside, Uncle and MacBain sat down, and I started banking up the fire.

'John, a drink for the barber-surgeon, if you will? It's been an arduous night for all concerned.'

I straightened my back and made to pour ale from the jug, but MacBain caught my eye and so I carried over a tot of whisky instead. The man pressed his fingers to the top of my arm by way of thanks. He took a gulp of the whisky and it brought colour to his wan cheeks. Then he made great play of rubbing his hands together in front of the fire, Nosewise at his feet. Uncle frowned at the dog's infidelity, but I was glad not to be the recipient of the vile beast's affections for once.

MacBain settled back. 'Here's the thing, why, when there are so many unchristian countries scattered about, would the devil choose to ignore those heathens and pick on us?'

Uncle opened his mouth to object, but the barber-surgeon waved him away and continued.

'Because the devil has no interest in them that's never been touched by God's hand. The devil's not concerned with the godless, for he already owns their misbegotten souls. He's only interested in taking back those who may have been touched by the hand of God – therein lies his filthy victory.'

MacBain cast his eyes at me. Doubtless, the charlatan was checking I was suitably shocked. I was shocked, but feigned boredom. MacBain made the most of the interlude by packing his pipe and lighting it with a cinder from the fire, puffing away until the pipe took hold of the flame.

Finally, Uncle James broke the silence. 'What a lot of rot, MacBain, and you've robbed me of a tot of whisky to hear it. And what was all that in aid of up at the Cummins' place, you old piece of mendacity?'

The barber-surgeon's eyes widened. 'I don't know what you mean, Pastor.'

'MacBain, you know fine well that the Cummins woman is sick. Clearly, she was just having some sort of fit, which you're more than capable of mending with a few shakes of this and that from the pouches hanging from your belt.'

At this, the barber-surgeon drained his glass and smirked at Uncle. 'Aye, of course, but you don't get paid nearly so much for fixing a fit as you do for ridding a body of the devil himself. Now, a man of the cloth should know that better than anyone.'

6

Jane

Sleeping Flowers

Sometimes in summer, it was hard to know what to do with all the daylight hours. Mam had no messages for me to run, and making daisy chains no longer appealed, so I sat quietly in a sunny spot in the garden, watching the daisies and determining to see with my own eyes when the flowers went to sleep.

Even though the shadows lengthened and the evening grew cooler, there was no detectable movement from the flowers. Perhaps they only moved when there was no one watching because they always closed their eyes and slept every night. But it seemed in the half-light of dusk that I must have taken an extra-long blink. In that sliver of time, the daisies must have bade goodnight to one another since their petals were now drawn close around them.

I went inside to ask the Reverend, as it was unlikely he had much to do, either. Mam was occupied with her sewing and Reverend Foster was hunched over his writing desk, but he wasn't writing. Praying Mam didn't look up and see me, I tiptoed to the desk and stood next to the Reverend until he looked up.

'Yes, Jane?'

Mam's head snapped up as soon as he spoke. 'Jane! Don't bother the Reverend when he's busy. Come away.'

'Oh, I could use the break, Annie, my sermon eludes me. Come, Jane, what's on your mind?'

'Reverend Foster, the flowers keep going to sleep without me noticing. How can I see them opening and closing?'

'Ah. Truly a mighty problem. Perhaps mightier than trying to write my sermon. Let me ponder it ...'

I concentrated on not fidgeting while the Reverend thought. Mam often explained that it made him cross.

'I think the only way to observe them properly is with ink and paper. Draw quick sketches and sketch a new picture every few moments. Trust your eyes and draw only what you see. By looking back through the sketches, you'll see the flower's movements.'

Although this wasn't a heartening instruction, I scrubbed the doubt from my face. 'But, Reverend, that will take even longer than looking at them. When I'm looking at my paper, they'll quickly close their eyes. And I haven't even got any paper, only my slate.'

He reached into his desk. 'Take these scraps saved from my schoolboys. They've practised conjugating their verbs on one side, but you can use the other. And you may mix some ink, but fetch it straight back afterwards.'

The small squares of paper were filled with close and spidery writing, but I couldn't make head nor tail of it.

'Off you go, Jane. Now, let me get back to my sermon.'

'Thank you, Reverend. Since you're so often right, I'll try it. But I'll practise with my slate first so I don't waste your paper and ink.'

I lay in front of the fire, clutching my slate and drawing. Tongue clenched between teeth, I rubbed and scratched. The sound drew Reverend Foster and he put down his breviary with a thump.

'Annie, is it not time for Jane's bed?'

The candle wasn't yet half-burnt, but Mam gathered her sewing together anyway. 'Come, Jane, time for bed.'

But I began to rub and scribble faster.

'Jane! Do not defy your mother.'

'Sorry, Reverend Foster.' With downcast eyes, I left my slate and allowed Mam to shepherd me to bed.

* * *

The next evening, propped against the reassuring bark of the rowan tree, I started drawing a daisy. Its face was upturned to the sun and its white petals were held out in supplication. It wasn't as detailed as I'd have liked, but I placed the paper under a stone for safekeeping. The next drawing didn't appear much different, but Reverend Foster had made me promise to trust my eyes and draw only what I saw to reveal the truth.

By the time Mam came outside to seek me, I was straining my eyes to complete the drawing of the newly closed daisy. Its pink undersides now reached for the moon. And its own internal sun was tucked away until morning.

'Jane, you should have been in long since. The bats are out now and you're lucky they haven't tangled in your hair.'

How had I not noticed their silent swooping? There were goose pimples on my arms.

'Sorry, Mam, but I've nearly got it and I want to show Cuthbert.'

'Not tonight, maid, for *Reverend Foster* is writing his sermon, and you've disturbed him enough of late. Come on, milk and bed. Your flowers will keep.'

* * *

First thing in the morning, I was back outside, wrapped in a shawl and trying to keep the paper clear of the morning dew. Reverend Foster stuck his head out of the door and haled me.

'Jane, don't let your mother catch you getting damp clothes. What are you about at this time of the morning? Has the fox been in at the hens again?'

'No, Reverend, they're all well. Sir Jack is protecting his ladies as well as ever. I'm still trying to see when the flower changes. One minute it's one thing and the next it's something else.'

He laughed. 'When you've finished, bring your drawings to me and we'll work it out together.'

I reversed the process, watching the daisy yawn, stretch and open herself to absorb the strengthening sun. But it still seemed impossible to grasp that moment of change. Each time, it slipped through my fingers, whether they were holding a quill or not. When I finally went inside, the Reverend was flicking back and forth in his Bible and making notes.

'That's such a lovely sound, Reverend, the pages rustling. Might I have a turn?'

'Go on then, you have a turn while I look at your drawings. Only mind you don't tear the pages. Look, spread your pictures out here.'

He cleared a space on his desk and I set out my drawings.

'You see, Reverend, the flower changes from open to shut and then open again, but it's impossible to see the change. Perhaps I have slow eyes.'

He studied the drawings closely. 'These are exquisite drawings, Jane, and you've a gift for recording nature most faithfully. If your eyes are slow, your hands are deft enough.'

But I wasn't interested in compliments, only in finding out at what point one thing became another. While waiting, I flicked through the Bible with my fingernail, watching the centuries rushing past with the rustle that only thin Bible paper could create. Although my feet managed to keep still, my toes wriggled, willing the Reverend to hurry up. Eventually, he turned to me and held out his hand.

'Jane, give me my Bible and pick up your drawings in the order you drew them.' He placed one piece of paper on top of the other, squaring the corners as he went. 'Grip the left-hand side firmly and fan them under your fingernail as you just did with the Bible.'

It took a few tries to manage it because the paper was quite coarse. But once I got the hang of it, the daisy furled and unfurled her petals, and I repeated the action many times.

'Father, this is wonderful, thank you!'

'What does this tell you, Jane? Think before you answer.'

I continued flicking the paper. 'That there's no time when the daisy isn't changing. She's always moving.' I looked up to seek reassurance that this was right, and the Reverend nodded. 'But why can't I see this when I look at the daisy?'

'Because, Jane, we have such impatient eyes. We think everything must move at the same speed as us. But sometimes, we need to slow right down or speed right up if we are to see things as they truly are.'

He was using his sermon voice. It was harder to like him so much then because it was harder to understand him. His words sounded as though he was telling a story, but the way he said them disguised the meaning. I began to twirl a lock of my hair, and then stooped to pick up Gyb, who was coiling himself around my legs. The Reverend paused.

'So, Jane, what it means is that everything around us is moving and changing all the time. Kittens grow into cats. Little girls grow into women. And young men grow into old men.'

This made me laugh. 'You're not old, Reverend, you're barely old enough to wear the vestments – that's what Meg Wetherby says, anyway.'

He rubbed Gyb's ears and stood up. 'Ah, well, Meg is one to be listened to, so she must be right. Come, put Gyb down and tidy your pictures away. Then you can race me to the church as I'm so young today.'

'But what about Mam?'

'Let her sleep. Your mother was up all night with Driver's wife.'

I fell into step beside him as we crossed the graveyard.

'And how does the Drivers' baby go?'

'God has taken the little girl to His breast. Goodwife Driver's fate rests in God's hands. Your mother can do no more.'

My shoulders drooped. It was unbearable to imagine the Drivers' tiny daughter in heaven. There was a question in my mind, but it might sound like I doubted God's word and that might mean I was destined for hell. But it worried me that God took babies and mothers so often unto His breast. And yet in winter, people didn't go straight to heaven, but went instead into the cold crypt. It was easy to hide behind the big tombstones and watch Bill and Tom Verger carrying people on boards, wrapped in old sacking. The dead people all stayed down there until spring. It was horrible thinking of babies down there, especially those without their mothers. It made me shiver just thinking about it.

'Jane, are you cold?'

'No, I was just thinking that I don't like the crypt.'

'Well, Jane, I don't much like it, either.'

'Bill Verger must be used to it, but his Tom pulls strange faces, especially when the ground thaws and they carry people back up for burial. Reverend, do the crypt people get fly-blown like meat that hasn't stayed properly cold?'

He cast his eyes towards the crypt and then back at me. 'Well, perhaps that's enough chatter, for now. It's time for me to think on my sermon.'

There was always a nasty smell in the air at the start of spring and the Reverend used more incense than we could afford because Mam was always telling him off. The nasty smell was the same as when I'd found our last cat, dead and rotting in the mint garden. Mam said the cat must have been poisoned because she'd have been picked clean otherwise.

'Reverend, why would anyone poison a cat? Do you remember our first Gyb? She took herself off with a bellyful of kittens, to make herself ready. The kits hadn't even seen daylight, and they lay dead and stinking inside Gyb's gut.'

'Jane! What madness whirls through your mind? Have you no errands to busy you? I must think on my sermon.'

'Sorry, Reverend. But it's summer and I'm glad because the Drivers' baby will be put into the warm earth and her tiny soul will fly straight to heaven.'

Reverend Foster stopped walking and looked at me. 'Is that what this has all been about? Come, we'll run the race I promised you, and then we'll say a special prayer and light a candle for the Drivers' child.'

* * *

Mam needed eggs, so I went out to see to the hens. I held a warm egg in each hand and placed them into the basket before ducking into the coop. The hens ruffled themselves while the cock strutted about outside, keeping a wary eye on me.

'Don't mind me, Sir Jack, your pretty ladies will all be left in peace shortly. Sh, ladies, it's only me, don't make such a fuss.'

Back in the kitchen, Mam took the basket from me, removed each egg, wiped it clean and placed it in a crock.

'Oh, Mam, you look so pale. You've been out all night again. That's twice this week. Are you tired?'

'Aye, Jane, I'm ready for my bed. The Green baby was very hard to deliver.'

'Why?'

My mother flinched and crossed her fingers behind her back, but I still saw her and wondered whether it was for luck, or to save her soul against telling a lie.

'Oh, because of the mother's age – she's not the right age for birthing. It was difficult, with only the girls to help.'

'But, Mam, you should have woken me up. I could have helped. And I haven't seen May for ages.'

'No, Jane. Green didn't even want me there, let alone you. But little Tilly ran over in the night for me. Green himself was fast asleep after too much ale. The man wants hanging.'

This was a dreadful thing to say. 'Mam! What for? Having too much ale?'

'No. For … for getting the baby's mother in the family way.' Mam shook her head and put the last of the eggs into the crock. 'I'm going back to bed. Let me rest awhile, and I'll be up by and by. Can you make sure the Reverend has something to eat?'

There was no time to get a hot meal ready, but there was a cold cut and some vegetables from yesterday, so we made do. And if Reverend Foster minded the makeshift meal, he never said so.

'Your mother, is she well?'

'Just tired. After birthing the Green baby.'

'Ah. Well, your mother's a right to be tired. I'll be in church again this afternoon, so how will you stay out of trouble?'

'I'll clean Mam's birthing tools and put them all away properly. She was too tired when she came in.'

He pushed his plate away from him, frowning. 'Very well. Hopefully, your mother will be well again by this evening.'

'And if she's not, I can make supper, Reverend.'

He looked upwards. Was he casting his eyes to heaven, or was he pondering Mam's health? 'Ruled by his stomach, that one.'

That was what Mam always said. I tidied away and then hurried out to the pantry. Mam's satchel was stowed outside, which meant it was soiled. Nothing unclean was allowed across the threshold of the pantry. Sighing, I carried the bag at arm's length to the scullery.

7

John

The Hellish Circle

It was the night of All Hallows' Eve and, unbeknownst to Uncle James, I found myself at the outer reaches of the kirkyard where the unholy ones were buried. It was strange being out when spirits walked the earth. Everything was made eerie by the night creatures waking and their amber eyes shining. I was glad of the full moon, which made everything silver instead of grey, and it took away some of my trembling. Even so, the bole of the old oak tree was much less comforting at night than it was in daylight, but it was the best hiding place by far. As Uncle James had taught me, I closed my eyes and prayed to God to help me in my endeavour, and this made me feel a little braver.

Kirstie Slater finally appeared in the kirkyard, carrying a small lantern. Her father was no longer lying at death's door, and the village was alive with gossip about how this had come about. I supposed Kirstie a witch and was determined to reveal her secret. But then thoughts of the child in her belly preyed on me. It was an ill-gotten bastard, but the child was hardly to blame, and it would be orphaned if she was put to the flame. I thought of my own orphaning. It was a terrible state to wish on another child – perhaps a boy like myself. But what if I turned a blind eye to this nocturnal magic-making for the sake of an infant? What then? Might it become indoctrinated into Kirstie's dread practices? The thought of a new witch being created made me shudder. It would be an act beyond forgiveness to let another witch be born. If I was to rid the world of this evil, then I must be resolute. When Kirstie was put to the flame, God would save her infant from darkness. It was my duty to spare the innocent soul.

As Kirstie picked her way through the undergrowth, her big-bellied body undulated and cast freakish shadows under the moon. She paused and brushed away some red-veined dock leaves, revealing a flat rock. It was hard to see properly without leaning right out of the tree, but I did my best. The rock had to be one of thirteen witching stones reputed to encircle the village – one stone for each moon of the year.

Uncle had told me that, in old times, cunning women anointed the stones with blood from their womb in an act of hellish consecration. Once the blood was painted onto the stone, it was planted, blooded-side down. This practice passed from crone to mother to maid, to preserve the so-called sanctity of the land, irrespective of whose kirk graced the ground. But Uncle was not able to show me these stones, as no man had ever found them, and he warned me against seeking them. But here I was, through no fault of my own, so Uncle could hardly castigate me.

Was Kirstie Slater to become the latest guardian of the stones? If I watched for long enough, would I see her anoint the stone with her moon blood and turn the stone blooded-side down to seal her fiendish gift between stone and earth? Tonight was blood moon, although it was unseasonably warm for the time of year.

How did Kirstie remember which stone came next when there were so many of them and they were so far apart? Perhaps the devil lent his strength to her memory. My uncle said each stone in the circle gave off its own energy, but that each one must be nourished with dirty blood once a year. By the time the thirteenth moon approached, there would be a weakening at that point in the stone circle, as if a sentinel were readying to falter. I'd struggled to absorb this information and Uncle was forced to repeat himself.

'It's very simple, John. Thirteen moons pass between your birthday and the next one. The time between the twelfth and thirteenth moon is when you are at your weakest and most open to evil influence. As if you were a fort and a wall had fallen down.

That's why you were out of your rightful humour just before your last birthday. Do you see?'

I'd nodded, but didn't really understand a word of what the old man said, because it made no sense to me. But under the moonlight, I wondered. Kirstie was casting sidelong glances at the stone. Then her hand slid out and touched the stone, before withdrawing. What had she felt? Did the stone give off a force – even if only a weak one that was getting weaker? Once the stone was lifted and the blooding done, would the stone gain in strength? Would it sigh as it rested back in its hollow, newly strong and alive, strengthened by the ripe blood, the full moon and the dark spirits roaming the earth?

Kirstie placed her hand back on the stone and closed her eyes, as if waiting for some sensation to grow in her hand. Was it just a trick of the night, or was there a growing warmth, a light coming from the stone? This was most certainly the work of the devil, and my eternal soul must surely be in peril. I altered my position to pray, but my movement made Kirstie turn and stare at the tree. Certain that she'd seen my eyes shining, I closed them quickly, trying to keep my breath steady as I heard her moving nearer to my tree.

'Who's that? Who's there? It'd better not be you come back to get me, Arthur Murray.'

Arthur Murray. Kirstie's rapist, according to the justice, who'd seen the man swing for it. An innocent man bewitched out of his wits, according to my uncle. Either way, she was a brazen girl, out in the moonlight when she might be at home tending to her siblings. She was both brave and foolish since many women had been burnt for less. Yet, she sounded afraid, even though she must still be standing within the protective bounds of her evil master's stone circle.

It was not such an obvious circle that I could see it. According to Uncle, the vast spaces between stones meant they didn't announce themselves. And these were not tall, manly stones that demanded men's notice; they were only flattish rocks, weighty enough to make a hollow for themselves, but light enough that they could be lifted by a girl. This was the only stone from the circle that I'd seen, which made me wonder where the others might reside. Perhaps Kirstie would lead me to one at the next full moon.

When I opened my eyes, the witch was still distracted from her task and loomed ever nearer to my tree, her face as white as the moon. My heart raced as she moved towards me, this pale wraith, with tiny moths fluttering about her. She raised her lantern and peered into the darkness. I turned my head lest she catch a glimpse of my eyes. But then she went back to her stone.

In the silvery light, Kirstie knelt before the stone and removed a jet bowl from her skirts. She held the bowl up to the light of the moon. Collected there was little more than a spoonful of liquid. Her womb blood was the colour of jet and seemed only a slightly more viscous part of the hollowed bowl. I knew little of women's menses, but innocent blood was scarlet and ran freely, so some demonic influence must be at work. She heaved up the stone, laid it on its back and then waited a few breaths – perhaps to let the tiny creatures underneath make away.

Jet was used in birthing bowls to purify, so the bowl would remove any influence from the blood by absorbing into itself any evil. This confounded me. If this womb blood was a satanic offering, why would Kirstie remove the taint by using a jet bowl? The blood itself was a small offering, and one with no great sacrifice attached, but then so much blood had already been shed here, not much more could be needed. Kirstie dripped the contents of the little bowl onto the bottom of the stone and began muttering.

'Stones so old. Stones so wise. Stones so hard. Drink this moon. Drink this night. Drink this blood. Bound us safe. Bound us strong. Bound us hale.'

Then she raised the stone and let it drop back into its hollow.

My blood sang in my ears and I feared for my soul as Kirstie began to walk widdershins about the kirkyard. What would happen if this hellish circle were sealed with me inside it? Before she was able to complete her third circle, I leapt from the tree and gave a mighty roar. Kirstie jumped a foot in the air and her lantern smashed on the ground. She clutched her belly, and for a second it looked as though she might fall down dead. But she recovered herself quickly, no doubt abetted by her dark master.

'Bless me! John Sharpe! What do you think you're doing jumping out of trees in the dark? I nearly lost the bairn with fright.'

'Never mind what I'm about, Kirstie Slater! You were pouring your filthy womb blood onto stones and casting spells. I jumped out of the tree to prevent you opening the mouth of hell by walking widdershins about the kirkyard at midnight.'

Kirstie frowned at me. 'John, how can you say such a wicked thing? Are you feeling all right in yourself, laddie?' She gave a nervous laugh and put her hands to her belly. 'And what womb blood can you mean? You know full well I'm with child. And it's not anywhere near midnight – why, the sun went down barely an hour ago. I was only collecting elderberries to make cough linctus as I do every year. See down there, you've made me spill my baskets by giving me such a fright. Help me pick them up and then I'll walk you back to your uncle's house. You look feverish and in need of a lie down.'

Indeed, there were two spilt baskets of elderberries on the ground. But I shook my head, knowing full well what she'd said and done here tonight. I backed away from Kirstie and started running.

* * *

When I raced into Uncle's house, Nosewise leapt at me, his volley of barks almost as terrifying as what I'd witnessed in the kirkyard. Perhaps Uncle saw something in my face, for he snapped at Nosewise and the slobbering beast slunk under the table to rest his misshapen head on his great paws. And Uncle didn't chastise me for being out in the night – let alone on such an unholy night as this.

'Sit down, lad, you look lathered. Take a deep breath and try to explain what has put such a stricken expression on your face.'

After I told him, he stroked Nosewise's ears, for the dog had now flopped its brutish head onto Uncle's knee.

'Are you certain that you saw and heard what you report? It being dark, is it not possible the girl was just picking berries from around the kirk? Many favour the graveyard, as there are always bountiful crops there. Although it is a strange night to be out berrying. And Kirstie Slater has reason enough to watch her step in these parts as it is.'

'Uncle, I didn't dream it or make it up. I could see everything under the moon.'

Uncle sat quietly for a while, petting Nosewise. 'Well, this land hereabouts is fat with the blood of sacrifice, with ritual victims sleeping layer upon layer in the quiet earth, silently remembering the old ways through the deep soil. The locals say this rich earth means the flora hereabouts contains exceptional healing powers.' He paused for a moment. 'In the morning, John, you will take me to see this stone.'

* * *

In the morning, there was no sign of the flat stone, and it was clear from Uncle's face that he didn't believe me.

'Well, if you can't find the stone, John, go and stand where Kirstie stood.'

I stood in the place where she'd spent most of her time. 'About here, Uncle.' He didn't seem to hear me, so I raised my voice and shouted. 'About here, Uncle.'

'Very well, John, very well. So she was within arm's reach of the elder bushes. Now, if I put myself next to the oak tree, here …' He walked over to my tree and climbed inside, where his voice became muffled. Then he climbed out of the tree and walked back to me. 'Now, if I were inside the bole of the tree as you say you were, it would be very difficult to see or hear Kirstie.'

Tears pricked my eyes. Uncle thought me a romancer.

'Look, laddie, is it not possible that Kirstie was just gathering berries, and the moonlight and the excitement have turned it into something else in your mind?'

Tears dripped from my eyes. 'Uncle, there is no mistake. As God is my witness.'

Uncle's face softened then. 'Have no fear, John, for if there is truth in Kirstie Slater walking widdershins around the kirkyard with a misbegotten child in her belly, then that alone might be enough to put her to the flame. And God will look down on you kindly for doing His will.'

8

Jane

A Terrible Question

I turned from Mam to eye the glories on the market barrows. The hams and gutted rabbits were hung high, and chickens pecked in wooden crates. Gossip chittered through the air, seasoned here and there with a pinch of salt. My nose filled with savoury smells from broth bubbling over open fires and fowl roasting on spits. In the distance, cattle lowed, snorted and stamped. My mother was on a special errand today, so I tried to ignore the stacks of preserves. Besides, Mam's own pantry would more than see us through. Still, my mother clicked her tongue at the prices called by the market wife and shook her head.

'It's terrible what these rains have done to the harvests lately.'

The market wife rubbed her hands and stamped her feet. Her face was chafed, and I didn't envy her.

My mother paused at the woman's stall. 'A pot of berry preserve, please.'

'Bless you, Annie Chandler.'

This extravagance made me gape, but one look from Mam stopped me asking why she was paying for jam thinner than that at home. The market wife nodded her thanks and we moved on.

'Mam, what did you do that for?'

'Charity, Jane, charity.'

'But, Mam!'

'Whisht, lass, whisht.'

I frowned, but held my tongue while Mam passed the time with local women and stopped to trade snippets with the known and trusted. During these pauses, I hopped from foot to foot, trying to keep warm without earning Mam's displeasure. At the far side of the market, William and Walter Green ran past, a gangly puppy in their wake, and fog streaming from their mouths.

'Mam, can I–'

'No, Jane, not with those Green boys. There's always bother when that family's around. Stand still. I won't be a minute.'

But a minute on a cold morning felt more like an hour and it was unlikely that Mam would only be a minute. Even hopping from foot to foot couldn't stop my numb feet from spreading their chill up my legs. Chasing after the rosy-cheeked Green lads was sorely tempting, but I couldn't ask again.

A woman approached Mam. She was heavy with child, carried a babe in her arms and three small bairns toddled at her heels. She was gaunt and looked fit for falling down. She and Mam began speaking in low voices. They chattered at such speed that my head span, their voices like knitting needles clicking away, creating some new weave of a story. Just then, the Green boys collided with a barrow, upending it and setting turnips rolling. Lucky for them that the barrowman wasn't there and his nephew, Andrew Driver, was minding the barrow instead. Andrew waved his fists, but the boys and their pup scampered off. I closed my eyes and whispered thanks that they'd not upended the potter's barrow, or they'd have been flogged for sure. I tugged at my mother's arm.

'Mam, can I go and help Andrew? The Greens have upended his uncle's barrow.'

With a quick glance at the mess, Mam nodded, so I skipped over to the sprawl of turnips and began gathering them into my pinny.

'Good lass, Jane, good lass. Those little buggers'll come to a bad end if they don't watch themselves.'

'Is that right, Andrew?' I smiled at him and settled the turnips onto the barrow, before bending to gather more. The turnips looked withered, whiskery and far too soft. The ones at home weren't any better though.

'Aye, hinny, you might well wince at them. Another blight like the last one and us farmers will all be done for.'

It was funny when Andrew called me hinny. He was only a year older than me, but already deemed himself a grown man. I kept my head down and allowed myself another smile. When most of the turnips were returned to the barrow, Andrew offered me one.

'No, but thank you. Are you not hunting the day, Andrew? I thought you'd be away with Tom.'

He shook his head, which set his black curls dancing. 'No, I'm not as lucky as Tom.' He looked me up and down. 'More's the pity. Me da says I've to sell all these turnips for me uncle as he's bad with the ague. Look at them, though. I'm used to hoying better than these to our cattle.'

'Well, I hope your uncle is soon better, Andrew.' I rearranged the turnips, turning their wizened faces away so they couldn't be seen so well. 'It's not much better and most wives will squeeze them until the sun sets, but you have to try.'

'Thanks, Jane. The sooner I'm back out hunting, the happier I'll be. Can't have Tom Verger taking the best of everything, can I?'

He leered at me, and it made me take a step back from him. Tom was his oldest friend, but the look in Andrew's eye made me wonder now whether he truly liked Tom at all. I wanted to slip away back to my mother, but I couldn't think of a way to leave without seeming curt, so I changed the subject.

'By the way, how's your mother keeping, Andrew?'

'She's back to her old self. As soon as she started cuffing us all again, we knew she was better.' His smile slipped. 'She nearly wasn't, though, was she?'

I frowned, not really knowing what to say, and not wanting to mention the baby girl who'd died, so I contented myself with a small nod. Andrew touched my forearm and peered closely into my eyes.

'It's true, mind, if it wasn't for you Chandlers, we'd have no mother. Your mother is a blessing to have around the doors. And you.'

I scuffed my clog on the ground, trying to ignore the heat creeping up my face, and stooped to gather the rest of the turnips.

'Sorry to make you blush. Such a modest maid, eh? So, how's that old vicar of yours keeping?'

I gave a nervous laugh. 'You mean the Reverend? He's not mine and he's not old. He's not much older than Mam, really.'

A smile lit Andrew's eyes. 'Is that a fact? And you with no da—'

'I have got a da, Andrew Driver!' My eyes brimmed with tears, but I didn't want him to see them. 'My da was killed in the war. So he's dead. Right? He's dead. I wish I'd never bothered picking up your rotten turnips now.'

Andrew smirked. 'Oh, I see. And there was me and everyone else always thinking your mother was nothing more than the Reverend's common hearth woman and you no better than—'

At this, I let go of my pinny and the remaining turnips fell at his feet. I willed words to come to my mouth to deny this terrible slight. Mam told me my father died in the war and the Reverend took us in – my mother as his housekeeper and me as his charge. But I didn't know. I truly didn't know. And I couldn't ask anyone such a terrible question, because what if Andrew Driver was right? What then?

Before Andrew could speak again, I fled to the other side of the market, tears stinging my eyes. I kept my face down, but there was no need to hide as Mam and the woman were still going strong, voices lowered and heads close. Mam removed a small vial from her shawl and the pregnant woman tucked it into her own shawl before moving off. It happened in the winking of an eye and I wondered what the vial contained. Mam often gave these vials to women with big bellies. She'd always taught me everything she knew, but she'd never taught me the contents of these vials, or their properties.

Before I could ask the question, Mam hastened towards the haberdasher's barrow, which was my favourite stall, even if we rarely bought anything. I tucked my hands under my shawl, not so much to keep them warm as to stop myself tapping my mother's arm and asking her about my father and about the vial. When we reached the haberdasher's stall, he was busy serving a well-dressed lady. He pulled out the tiny drawers of his wooden travelling cabinet, which twinkled with shiny needles, pins, hooks, buckles, buttons, ribbons, lace and yarns. Normally, I would be entranced by these treasures, but I found myself staring into the distance. Andrew Driver had made me feel unhappy, and he'd tarnished my trip to the market.

'Come, Jane, you'll turn blue standing there. The haberdasher will be back again, and we might need to buy some bonny silks for Christmas.'

As we made our way home, my legs burnt on the steep hill, but it was a welcome pain as it warmed me a little and gave me courage. 'Mam, what did you give that woman with all the little bairns?'

'Nothing. I gave her nothing.'

'But, Ma-am.'

'But, nothing. Keep your eyes and your questions to yourself, or you'll cause heaven only knows what grief.'

Now Mam was rattled, so it was best not to push my luck. But what was in that vial?

* * *

The pantry got the afternoon light from the south-west, which made it perfect for drying herbs. There was a big mortar and pestle that we used to pound dry plants to dust and a wooden table that was scrubbed to within an inch of its life. An old chest held dozens of bottles, pots and jars. The brown bottles all looked the same, and it was a miracle that we could tell them apart. From the ceiling hung an airer, and from the airer hung bundles of drying herbs. Their smells fused together, and it was impossible to pull apart the different strands of scent to make out the individual plants. I looked up, checking that all were present. It was easy to identify them by sight because I'd been harvesting these plants from early childhood. There was feathery fennel for mother's milk. There was spiky rosemary for remembrance. There was hairy comfrey for knitting bones. There was heavenly lemon balm for bringing good cheer. There was silvery mugwort for the womb in all its phases. There was lavender for bringing sweet dreams to children and soothing mothers' tempers. It was used to clean and freshen, and it was the best herb of all, after fennel.

After I'd lowered the airer, removed the driest bunches and hoisted it back up, I rubbed the dry leaves and touched my fingers to my tongue. It always amazed me how the fragrance and flavour of each herb were so much intensified once they were in this dry and fragile state. Despite the fact that wet herbs came here to dry ten moons a year, it was a warm and dry room, heavily scented with a smell that always seemed the same, but which, in reality, turned with the seasons. The fresh smells of spring, of rising sap and delicate floral fragrances. Then summer, with its glut of bright colours and strong perfumes to entice the bees and other winged insects. Next, autumn, ripe with fruit, seeds and berries, bringing the warming and pungent smell of plenty. And finally, the produce from the astringent white months, when the sap fell in the trees and turned leaves brown, when nature went within herself, and we endured the time of bitter barks, hardened stalks and withered husks.

And so the great clock of the year wound itself throughout the seasons. Now that autumn was well under way, it was time to store the last sprigs of dried comfrey. The crock wasn't yet halfway full and we really needed more, for the villagers would find themselves in need of knitbone once the treacherous ice came. The next job was to strip the dried fennel flowers – this was the best plant and I inhaled the heavenly smell. Mothers' delight, since fennel tea could help bring on a late baby and it helped milk to flow. I ground the young willow leaves to the palest of green powder before pouring it into crocks and sealing them with wax. This was most valuable to the local women as it helped with the pains of childbirth and monthly menses, and it brought down milk fever. Even Reverend Foster would take a pinch or two when he'd been in his cups for too long.

When gathering willow leaves, I felt safe and protected under the rustling fronds. No matter how great these trees grew, they always made the effort to dip down to me. They were my favourite trees for dreaming under, and I was often found fast asleep beneath a willow. But one autumn, when I was smaller and without wit, Meg Wetherby found me underneath an elder tree. She woke me by digging her sharp fingers into the flesh of my arm, her face red with anger as she shook me awake.

'Lass, wake up! Wake up!'

'Ow! I'm awake, I'm awake.'

'Jane Chandler, promise me never to sleep beneath the elder tree again.'

I'd sat up, rubbing my eyes and yawning. 'Why on earth not, Meg?'

'Because the little folk will snatch you away. Oh, it'll look to all the world as though you're asleep, but really, you'll be away dancing yourself to death in the hall of the faerie queen.'

'Oh, but that sounds quite lovely, Meg.'

'It might seem lovely at first, dining on rose petals and dewdrops, but once the dance starts, it can never stop, for the faerie queen is an angry queen and it doesn't do to displease her. And you'd never see your Mam, nor Cuthbert, nor Tom again.'

At this, I bit my lip. The treasures of the faerie queen sounded like hollow and brittle fancies compared to the warm smells and sounds of home.

'I promise, Meg. From now on, I'll only sleep under the willow.'

'Hinny, you can have your pick of the trees, just leave the elder to her own devices and she'll leave you to yours. They call her the witch tree because only something wicked inside could spawn such dark berries.'

I smiled then, my terror forgotten. 'Oh, Meg, how can you say that when your own mouth is stained by elderberry juice?'

'I never said the fruit wasn't delicious. But stick to picking berries from the hedgerows. Leave these old trees to Meg.'

But even back then, I knew that the wilder and older the trees, the better the berries, so they were still my favourite picking trees.

9

John

Under Oath

The justice leaned over his bench. 'Is this true, Kirstie Slater? Did you walk three times widdershins around the graveyard on All Hallows' Eve?'

Kirstie opened her mouth, but nothing came out.

'Answer me, girl, for it is a simple question. But let me make it easier. On All Hallows' Eve, were you near the kirk?'

Kirstie swallowed. 'Yes, sire.'

The clerk scribbled a long time for someone recording only two words.

The justice continued. 'And might you have walked around the kirkyard?'

'Yes, but–'

'A simple yes will suffice. How many times did you walk around the kirkyard?'

Kirstie shut her eyes and counted on her fingers. Perhaps the numbers wouldn't stand still in her head long enough to be counted, requiring the use of her digits also.

'Well, Kirstie?'

She peeped at Ethel Murray. 'I don't know, sire.'

The justice frowned at the mendacious maid. 'Was it more than once? For instance, did you pass the kirk door?'

'Sire, I'm trying to recall walking around the kirkyard. Being under oath, I don't want to err and risk my immortal soul.'

Kirstie glanced at her father, who nodded. No doubt, the miraculously recovered man had counselled his daughter to be chary with her answers. Chary so that the justice couldn't give her words another meaning and chary so that she didn't imperil her soul. But justice would be served – of that, I was certain.

'How many times, Kirstie Slater, how many times?'

'More than once, sire.'

'More than once.' The justice held out a finger and then thrust out a second. 'So, at least twice.' He thrust out a third finger and tapped each finger in turn. 'Perhaps thrice? Think carefully, Kirstie Slater, for you are under oath. Did you pass around a third time?'

Kirstie pressed her hands over her eyes. 'Really, I … I can't be certain, sire.'

'You're certain that it was twice. Yet, you can't be certain that it wasn't thrice.' The justice consulted a scroll. 'Fortunately for us, John Sharpe watched you make three turns around the kirkyard. When he made himself known to you, he said that you "jumped a foot in the air". Do you recollect this?'

Kirstie blinked. 'I was surprised by little John Sharpe, but …'

Little John Sharpe, indeed. I opened my mouth to object, but Uncle James pressed his hand on my knee and gave me a stern look, which closed it.

'And did you jump in the air, Kirstie?'

'Well, not a foot in the air, sire, but he gave me a start, leaping out from the tree.'

'The reason John Sharpe was able to surprise you is that you were passing the wrong side of the oak. I put it to you, Kirstie Slater, that you were walking widdershins around the graveyard – on hallowed land. How say you to that charge?'

'No! I was only gathering elderberries.'

The justice smiled. 'Really? But your whole village is thick with elderberries, so why venture to the graveyard?'

Kirstie's chin quivered. Her own words were tying her in knots. It might go better for her if she remained silent. But she kept her eyes on her father, took a faltering breath and continued. 'Because those berries are the biggest.'

'So, you went hunting for berries from the witch tree? Not just any berries, but those growing lush in the graveyard, made fat by the flesh of innocent souls resting in sanctified ground. Not content with this macabre harvest, you walked widdershins three times around the kirkyard. To what end?'

Kirstie's shoulders heaved. 'I ... just that I wanted the juiciest berries for cough bottles. There's a hard winter coming that will clog many chests.'

'You were gathering witch berries to make a curative linctus? Not content to accept God's will, you determine to interfere with His intent by creating and administering your foul brew to innocents?'

Kirstie's father closed his eyes and moved his lips. Was he praying for her? Or making a charm against me?

The justice glared at the accused. 'Girl, attend when I speak!'

She flinched and then murmured her apologies.

'Kirstie, how are you so certain that a bad winter is coming?'

'Well, sire, because I read the signs and they tell me what to expect.'

'You "read the signs". What signs are these? Might anyone read them?'

'Yes, sire, anyone with a mind to.'

'I see. Please furnish me with instances of these signs.'

I sat up. So many examples to give. Which might save and which condemn?

Kirstie pleated her shift between her fingers. 'Well, sire, the holly trees are bending under the weight of berries, the onions have put on their warm coats, the squirrels are nesting low and the cows' necks have thickened. All these are sure signs of a hard winter coming.'

Kirstie tried to catch the eye of her neighbouring farmers. If she hoped one would nod in recognition, she was sorely mistaken, as none would meet her eye. Findlay examined the toe of his boot and Reid gazed past her. Uncle James shifted in his seat, and I heard him utter a soft prayer.

'So, you look to flora and fauna for signs to predict something that only God should know?' The red in the justice's eye had swallowed much of the blue and his eyes blazed. 'So that you can interfere with His mighty plan?'

Despite the cold room and Kirstie's scant shift, sweat trickled down her face. A definite indication of guilt.

'No, please, sire! You make it sound worse than it is. Everyone keeps an eye out for signs to prepare for what's coming. Just as dandelion seeds aflying when there's no wind is a sure sign of rain coming.'

Kirstie looked to the women. She could expect nothing from Ethel Murray, but Goodwives Findlay and Reid should be grateful to her. Would they come to her aid? Would she remind them of help given and gratefully received? These weak and foolish women had fallen prey to Kirstie's interference in God's will, but she was on trial, not them.

'Kirstie Slater, I put it to you that you were picking bewitched fruits made gross by the blood of the dead in an effort to commune with the devil, there to gain illicit knowledge to concoct your foul wares.'

The justice pointed at Kirstie, and she trembled before his unwavering stare.

'I put it to you that you are a diabolical dabbler, interfering in God's great work. I put it to you that by walking widdershins three times around the kirkyard, you were opening up a hole into hell, so that the evil one might make his approach and lie with you, to fill your belly with imps.'

At this, the justice slammed his hand on the bench, making Kirstie flinch. It even made Uncle James sit up, and he had God on his side.

'I put it to you that you are both witch and willing servant to Satan. That you give him suck and in return he gives you arcane knowledge.'

A smile crept across Ethel Murray's face, though she'd little to smile about.

The justice looked around. 'We've heard the charges, so will anyone now speak for the accused?'

The room was full of people Kirstie had grown up with. But none would look at her. There were only blank eyes. Perhaps the imps in her stomach were turning since she started panting as if to keep them down. Eventually, her breathing slowed and she stole another glance at Ethel Murray. There was an expression on the older woman's face, but what was it? Satisfaction. She looked satisfied.

Kirstie's father pushed his way forward. 'Sire! I'll speak for Kirstie.'

'What? You will speak for your own progeny?' The justice sniffed. 'You may have bias, but since none other will speak, pray continue.'

Kirstie's father straightened his jerkin. 'My daughter is no witch. What has passed today is madness.'

The justice frowned. 'Beware, man, of slandering these decent people.'

Slater continued in a voice so low that even the justice was forced to lean forward to catch his words. This surely wasn't his everyday speaking voice. Perhaps he was also a witch and this was the voice he kept for voicing his private incantations. I would raise this question with Uncle James later and seek his opinion.

'Kirstie was gathering berries to prepare syrups, something she's done every autumn since she could walk. These syrups restore the humours of sickly children, and keep men working and feeding their families throughout winter. Is there anyone here who has not sought help from Kirstie or her late mother, God rest her?'

He looked at Findlay, Reid and Smith. After considerable shuffling and mumbling, there were a few nods. Then Slater turned to Ethel Murray.

'You there, Goodwife Murray. Have you not sought help from Kirstie?'

'I am Widow Murray, thanks to your haggish daughter. I've sought nothing from her. And you'll not use your clever words to despoil this court's purpose. Your young vixen bewitched my Arthur out of his wits, so she could steal him.'

Kirstie drained of colour, and she pressed her hands to her belly.

Slater continued. 'But Widow Murray, Kirstie is but a maid, and a wronged maid at that.'

'A maid who bewitched my Arthur into coupling—'

Slater's voice rose. 'And now she carries that terrible man's child!'

Ethel threw up her arms. 'As I am a devout and healthy Christian woman who did my wifely duty as often as God required it, were there to be any issue from my husband, I should have been the one to bear it. Your she-devil carries the demon's seed and not my Arthur's child!'

Kirstie's father dipped his head. 'May God have mercy.'

But Ethel Murray hadn't finished. 'The Slaters are a hex on this village. Our crops have failed, the beasts have lamed, and we've gone from a prosperous farm to one withering. Once she's gone, the curse will lift and our goodness will return. It's not right that she stalks the town with a bellyful of imps when it's clear that she should have swung and not my Arthur.'

Slater shook his head. 'Widow Murray, your husband was found guilty and hanged accordingly.'

Ethel Murray pointed at Kirstie. 'This spiteful slattern took my husband's goodness, and with it, my happiness.'

Kirstie put her hand over her mouth as if she were the wronged party, when Ethel Murray's man had swung for the sake of Kirstie's fiendish desires.

But Slater was not done. 'Sire, we must see sense. The country has been under deluge in years past, and crops have failed in successive summers. This tragedy may be due to God's displeasure, plain misfortune, or the whim of the weather. But it's not due to my daughter picking berries. Kirstie seeks only to help others.'

He paused and stared at Ethel Murray. 'Widow Murray, did you not seek powders from Kirstie last spring? Didn't Kirstie's poultice draw the poison from your eye? Didn't my girl save your sight? Without her ministrations, might you not be half-blind?'

Ethel put her hand to her left eye and her face reddened. People were nodding and murmuring. The justice knocked his gavel against the sounding block. The loud bang sobered the crowd and returned them to silence.

'Slater makes a strong case, although it goes badly for him that he's revealed the travails of the Widow Murray to do so. But his girl has still confessed to behaviour of a most suspicious nature—'

Slater interrupted the justice. 'Sire, there's no witching in Kirstie. She's done only kind works in this village, providing remedies for those who can't afford the barber-surgeon. All present must have short memories. Without Kirstie, those unable to pay MacBain would go without any help. How many would be sitting here today without the ministrations of Kirstie?'

He paused, putting his eye on various members of the courtroom.

'How many of you have Kirstie or her late mother to thank for delivering your children, saving your lives and easing your pains when you lacked the coin to pay? Yes, you might well hang your heads. Findlay, you'll recall your goodwife recently giving birth, when mother and child were both spared thanks to Kirstie's intervention. Reid, was not your ague relieved by Kirstie? And you, Smith, when you turned yellow with your own bile, did Kirstie not set you back in your right humour?'

Was that a smile playing on the witch's lips as she watched the grudging nods of agreement? Perhaps Slater possessed juicier ailments, which he'd reveal to save his daughter. For the first time, I worried that he might turn the justice's mind.

Slater continued to eye the crowd. 'It's useful to jog the old memory, is it not? How many of you here today–?'

But the justice banged his gavel again. 'Enough! That is enough, Slater. You've made your points and you've made them well. A case has been made that Kirstie Slater is no witch, but merely a cunning woman keeping her neighbours hale. But that can't be an end to it. We must have proof absolute that she is no witch. Your testament will not suffice without physical evidence. We'll fetch the barber-surgeon since he's well versed in testing witches.'

Kirstie's father frowned. 'MacBain? In this weather? The big sawbones will not like being drawn from his fire. He's as honest as a bereaved dog, but energetic he is not. If he's not lying down, he's hugging the fire and dreaming of lying down. Yet, my girl's life hangs on the man's abilities.'

'Enough, man! MacBain is the best man for the job. We can trust his judgement. This hearing is adjourned until the barber-surgeon reaches us.'

* * *

At the reopening of the trial, Slater and a bailie were stationed at the door, peering through the window, waiting for the barber-surgeon. I was back in my seat, with Uncle James at my side.

The bailie grinned at Slater. 'Here comes MacBain, picking his way down the path, as delicately as a thin-boned bride. Clearly, a man who doesn't want to miss pricking a maid because of a snapped neck. And there's his vast bag, no doubt filled with dreadful implements that even the devil would blush to use.'

Slater turned a grim stare on the man.

But still the bailie babbled. 'No doubt the usual selection of pincers, clysters and flenching knives.'

Slater put his hand on the bailie's shoulder and squeezed his bones until the man continued in a less excitable manner.

'Although there's no relish in MacBain for the job. It's not a task he takes lightly, I hear, and that may go well for your Kirstie.'

Slater looked at his daughter. 'I pray you're right. For there are stories of wicked men who take pleasure in pricking maids and sending them to the flames.'

The bailie shrugged. 'Doesn't bear thinking about. Though better that than a witch roaming free.'

Slater looked ready to strike the bailie, but a sergeant lifted his club, which settled him. The two men turned to watch MacBain's progress down the slippery path.

Uncle James turned to whisper in my ear. 'This pricking business is worrying, much more worrying than Slater's words. MacBain is a just man. Misguided, of course, but just. Even though Slater paints him as a man who wouldn't act unless there's coin to be paid, I know he's given poppy milk to many when they were weak with pain from canker – coin or no coin. Plenty here will take heed of him.'

Before I could reply, the door opened and a blast of rain entered the room, followed by MacBain stamping mud from his feet. Slater took his wet cloak. Kirstie looked at MacBain, but he didn't smile at her. This cheered me. The barber-surgeon nodded to the justice and to Uncle James, and then crossed the room, leaving footprints in his wake. He placed his bag on the table before beckoning Kirstie and taking her hands.

'Kirstie, lie on this table, and we'll make this as swift as God permits.'

While MacBain blew onto his cold hands, Kirstie was lifted onto the table by two sergeants. The barber-surgeon turned Kirstie this way and that, gently lifting sections of her shift, moving the garment one way, then the other, before turning her onto her front and repeating the procedure. He was modest and shielded the girl with his own body, careful not to reveal her form to voracious onlookers since she must be naked as venison beneath her shift. After MacBain examined Kirstie, he straightened her shift and cleared his throat before addressing the bench.

'Sire, after a thorough search, I conclude there is no third teat, or anything untoward on this maid that would give suck to the devil, or to his imps.'

A flicker of disappointment crossed the justice's face. 'If you're certain, MacBain?

'Quite certain, sire. The devil's mark is well known to me.'

Uncle James spoke up then. 'Continue with the pricking, MacBain. The devil may have left his stain invisible about her person.'

The justice flushed, but he was not about to argue with a man of God. 'You heard the pastor, MacBain, he knows of what he speaks. You may continue.'

The barber-surgeon inhaled deeply and then he turned to his bag and removed a blade. He nodded to the sergeants, who held Kirstie down.

'I'm sorry for this, lassie, but it'll be over soon.'

She closed her eyes. MacBain raised Kirstie's shift to her thigh at the side furthest away from the crowd and forced the blade into her. She screamed and a gout of blood spurted from her leg. This was a disaster. What trickery was afoot?

The barber-surgeon began to dress the wound he'd made. 'Sire, this maid has no third teat. She screamed and bled copiously upon being pricked. Therefore, she can't be a witch, or a consort of the devil.'

I was tempted to interject, but the justice stood up.

'MacBain, it is for the justice to pronounce guilt or not, it is not a job for a mere barber-surgeon.'

71

MacBain tightened the dressing. 'Surely, sire, it is for the justice to consider all the available evidence before pronouncing guilt or not.'

'Silence, MacBain! Do you hold my position in such contempt? Prick her again. Or I'll find another who is willing and perhaps more capable.'

Kirstie was forced backward onto the table once more, her arms pinioned. Her leg still oozed the treacherous blood. She was pale in the face, no doubt hoping to fall into blackness at any second, so her dark master could save her. But no, she was staying with the light, and her eyes were wide open.

The barber-surgeon closed his eyes for a heartbeat – perhaps he was praying for her. He stuck Kirstie in her arm, but this time the blade didn't go so deep. Even so, she made sure to jerk mightily and to shriek, and she'd surely prayed to Satan to make her blood run free again, as blood trickled from her arm and pooled on the table. There was not so much blood this time, but it was blood all the same. MacBain made to dress the wound on her arm, until the justice interrupted him.

'Again, MacBain! Prick her again. She has four limbs, does she not?'

'Sire, I've pricked this girl left and right, arm and leg, and she's bled a great deal. I can't find a spot on her that will not bleed. I'll kill her if I continue.'

I leapt up. 'Pure trickery! The witch has found a way to outwit MacBain.'

The justice sighed. 'Sit down, John Sharpe. Pastor, control your charge, and we'll get to him in turn.'

Uncle turned a cold eye on me. I had displeased him with my outburst, so I shrank down in my seat.

Slater stepped forward, still clutching the barber-surgeon's cloak. 'The sawbones has pricked Kirstie – she's half dead through bleeding – and before witnesses. Plenty of witnesses, who can vouch that my girl bled red and true from two wounds on the opposite quarters of her body.'

The justice looked from Slater and then to MacBain. 'Very well. We shall say no more. MacBain, continue dressing the girl's wounds while I consider my verdict.'

MacBain bound her wounds tight. He'd cut her left arm. Was it because that was the devil's own side? Or, did he spare her right arm so she could continue to work? It would pay to watch this man. When MacBain was finished, he helped Kirstie down from the table and held out his hand for his cloak. Slater helped him into it.

'Get her home, Slater, and keep her warm, for the terror of the proceedings and the cold will be more likely to kill her than any knife, especially given her frail condition. And get her away from here. Ethel Murray, John Sharpe and the pastor will see your Kirstie burnt one way or another.'

MacBain's comments made my uncle bristle. 'The impertinent man. He cares not a whit whether I heard him or not! He is perhaps a man who warrants further investigation himself.'

The barber-surgeon left as the justice got to his feet. He tapped his gavel, and all eyes turned from Kirstie to the justice. My heart raced. Would the witch be cast from this world, or would she be set free to devour yet more souls?

'I have reached a decision on whether Kirstie Slater is a witch and consorter of the devil.' He paused and looked at me. 'The case against Kirstie Slater is found not proven on both counts.'

I couldn't take in this revelation. The justice claimed Kirstie Slater wasn't guilty. By the looks of her, the witch's humours were fully restored now that she'd cheated the flames. I dared not turn to look at Uncle James. But I'd see my day with her and her kindred, and then Uncle would be proud of me.

The justice stood up. 'Let everyone here present note that questions remain about Kirstie Slater's behaviour. It ill behoves her to come before me again, as she may face a less lenient judgment next time. But on this day, she may go free.'

Kirstie put her head down, no doubt fearing the justice would alter his decision.

Uncle clasped my shoulder. 'Let this be a lesson to you, John, about how fickle people are, that they call for a girl's neck one minute, and allow her freedom the next, their humour changed only by a few words uttered by one man or another.'

I nodded, weighing his words carefully. This is something he wanted me to watch out for in future trials – men with worthy intentions, but with too many clever words in their mouths.

Part Two

10

Jane

Time of the Moon

My first bleeding caused me to double up. Mam nodded and beckoned me away from the fire.

'Oh, Jane. Come here, pet.' She took a wooden box from behind the curtain and opened it. Inside, were clean pieces of rag. 'You've started to bleed, just like I told you. These rags'll soak it up a bit. Change them once they fill. And once they're soiled, soak them, scrub them and air them before they go back in the box, otherwise you'll end up sore, or you'll have dogs following you.'

The pain sickened me, so I could only nod while I clutched my stomach.

Mam peered outside. 'Nearly the full moon, so that's your moon time, same as when you were born. You're to let no lad or man near you. Especially at the dead moon. Do you mind me?'

'Yes, Mam.' She didn't need to tell me as we'd both seen the end result too many times.

'Men aren't all polite and some will take what they want if they think they'll get away with it. And some even if they know they'll swing for it. Look, get away to bed with you. I'll warm up a stone and fetch it to you. It doesn't get any easier, but you'll get more used to it as time wears on.'

I mutely accepted the wooden box and made my way to bed. This wasn't the box Mam used – that came and went often enough as the moon grew fat and then died. Mam must have prepared this gift in readiness. She must have been watching me. I'd noted my own budding breasts, swelling hips and narrowing waist, the troubled complexion and a sharpening in both odour and temper. So Mam must have noticed the very same.

The rags were clean now, but they would soon stain and never be this clean again. Tears slid down my cheek in mourning for the childhood that must be put away. This was my entrance to the world of women. A mixed blessing of the magical, the mysterious and the meanness. This baptism in blood would only lead to more, as blood was begot by blood. So many girls and women died when birthing and soon after. It was cruel work being a woman. But still better than being a man, who could be sent to war.

* * *

I was at the window, watching Bill and Tom Verger carrying shrouded forms to the crypt door. It was grey outside and it was hard to tell whether it was day or night. There was just enough light to see them pick their way through the graveyard, but just enough darkness to make it hard to see exactly what they were doing.

'Jane, get away from that window. You're letting all the cold in. And put that curtain back down.'

'Mam, what are Bill and Tom Verger doing out there?'

'You know full well that they're doing God's work, Jane, so stop gawking and help me make supper.'

But my mind continued working, even as I peeled and chopped roots for the pot, hoping there would be bacon to add.

'Shall I add split peas and barley, Mam?'

'Yes, you do that, and I'll go to the larder.'

My mouth watered. Split peas always meant ham. There was a hock in the larder, and I was already imagining a salty supper. Mam placed the hock on the table with a dull thud.

'You'll have no luck cutting that, Jane. It's so cold, it's near frozen. Let it soften before you try. Here, add some extra roots to the stew and we'll get a few days out of it. And fetch some sage and onions from the pantry. No salt though, as there should be plenty on him already.'

'Oh, Mam, don't refer to our meat as "him". I know where it's come from, but I prefer to separate the poor soul who lived in the pen all year from the tasty meat this hock will make.'

But Mam only laughed. 'Oh, Jane, you'd soon enough take a bite from a living pig if you were to go without meat for more than your six weeks of Lent!'

Head hanging, I went to the pantry. Mam was right. My favourite day of the whole year was Easter Sunday, when we'd have crisp and fatty lamb, brushed all over with salt and rosemary. My mouth began to water anew at the imaginary smell of lamb and rosemary roasting over the fire, with the fat crackling and sizzling when it hit the flames.

In the pantry, I first cut a pair of onions from the string along the wall. Their fragile skins reminded me of Bible paper. Then I opened a crock and took out some sage. It was so dry that it would crumble easily between my fingers and it would most likely turn to dust on the journey back to the kitchen.

Back in the warmth of the kitchen, I crumbled the sage into the bubbling pot, then peeled and chopped the onions. My eyes stung and tears rolled down my face. Wiping them with my elbows only made them worse.

Mam pursed her lips. 'How many times, Jane? Make sure the knife's sharp, and try whistling while you work so you don't cry.'

I smiled through my tears. 'But I enjoy it, Mam, since a good keen makes me feel better, even if I'm not sad.'

'You're a queer girl sometimes, Jane. Now, if you can manage here, I'm going to see to the church for an hour or so.'

When Mam left, I threw the chopped onions and roots into the pot over the fire. Even though there was no meat in the stew, it gave off a savoury scent and my stomach rumbled. It was hard to look at the hock of ham without seeing it for the leg it was. When I pressed my fingers into the cold flesh, it was still stiff, with very little give. My fingers didn't even leave an impression. It was tempting to move it nearer to the fire, but it could spoil and then there'd be no meat.

The stew could mind itself for a while and the hock wasn't going anywhere anymore, so I crept back to the window to see if Bill and Tom were back. A little breath of cold air chilled me when I lifted the curtain, cold coming in waves from the glass. It was too cold even for snow. Through the murk, it was just possible to see Bill and Tom come out of the crypt door, closing it behind them. This was the only time Tom didn't wear his big grin, when he was doing his duties for the departed. If he would only smile, though, and make the dimples wink in his cheeks and the crinkles appear around his green eyes.

The door opened then, letting a blast of winter air in, and Reverend Foster appeared, closely followed by my mother and Meg Wetherby. Reverend Foster rubbed his hands together, reminding me again of Bible paper.

'Enough tittle-tattle, Annie, I've a sermon to deliver. But first, let's have some warming sustenance.'

Meg headed straight for the hearth cracket, 'Aye, Reverend, sometimes the Lord's work needs hell's furnace under it, eh?'

Mam sniffed. 'I'll thank you not to compare my hearth to hell's furnace, Meg Wetherby. But the stew is nearly ready so you'll be staying, I take it?'

Meg's face cracked into a smile. 'No harm meant. You should know my bad ways and words by now. Just take your time, Annie, take your time. Now, Jane, come and have a look in my sack.'

I left my station at the window and went to join Meg at the fire. 'Hello, Meg, what have you got?'

'Well, since it's the eve of Twelfth Night, I've brought some candles to sell for the wassailing, see.'

Meg opened the sack and a dank smell wafted out. My nose wrinkled at the smell of the candles. These weren't the pleasant candles that Mam loved to light in church – those candles were made of beeswax and were too precious for every day.

Mam looked inside the sack and took a step back. 'Meg, these candles are nasty tallow. Have you no beeswax? Even without them being lit, they give off an unsettling smell of rotting flesh, which turns my stomach.'

I peeped into the sack. They were ugly candles, varying in shade from light brown to night black.

Meg turned from the fire. 'Oh, give over and don't be so fussy, Annie. The light from these beauties is just as bright as anything from your fancy church candles.'

Reverend Foster's voice came from his corner. 'Sincerely, madam, I doubt that very much. Filthy, smoking stems from that heinous butchery in the town, no doubt. Although, as is so often the case with you, Meg, it's perhaps wiser not to ask.'

'No, Reverend, you're right, they're from the tallower in Newcastle.'

'Then a murkier provenance these lights could not have.'

Meg ignored him and turned to me. 'Come, hinny, help me up from this cracket before these candles melt. We'll settle at the table and busy ourselves awhile.'

She emptied her sack onto the table and then produced a pouch full of iron nails. 'These are only feeble nails, Jane, useless for mending a roof or the like. But useful for keeping away evil spirits and waking people up. See, we'll press them into the candles a little way apart from each other, like this.'

Reverend Foster passed the table. 'Be careful, Jane, lest your warm hands revive the fat back to something animated, albeit most foul. You'll have the vile stink of death on your hands, as surely as if you'd plunged them into a beast's corpse.'

I shuddered and lifted my hands away from the candles.

Meg turned from her work. 'Give over, Reverend, and stop trying to work the girl into a state. The wind will change soon and you can't bless bairns with that face.'

Meg's pertness made me giggle, and the Reverend's face was twisting with the effort of not smiling.

'Don't speak to me of faces, crone.'

I blinked. 'Reverend Foster, you mustn't call Meg a crone!'

'Meg knows I mean her no harm. Look at you, content as a fish, having Meg and Annie at your side. Maiden. Mother. Crone. Twas ever thus. Together you form a trinity – not entirely holy and not entirely unholy – but a trinity, nonetheless.'

It was hard to understand the Reverend's meaning. Perhaps he'd taken too much of his special medicinal compound. Whenever he did, he got funny ideas. I rooted in Meg's sack and pulled out another candle, crude, discoloured and misshapen.

Then I pierced its length with nails, shoving them in with my thumbs.

Reverend Foster wrinkled his nose at me. 'It's an effort not to vomit at the sight of such ungodly creations.'

But I glared at him. 'See, Reverend, this nail is for when it's time for my bed. And this one is for Mam.' I moved my finger along an inch to the next nail. 'And this one is for your bed.'

Hands behind his back, he leaned forward to inspect my handiwork. 'And what of these nails, Jane? Why, then, the very long gap after my bed?'

'That's so you can wake up in the morning, Reverend. The candle burns down, the nail falls out, you hear it clatter and then you wake up.'

'Very clever, but who has money to waste by leaving a light on all night? And who could bear the hellish stench from such a candle in their chamber while attempting sleep? Lying there unguarded, the dreadful miasma would surely inflict itself upon a passive soul as it lay in repose.'

Not all of his words made sense, but a tear wavered in my eye as suddenly as if he'd cut open an onion in front of my face.

Mam clicked her tongue. 'Reverend, that was hateful of you. Sometimes, you'd do better to keep your own counsel. And perhaps no more to drink today.'

I wiped my eye and looked to Mam. 'Can we afford candles like these to wake us up?'

She shrugged. 'Not us. When we go out, so does the light. And we rely on Sir Jack to wake us up.'

The Reverend laughed. 'Yes, good old Sir Jack. The scoundrel in charge of this neck of the woods. And also impudently – perhaps dangerously – the scoundrel in charge of the hen house. Pompous old cocks both.'

'Reverend, please!' Mam was red in the face.

I turned back to Meg. 'Who does need these candles to wake them up?'

'Well, those who don't keep cocks, or live near one.'

I thought about Meg's words. 'But that must be no one near here. Sir Jack can be heard as far as Shotley Bridge.'

'Aye, hinny, but everyone needs iron nails to scare away dark spirits. So there's my market. Now, you should always keep a handful of iron nails handy, because you never know.'

I returned my completed candle to the pile next to Meg. Some were packed with many nails, others with only a few.

Meg sorted the candles into two separate piles. 'There, you see. Large families and small. All sizes provided for, providing they can bear the cost.'

Reverend Foster winked at me. 'Have no worries about who will bear the cost, Jane, since Meg has a certain way with words. People often find themselves charmed into parting with money, produce or belongings they can ill afford.'

Mam placed a bowl of stew in front of the Reverend. 'There's no meat in it and there won't be any, so don't waste your breath complaining. Besides, you're forgetting what people really want to buy from Meg.'

The old woman grinned then. 'Aye, for I hold something else, something desired by the high and the low alike.'

I frowned at the riddle. 'What do you have, Meg, aside from candles and cats?'

'My old woman's almanac for the coming year, carried about in my head, and snippets passed on for small favours and considerations crossing my palm.

'What's an almanac, Meg?'

Mam put a bowl of stew in front of me. 'Jane, Meg knows just when to plant and when to reap, and all the farmers and good-wives value her advice. Eat your supper and get to sleep early, for the morrow, there'll be wassailing to keep you from your bed.'

11

John

Foul Temptress

A hush fell over the kirk as men waited to hear Uncle James speak. I stood at the front, still and quiet. The kirk was always full when he spoke, perhaps because his speaking turned so quickly into ceaseless ranting. I wondered at the fires that must burn inside my uncle to keep him going. This public preaching man was not the same man who'd shared his hearth with me for so many years. There were scores of men here. I was of a height with many of them nowadays and it pleased me. Uncle stood up to speak, no doubt readying to aim his words at me as he so often did. He'd been kind to me over the years and had never once raised hand or foot to me. All the same, the twists and turns of his mind troubled me. My stomach roiled at the thought of what was coming. While Uncle James had shown his love by putting a much-needed roof over my head, he also liked to punish me for my failings. And he did not shy away from revealing them in public. Although it was sinful to think it, I looked forward to returning to my own home and my wife, and away from his jibing tongue and low opinion of me.

'Today, I'll speak of women and the dangers they bring. It will be hard for you to stomach, because you will be thinking of your own wives, daughters and mothers. But it's important that you see them as they really are. Shaming it is that boys and girls are born in equal number. For daughters are of little use, yet still require food and shelter. Even the lowly, cloven-hooved females are more useful in the giving of their milk, their hide and their flesh.'

Uncle paused, but only for effect, and he soon continued.

'God wishes mankind to multiply and so the lower sex is necessary to his future survival. It's a conundrum, and I'm not one to question God's judgement. But these daughters of Eve are formed from sin, there to tempt decent men from God and labour. And however foul their temptations, we allow them to move freely amongst us, to work and even to worship. Beyond their usefulness in procreation, their purpose confounds me.'

Uncle James wagged his finger at the assembled men and paced before them. The very word 'procreation' made my heart sink, since it was plain to me what direction his words would take.

'Being such physical creatures, women are much closer to the earthly world and to the devil. Women's small brains mean they can't be blamed for obeying their nature, as they are little more than beasts of burden. But I warn every man here to be on his guard against the dread darkness inside every woman. They will create a fire in your loins that should rightly be used only to create God's children.'

Uncle's eye rested on me. Against my will, I looked down. This was akin to a confession of using my wife without creating any children. If only Uncle wouldn't put so much emphasis on women just being there to make children. I felt he was judging me, as I'd not yet managed to get a child on my wife. Uncle would often comment on Lucy's flat belly, and it slighted my manhood every time he raised the matter. Was Lucy filled with darkness? Was she not, after all, the respectable and plain blessing from God that I deserved? Soon, I would have a child of my own, and Uncle James might then shift his sermons away from the difficult subject of procreation and childbirth. Finally, he shifted his gaze to another unfortunate member of the congregation.

'First of all, let me clarify women's role on earth. A woman is here to serve a man as his helpmeet, to act as the receptacle to receive his sacred seed and to nurture his child until it is ready to enter the world of men.'

It pained me to think of my own mother described only as a receptacle for seed, sacred or otherwise. But men around me were nodding and grunting assent. And then I thought again of Lucy, who had failed to provide me with an heir. Whose fault was that? It certainly could not be mine, as I feared God and did my Christian duty. Perhaps it would do to examine Lucy's habits more closely, to be certain that she was not interfering in God's will. It was hard not to feel a grain of resentment towards her, whether she was thwarting my efforts deliberately, or just through lack of care. If Uncle said that it was her role in life to receive my seed and grow a child, then I must do everything in my power to make sure she fulfilled her duty to God. And it would perhaps persuade Uncle to focus his sermonising elsewhere.

'Since women are only here to deal with the more carnal aspects of extending God's family, they are connected to the hidden, the sinful and the maligned. It pleases me, as it pleases the Lord, to hear the creatures' guttural screams in the pain of childbirth. Through this pain, each daughter of Eve comes to know that she was born in sin, and that she will pay for that sin in perpetuity. Yet, this pain is still not enough to punish that foul temptress whose fault it is that mankind was turned out of paradise to live meanly outside of Eden.'

Uncle's words troubled me when I held them up against the memory of my mother. He couldn't mean my mother, who was his own sister. He must mean other women – unworthy women. I reached for the milk teeth in my pouch and rubbed them. If I held his words up against unworthy women like Kirstie Slater, then they seemed more fitting. The justice said Kirstie was not guilty of being a witch. But certainly, that hussy once lured an honest man into coupling outside of wedlock. Did all women have this power in them, handed down from Eve, to tempt innocent men into evil? Arthur Murray paid dearly for a weakness of the flesh, which had been excited by Kirstie Slater. Did all women have something of the witch about them? I was certain there was no badness in my mother. I was less certain when it came to Lucy, whose inability to get a child was the bane of my life of late. After all, my mother had managed to give birth to a child, and she had fulfilled her duty, even though it cost her life. A shaft of light came in through a high window and distracted me from my thoughts. The light must have dazzled Uncle, but he didn't shield his eyes or turn his head, and still the words tumbled from him.

'But do women seek redemption through their necessary suffering? No, they do not! These sin-ridden creatures seek only to reduce the richly deserved agonies of childbirth. Their midwives ply them with unguents and charms to lessen their pain. It's nothing short of evil to deprive women of the vital lesson of their birthing pains. And even more evil is afoot when these haggish midwives intervene to prevent the Lord from taking His chosen ones to Him.'

There was so little air, it was hard to remain upright and I shifted my weight. Others in the room were also restless, so my uncle must cease before long. The lack of air made it even harder to work out the rights and wrongs of what my uncle was saying. Dora Shaw hadn't managed to prevent my own mother being taken to the Lord. Of course, it pleased me that God had chosen her, but I still felt sad that she was taken from me, leaving me to face the world alone. It worried me that the Lord might also take Lucy. My wife was not yet with child, but it must happen soon and when it did, I'd secretly pray that she not be taken from me, for I would need her to raise the child. My selfishness made me feel ashamed, but a glance around the room didn't reveal any other men looking ashamed. Many were nodding in agreement.

As if reading my thoughts, Uncle James turned his gaze on me. 'So, women in childbirth are not the worst grade of sinner by any means, for they are but weak of flesh and will. These weak vessels only seek to reduce their natural God-given pains. No, the finger of suspicion must point at those wicked hags, the midwives, who attend them with promises of removing the pain that God has decreed.'

Uncle paused. Had he finally worn out his inner frenzy? But he started shaking his head slowly. A faint sheen of sweat coated his face, and he jabbed the air with his finger, directing his ire into the crowd. What drove the man?

'These hags, not content with spiriting away the pains of childbirth, also traverse the countryside, offering to take away God-given ailments and sickness. There is no greater disobedience to

God than interfering with His will. It is whispered that these midwives ease the pain of menses in maids. God clearly intended that Eve and her descendants should be reminded of their sin with every turn of the moon. Instead of accepting this reminder of their sin, maids visit the hags for powders to abate the pain.'

At this, he looked straight at me. I rubbed at my chin. He must be referring to my time with Dora. Perhaps he even accused my own mother. Nowadays, I felt Dora's presence in my life like a stain on my soul. On the odd occasions when she haled me, heeding my uncle's instruction, I turned my face from her. I had cause to wonder at her seeming kindness towards me. Had she really cared for me? Or was she – as my Uncle was fond of saying – merely trying to make good her bargain with Satan? After all, my mother had died at her hand, and there was still suspicion over my father's death. I myself only lived because of Dora Shaw's hellish intervention. I dropped my gaze, and my uncle looked away from me and continued.

'Do they not realise that God has created this punishment for their own betterment? For He removes the cause of this pain as long as a woman is carrying a new soul or feeding one. Thus, a woman who is with child or suckling a child is in a temporary state of grace, free of the filthy curse and its concomitant pain.'

I considered the pains I'd borne during my life. Did Uncle expect men and boys to bear their pains? And were gentlemen's physicians included in his scolding? And barber-surgeons, too? Perhaps not, since he seemed to believe that only women should suffer, in light of Eve's transgression.

'When these hags anoint women during their travails, it's a hideous parody of God's servants using holy oil to bring His protection. These denizens of the night smear innocent flesh with unguents tainted by the devil's kiss so that they can spirit away pain. All of which allows the passage of the child into the world without its mother accepting her rightful allotment of suffering.'

Uncle leaned closer to the men at the front and rested his gaze on each of us, lowering his voice.

'We must have fear in our hearts for the souls of babes born so easily, since the devil must surely find their tender souls already primed for the taking. We must look to our own hearths to root out this evil. We must rid the world of these fiendish midwives who would take away the righteous pains of birth decreed by God.'

Several of the men in the front row stepped back at this pronouncement, as if wishing to dissolve into the rows behind, but the rest of the room broke out into ringing cheers. Uncle folded his hands, looking as pleased as I'd ever seen him.

12

Jane

No Smoke

My hands were cut to ribbons, as it was impossible to cut holly properly with mittens on. But the scratches were soon forgotten and my heart skipped when Tom Verger appeared at the top of the hill, his red hair bright against the blue sky. I waved to him.

'Hello, Tom.'

He ran easily down the hill. 'Hey, Jane. 'Wouldn't you be rather be at home, keeping nice and warm on a day like this?'

'Yes, but I need to start making wreaths for the church.'

'Already? Here, I'll lend a hand. Mind, the holly trees are fair weighted with berries this year.'

'Meg says the more berries, the harsher the winter.'

Tom grimaced. 'It'll be hard enough hereabouts, even if it's not harsh.'

'I know; everyone looks thinner and their clothes more patched than usual.'

Tom folded his arms over his patched jerkin. 'Thanks.'

I touched his arm. 'Sorry, Tom, I meant nothing, just, you know ...'

He smiled down at me. 'Aye, I know. Besides, you're looking well-patched yourself of late!'

My frock was too short and my bodice strained. Our eyes met, and he turned away to hide his thoughts.

'Mam says it would be wasteful to make a new frock just yet. She hopes it'll do another winter. But it's hard to lift my arms without making ripping noises.'

To prove it, I raised my arms. Tom grinned and then looked away again.

'Tom Verger, are you blushing? Whatever for?'

But Tom's words deserted him. He pushed past me, pulled his own knife from his belt and began hacking at the tree. His hands were big and hardened, and he ignored the holly scratches, but one deep scratch drew blood. Frowning, he held his cut hand before my face.

'See what you've cost me now. A pint of good blood!'

Before he could stop me, I grabbed his wrist and put his thumb into my mouth. But the look on his face was terrible and he reared away, tucking his thumb firmly under his oxter and out of harm's way.

'Pack it in, Jane, there's an act that would send an angel to the gibbet.'

'Tom Verger! Don't you go wishing bad fortune on me.'

'Well, witch, stop dining on the blood of innocent lads.'

'Quiet, villain, or you'll have me taken away!' I made to cuff his ear, but he laughed and dodged me. 'Here, if you've finished bleeding, cut some of those high boughs and I may forgive your slanderous tongue.'

He came and stood close and stretched over me to reach the high branches. There was a new smell from under his arms, and when I breathed deeply, his face looked hot again.

'So, do you plan to stop growing this year, Tom? Or will you eat your father out of house and home?'

'There's always plenty of hunting in these parts, so me and Da will never starve.'

When he passed me the boughs he'd cut, our hands brushed and my heart leapt. He looked at me until I dropped my gaze this time.

He frowned. 'Jane, where's Meg? I've not seen her lately. Is she on her travels again?'

'Meg? Not that I know of. She came round last week with berries.' I put down my holly and looked at him, torn between worrying about Meg and enjoying being alone with Tom. My hand still tingled where he'd brushed it with his and it made me warm inside. But guilt made me push down the happiness welling inside me.

Tom tucked away his knife. 'I generally see her on my hunting jaunts, but she's not been around for days. Most likely, she's just on her travels.'

'No. She'd have said something. Meg always tells us when she's going away. I'd better go and check on her. We need to stock up on bitters anyway as there's so many women due to be confined. It'll save Meg the walk.'

Tom looked at the sky, perhaps weighing its intentions. 'You're not setting off at this hour? It's dark nights, mind. You'll not make it there and back by nightfall.'

'Oh, it's dry and it'll be fine. Can you take this lot home and let Mam know where I've gone?' I shrugged my cloak around me.

'I'll do no such thing, Jane Chandler!' He put his hand on my shoulder and smiled. 'I'm coming with you. And don't waste your breath arguing, because you don't know who might be abroad. Besides, if Meg has taken bad, then I can help.'

'Tom! Don't let Meg hear you offering to help her, or she'll have your ears.'

He grinned. 'I'll chance it. Come, let's get our legs going before dark and we'll soon see what ails Meg.'

Although Tom was only walking, he had such long legs it was impossible to keep up and my lungs burnt with the effort.

'Are you all right, Jane?'

'No, I can't match your great strides. You're so long of limb these days.'

'Sorry, I was just hurrying to get to Meg. I'll slow down a bit. But not too much. I want you out of these woods before dark.'

* * *

It was nearing dusk when we approached Meg's dwelling.

Tom frowned. 'Look, there's no smoke from the chimney. Meg never lets her fire go out unless she's away. And the nights are freezing.'

We began to run. But Tom reached the dwelling first and pushed himself between me and the door.

'Let me in first, Jane. Just in case, you know …'

I closed my eyes and said a silent prayer. 'Thank you, Tom. But you're very close to Meg, so you don't want to be the one to find her.'

But he shook his head. He pushed open the door and went in.

I followed behind and a bad smell emerged. This wasn't the usual aroma of wood smoke and herbs. We edged towards a pile of rags on Meg's bed. But then came the sound of laboured breathing, and Tom knelt at Meg's bedside.

'Meg, it's Tom. Tom and Jane. Can you hear us?'

When I managed to speak, my voice was wavery. 'Meg, it's me as well, Jane.'

Her rheumy eyes flickered and she croaked something. Tom's eyes scanned the room. 'Meg, you've no clean water and no fire. And it's so cold in here.' He looked at me and all the colour had drained from his face. Even in the gloom, his face was pallid. He stood up. 'Meg, I'm going to fetch wood and get your fire going while Jane sees to you.'

Meg's mouth was moving, but no sound came from her. I clutched his sleeve and shook my head slowly.

'Come, Tom, we must stay by Meg's side. Take her other hand.'

Tom took Meg's hand. She was cold, and I swallowed back tears as the woman who'd been a grandmother to me slipped away into the night.

Eventually, Tom let go of Meg and took my hand. He was trembling and he would not meet my eye. Instead, he peered out of the door.

'Come on, Jane. We need to get going. It's already getting dark. I'll come back with me da at first light, and we'll fetch Meg.'

I glanced at Meg and felt fresh tears welling. 'But, Tom, we can't just leave her unwashed and unburied.'

He looked at me in the half-light, and I saw his wet face. He took both of my hands and spoke quietly.

'There's no choice, Jane. We need to get Meg brought to the church for a proper burial. I'll fetch Da, and we'll bring her back.'

93

I laughed sharply. 'A proper burial? Meg won't have it. She'll get up and walk at the thought of being buried in the churchyard.'

Tom frowned at me. 'It won't be up to us, anyway. Or Meg. The Reverend and me da will decide what's best for Meg. Come on, let's say goodbye to Meg, and then we have to go.'

* * *

The sound of a twig snapping made me flinch, and Tom stopped and looked at me. 'You're very jumpy, Jane. It's not like you. Is it because of Meg?'

I nodded.

We continued through the woodland maze, but I paused to look over my shoulder.

'Tom, wait. Please stop. I've got the curious feeling of eyes on me.'

He stopped and turned to face me. 'Eyes, Jane? Why there are thousands of eyes upon us. The whole wood teems with creatures getting their pantries ready for winter.'

'But Tom, it's not the creatures I fear. There's no danger from a bury of rabbits. I fear we're the prey.'

He looked around, one hand on his knife. 'I can't see or hear anything.'

'Sorry, Tom. I'm still upset about Meg. And the dark wood is making me skittish. Or perhaps my conscience pricks me. We shouldn't be here alone.'

He held his breath and listened. 'Sh, Jane. There! You're right, branches snapping. Most likely a deer followed by poachers. But quick, get up that old oak.'

Tom linked his hands for me to step on, and he hoisted me up so I could reach a decent foothold, and then he scrambled after me. Breathless, we rested near the top of the tree. I rubbed my damp palms on the rough bark.

'Tom, I feel scared. My heart's hammering.'

But he was busy inching along a bough so he could peer down. 'Jane, look.'

I heard animals crashing through the undergrowth. A red

doe appeared, followed by a white fawn and a brown mare. The mare's hooded rider pulled an arrow from his quiver.

'Oh, no!' I put my hands over my eyes and would have slipped from the bough had Tom not steadied me. He put a warning finger to his lips and took out his catapult and a handful of pebbles. He lay along the branch, narrowed his eyes, drew back the catapult and let fly the stone. The stone found its mark. The mare reared and she tore off, with her rider barely managing to stay on.

'Tom! You saved the white fawn.'

His face flushed and he fidgeted with his catapult before putting it back in his pocket. 'It's naught. I wonder if it's related to the one you saw being born?'

'It must be, Tom. It might be her granddaughter. You know, Meg told me a white fawn is a sign from the other world.'

Tom raised his brows. 'Other world? Don't let the sergeants hear you talking like that, else they'll have you off to the assizes.'

'Tom, please don't say that. But Meg said it was a warning of danger coming.'

'You're touched in the head, Jane. And I don't want to speak ill of the dead, but so was Meg. Look, I've never seen a white deer before. Let me try and get a closer look.'

I pinched his arm. 'If you want a closer look, I'll push you out of this tree – just say the word.'

'Fighting talk, eh? At the top of the tree and all?' He plucked a sprig of acorns and handed it to me. 'Come on, let's stop fighting. Here's peace.'

I held the sprig to my face. 'Thank you, Tom. I miss Meg. Do you?'

He nodded and looked down, but not before I noticed his chin quivering, 'Aye, and always will. But let's get down and see what's what.'

'Is it safe? What if that hunter comes back? We've deprived him of a great prize and he might be angry.'

Tom shrugged. 'He'll be long gone. I doubt he'd think to blame a lad in a tree, so the innocent mare will have no oats for her supper.'

Even so, we set off at a brisker pace and kept our silence so we could listen for anyone following.

* * *

On the homeward walk, Tom suddenly stuck out a hand to stop me and stepped in front of me. I followed his gaze and saw the red doe lying in the clearing. Her throat was gashed badly and there was a lot of blood.

'Oh, Tom! The wastrel didn't get the fawn, but he killed the mother, anyway. Or, what if he did get the fawn?' I hurried to the doe and ran a hand across her pelt. 'She's still warm, so he–'

The words died in my mouth as an arrow flew past, slashing Tom's leg on its flight. His hands went straight to the wound, and instantly they were soaked with blood. I made to run to him, but he held up a hand to warn me off. I saw a shadow slip down from a tree and silently make away. Tom glared at me, trying to get me to heed my own safety. But I ran across the clearing.

'It's all right, Tom, he's gone. I saw him go. He won't be back. And I'm not going to leave you untended, bowman or not. Stop thrashing and lie down, or you'll bleed more.'

My voice was filled with tears, but I pressed his wound firmly, staunching the flow.

When Tom looked down, his eyes widened at the pool of blood at his feet and he sank to the ground. He lay still while I untied the rope holding his breeches and fastened it around his leg. He flinched when it pulled tight.

'Careful, or you'll have me leg off.' He smiled, but his voice faltered.

I paused. 'You've killed enough game in your time to know how much blood you can stand to lose.'

He nodded. 'Pull it tight, Jane, else who will save you then?'

I sat holding the knot. It sickened me to see blood running from him. It was too much blood to lose so quickly. It would've been better had the arrow lodged in place. After a time, the blood slowed a little, and Tom's eyes fluttered and then closed. He had either fallen asleep or fainted and there was no time to ponder which. But I kept talking to him, hoping that my words were getting through.

'I must find something to help your leg knit.'

My heart pounded as I ran about looking for suitable plants. The only time I'd seen this much blood was when Ma Thompson bled to death after birthing. But Tom was bigger than most men and must have more blood than a short woman. I hoped not to find out and continued searching for woundwort, sphagnum moss, oak leaves, anything to staunch the blood and knit the wound. My eyes fluttered left and right, always finding their way back to Tom, who was awake again. His groans grew further off as the circle of my search increased.

Eventually, I stopped and recalled Meg's advice. 'Still your feet, still your heart and still your breath.' Although my body urged me towards hectic activity, frantic searching would only waste time. So I held my breath, closed my eyes and saw in my mind's eye what was needed. As my mind stilled, my eyes opened and I let them haze before blinking them into focus. There, on the periphery of my vision was a clump of dry yarrow – woundwort. I ran over and began scooping handfuls of dry flower heads into my pinny before racing back to Tom. His breathing was laboured. Tears stung my eyes as I began to pack the wound. At first, despite the rope, Tom was still bleeding, but then the woundwort started taking up the blood. As I pressed more yarrow into the wound, the blood gradually stopped seeping.

The rope round Tom's leg was a worry, but it wouldn't do to loosen it until the yarrow did its work. But it would need slacking off soon, or Tom's leg would be lost. I packed the wound with more yarrow and then pushed my knee into the freshly padded wound, causing Tom to groan. Slowly, I unpicked my knot, careful to pull on the ends so that the bite wasn't lost as soon as the knot was loosened. The woundwort turned red as the pressure of the rope lessened, but the compress seemed to be holding the blood back. Tom was shaking. He had to be kept warm, so I unwound my shawl and covered him as much as possible. Night would fall soon and he couldn't walk like this, so it was best just to keep the cold off him. He needed something hot in him, which meant finding dry wood. I slid my hand into Tom's pouch until my fingers touched cold metal. Tom's fire steel. His most treasured possession. And there was the piece of flint and the little tinder-box.

There was plenty of dry yarrow remaining, so I prised open the tinder-box and took out some dried moss and a square of char-cloth. I folded the cloth over twice and then clamped it over the piece of flint. Closing my eyes, I murmured a quick prayer and then began striking the fire steel's hard edge against the flint. Eventually, one of the tiny sparks caught the tinder. I tucked the smoking tinder into a nest of dried moss, held it above my head and blew air into it. Once the flames caught, I set the burning nest into the dry yarrow stalks and guarded the little fire until it was well away.

It was tiring work, gathering wood and dashing back to check on Tom. The yarrow poultice had moved a little, but there was no new blood. It was important to get him under cover. There wasn't much in the way of shelter, but there were plenty of branches to cut and there were dry leaves everywhere. Providing it didn't rain, Tom would stay warm and dry.

Exhausted, I wanted to crawl next to Tom and sleep, but he needed hot liquid in him. He'd borne up well so far and I had to keep going for his sake. The stream was nearby, which meant an abundance of herbs even so late in the year, and Tom's flask would hold plenty of water. First, I gathered the herbs. It wasn't the best time for picking, being neither sunrise nor sunset, so I mouthed charms to make up the shortfall in strength. Meat would be best to bring up Tom's blood, but meat would be too hard to eat and there'd been enough bloodshed for one day. A brew of nettles would have to do.

When I knelt at Tom's side and stroked his brow, he smiled at me, but it wasn't a proper Tom grin and he was in a bad way. He was so pale to begin with; his only fire lived in the red of his hair, but his complexion now held a strangled hue. He looked at me with eyes I'd never seen before. There was no green there, only black holes surrounded by white. It may have been the fire, but whatever had flared in Tom's eyes made me scared. First Meg and now Tom. It was too much to bear.

'Tom, I'm going to get water to keep you warm, please hang on.'

I found two flat stones to pulverise the herbs, and then I added these to the flask and hung it over the fire to boil. Once it cooled,

Tom could manage small sips, but he was barely awake when I fed him the astringent brew. It was a slow job, but sip by sip, I got a flask of tea into him. So far, he was keeping it down.

Tom's face glistened in the firelight, so his face and his hair both seemed to be alight. Fever? But I had to leave him to get help. I banked the fire in the hope it would last. Then I dropped a dry kiss onto Tom's slumbering forehead, promising not to be long. As I wended my way through the wood, my heart raced. I peered into the darkness, watching for movement in case the hunter came back. But he must have gone for good, as he'd not want to risk the villagers' wrath and be hanged for near killing their favourite lad.

* * *

Bill Verger and Jim Driver carried Tom up the hill on a board as though he were no weight at all. When they took him into Mam's pantry, I wanted to go and help, but Mam would hear none of it.

'Jane, you've saved Tom's life and his leg. But you will go to bed straight away and I won't hear another word from you about it.'

'But, Mam, he saved my life by pushing me up a tree out of the hunter's way.'

Bill Verger and Jim Driver exchanged glances. Jim addressed me.

'Jane, tell us what you remember of this man, for we must send up the hue and cry before he does kill someone.'

'We never saw him, just his brown mare – off and on like your Andrew's.'

Jim Driver leaned close to me. 'But it can't have been our Andrew, since he's been at Hexham the past two days.'

'Of course it wasn't Andrew. He'd have haled us. And he's Tom's best friend, so he'd never shoot him. It was just the same colour mare. But we never saw its rider.'

Bill patted me on the shoulder. 'We must send up the hue and cry then, for an unknown man riding a brown mare.'

Jim Driver turned. 'Aye, but first make sure that our Andrew isn't taken.'

'Of course, Driver. Come, we should go, although the man will be long gone if he's an ounce of sense, and we must fetch Meg.'

'Aye, but shorten your stride, Verger, as Meg Wetherby's not going anywhere.'

Once the men left, Mam held out a bowl. 'Here's some hot pottage. Not that you deserve it. Now, get it down you while it's warm and then straight to bed with you.'

The pottage was most welcome and it warmed me. 'But, Mam, I want to see how Tom is.'

'How many times must I tell you not to speak with your mouth full? Tom is perfectly well. He's a strong lad, and he'll recover nicely. He just needs his rest. And so do you. Now off to bed with you, unless you want to explain why you were out in the woods all night with a lad—'

'But it was only Tom and he's my best friend. And we had to check on Meg.'

'Well, perhaps it's time you got yourself a friend who's a lass. It might bring less mischief.'

My eyes welled as Mam retrieved the empty bowl. 'But Mam, Tom would never harm me. I can't just stop being his friend. Not on top of losing Meg. He saved me from being shot by that hunter.'

'And you saved him, so you're square – more than square. I forbid you from going out in those woods and you're to keep away from Tom Verger.'

'But Mam—'

'Enough. Do not disobey me, Jane. Say your prayers. Be sure to give thanks to God for your safe deliverance and then not another word from you.'

I opened my mouth, saw the hardness in my mother's face and closed it again. Eyes downcast, I kicked off my clogs and knelt in front of my pallet in the alcove, hands clasped before me. Warm, safe, with a full stomach and Gyb by my side, I tried to feel grateful. Yet God had played no part yesterday. Meg was dead and the only blessing was that she'd not died alone, even if she had suffered alone for days. God hadn't helped Meg. If Tom hadn't pushed me up the tree yesterday, who knows what might have happened? If I'd not kept my wits, Tom might have bled to death. And he must still be weak and sick from losing so much blood. He was home and Mam would heal him, but I wanted to see how he fared.

When my knees began to ache, I decided that God would forgive me for not being more grateful. Once in bed, even my concern for Tom couldn't keep me awake. My eyes wobbled, quickly followed by my mind, and I fell fast asleep, never mind the daylight and Mam's sharp words.

* * *

I slept all of that day and all through the night. My stomach woke me just before dawn – it was so hollow that it pained me. Quietly, I put on my clogs and crept into the kitchen. There was a heel of bread and some ale left in the jug, just enough to soak for pap as if I were still a bairn. It was tempting to bite straight into the bread, but it was as hard as the hobs of hell. These words made me smile. They were words that Tom would use about day-old bread, which made me blush, but I secretly enjoyed his impertinence.

While the bread softened in the ale, I went out of the kitchen door and brushed my hand across the dew-drenched fennel stalks. With fragrant, wet hands, I washed my face and smoothed my hair. The smell of fennel was refreshing and woke me up properly. I peered at Tom's dwelling. He'd be lying in there, suffering. More than anything, I wished to see him and tend his wounds. But he might be sleeping, and Mam would be crosser than she already was. The best idea would be to stay out of her way until she was calmer. Then she might forget about not letting me see Tom anymore. It gave me a sick feeling inside to think of not seeing him again. It was bad enough never being able to see Meg again. I hugged Gyb to me, because he was all I had left of Meg, and he gave me some comfort. And it didn't bear thinking about what the man in the woods might have done to me. Even now, I could be lying on the forest floor, stiff and still were it not for Tom. I had to thank him for saving my life. Surely Mam would come round in time?

13

John

Troubles of the Marriage Bed

Lucy followed me into our home, shaking the sleet from her coif.

'Oh, that was quite a storm, John, I can't believe so much snow was ever in the sky.'

'What? What's the weather to do with anything? Besides, you needn't worry about any more bad weather because that's the last time I take you into town. The men's eyes all over you. We've been scarce wed a year and already the sly smirks are coming in my direction.'

Lucy shivered and shook her cloak, taking care not to splash me, and then hung it on the door. 'Oh, John, people are too busy minding their own business to care about ours.'

'There are none so blind as those who won't see. They were ogling you freely, plain though you are, as if you were a harbour doxy.'

'John! What a wicked word to say.'

'Quiet, woman, and get these boots off me.'

I sat by the fire and extended my legs. Lucy knelt to pull off my boots, her fingers slipping on the wet leather. I could not begin to tell her the feelings of rage and humiliation that did daily battle within me at the thought of my manhood being called into question. She unhooked my boots and looked towards the fire, as well she might, since it was in danger of going out. It angered me to think of the fire going out, and how I'd been beaten by my father that night when we had no fire. It occurred to me then that my father must have suffered similar humiliation to my own as my mother was advanced in years when I was born. Perhaps it went some way to explaining his terrible temper and violence. These days, I often felt my blood heat and course into my fists and feet, and it was a struggle to hold myself back. Of course, I would never beat Lucy out of temper, even when she seemed determined to try my patience, but only for the sake of chastisement to keep her on God's path. Uncle James had taught me thoroughly about the duties of a husband.

Before Lucy had managed to take off my boots, I kicked them off myself and took her over to the straw mattress. She turned her face while I loosened myself. Then I untied her chemise. Although I was a spare man, she cringed when I lay on her. I leant over, grinding my hip into hers.

'John, why are you fishing around for your cloak?'

'To make us decent. The room feels filled with the eyes of my forebears.'

'Oh, John.' She smiled, but soon let it fall away.

'Aye, wipe that smirk from your face, before I wipe it for you. I'll not have my forebears gaze on this bare backside.' I drew the cloak over my bareness. 'There, no forbear can peer through wool.' Then I started fastening up her chemise, my cold fingers fighting with the flimsy laces.

'John, whatever's wrong?'

'I'm covering your womanly flesh decently in God's sight.'

'But, surely you don't think–'

'Yes! He's everywhere. And how might any man be expected to perform under God's eye?'

'But God can't keep watch over everyone, John. Besides, it's natural for married folks to–'

'Be quiet. The act of procreation is sanctified for making children and no more.'

I lay rigid my whole length, except the small length that mattered. It dismayed me. No child would ever be born this way.

Lucy began untying her chemise once more. 'Perhaps if we lie as God intended, you know, before the fall–'

I was forced to slap her. 'Have you lost your wits? First, lascivious behaviour and then blasphemy.' While it saddened me greatly that I had resorted to my father's ways, Uncle had made me understand my purpose as a husband, and it was surely my duty to knock this wicked taint out of her.

* * *

In the morning, Lucy awoke under my weight, although my member hung limply. When she protested, it was necessary to silence her before she made a sinful complaint, so I clamped my hand over her mouth until her eyes bulged. Something must have stirred me then and her cowering drove me on. Without intention, I twisted her left breast, which caused tears to spill from her eyes, but I drove myself against her unyielding body, chafing myself in the joyless process. Finally, I grunted, pulled away from her and sneered as I fastened myself away.

'See yon blood! Smear the linen and hang it out. I'll have no more sneers from the neighbours about my manhood.'

Lucy curled up, clutching her left breast. 'But, it's only moon blood.'

She slid from the mattress and there was not even a meagre trickle of seed on her thigh. Something must be done, but what? While she hung out the linen, I realised that no heir would leave my loins if left to nature. My shudder didn't herald life-giving seed. If anything came from me, it was as dust and too light to land, let alone take hold inside my wife and make a child.

* * *

After tending the beasts, I came home. Lucy flinched when I kicked the door shut. 'Those little snots, they mean me to overhear them. Soft-tail Sharpe they're calling me. Lads half my age laughing behind their hands.'

I took out my flask of whisky and swallowed a draft. Then I looked around me. At the sight of the untended room, the hairs on my hands stood like wire, a nerve jumped in my cheek and the skin tightened over my cheekbones.

'You wee slattern! You think you can keep the hours you want while I go unfed and uncomforted in this filthy hovel? While you – snivelling sloven that you are – do just as you please with the hours God gives you.'

She eyed the flask in my hand. 'What's come over you? This isn't the John I married.'

'Aye, well, it's the one you've got. Cut your whingeing, woman. A man shouldn't have to wait for what's rightfully his after a day's graft.'

My heart pounded so hard I fancied Lucy could see it thumping. My eyes bulged and a great sweat came upon me, as if I'd run a mile with a mastiff behind me. My member was stirring. Had my coursing blood set it twitching? When I took out my member, Lucy turned her face from the ugly bloom.

'Don't you dare turn away from what God made.'

I pushed her against the table, lifted her kirtle and rammed my soft flesh into her. She clawed at the table, but didn't cry. Did she think I fed on her terror? Had she decided to show me no more? I leant over and bit her breasts. It made her wail, which excited my blood further. Finally, I grunted and slumped on top of her, knocking the breath from her. Now that I'd unlocked something within me, I'd use her more roughly and not care what damage was inflicted if her cowering helped me get a bairn on her.

Later that night, I tried again to make a child, but to no avail. Lucy tucked herself behind me in our bed, her hand over my furious heart. It was beating too fast for sleep, so I deepened my breathing to fox her. She pushed away from me and turned onto her back. No doubt to stare at the rafters until the night was gone. But that night, the full moon shone through the window, so Lucy reached into the straw mattress for her dead mother's silver coin and turned it over as she did every full moon. At first light, I'd take her mother's coin and visit MacBain.

* * *

I stamped through the woods to reach the barber-surgeon's shack and a spire of smoke streamed from the roof, bringing with it a savoury smell that made my mouth water. Before I called out, the barber-surgeon opened his door.

'Sharpe. It's never good to see you. But get in and warm yourself.' He pointed to a stool near the fire.

I looked at the crocks jostling on makeshift shelves. The big barber perched next to the fire, stirring a bubbling cauldron – the source of the savoury smell.

'Why are you here? Have no fear. I may well dislike you, but your coin is as good as any man's, and your words won't travel beyond my home.'

The man was hardly convincing, but I was desperate for his help, and so I let the slight pass by unremarked. 'I … fear that my wife's womb is barren.'

'Then I must ask about the private workings of your wife's body. Do you understand?'

I nodded. 'Yes, I understand.'

'First, when does your wife bleed?'

'Now. At full moon. And her fertile time is dead moon. She reports a tiny pain and I notice the increasing strength in her hands.'

MacBain snorted. 'Aye, God giving women a fighting chance at their fertile time. Now then, you've lain with your wife at these fertile times?'

My cheeks were alight with shame and I didn't reply.

'Sharpe, I can see you wonder whether this old barber can help you. Well, set your mind at rest. I've helped more bairns be made than a body's a right to know. Now tell me, have you lain with your wife at her fertile time?'

I nodded. 'Since our wedding, I've not once escaped my duty. So, Lucy must be barren.'

'Come closer.' The barber grabbed my hands and studied my palms by the firelight. When he released them, they were strangely warm, despite his cold grasp.

'What were you doing, MacBain?'

'Reading your life, Sharpe. There's naught ails your goodwife that a kinder husband wouldn't mend – now, don't go getting all hot-headed at a dose of the truth. Tell me, how goes it when you lie together?'

I bit back my retort at his insult and answered him. 'Well … some thing isn't right. There's been no blood but her moon blood.'

MacBain nodded. 'So, John Sharpe can't get a bairn on his goodwife? Your prong is soft?'

My eyes widened. 'Watch your mouth, MacBain!'

'Oh, take that look off your face. Nobody ever died from a dose of the truth and false pride won't make a bairn for you.' MacBain ladled out a bowl of broth. 'Here, swallow this and get some meat on your bones. Eat up, that rabbit didn't give over breathing so you could let him cool and go to waste. It's just a taste and there's always plenty more rabbits in these woods. So eat up and let me think on.'

The barber gazed into the fire while I speared tender morsels of rabbit with my eating knife. I looked up. 'MacBain, this broth is salted and saged to perfection.'

He gave a grim smile. 'Always goes down better when you've not had to catch, kill and cook it yourself. While I mix my herbs, you get on with that broth.'

I concentrated on the broth, trying to make it last.

'Here, Sharpe, when you've done with the rabbit, heft the stew onto the embers and set that water to boiling.'

I swallowed my stew as if the mouthful contained an entire rabbit and the blood boiled into my face at being treated like a maid. But it wouldn't pay to anger MacBain, so I switched the crocks and the barber handed me a small pot.

'Here, rosehip syrup. Pour in one-quarter worth and we'll have us a fine drink.'

I trickled the red syrup into the hot water and a sweet smell rose in the steam.

MacBain eyed me, nodding. 'A man careful about what he gives away.'

'Don't speak to me in clever riddles, Barber, I know your hidden meaning.'

'Ach, Sharpe, you'll not be the first, or the last, to suffer from slow-running seed. Come, fill these bowls and we'll warm our bones.'

We perched near the fire, hugging hot bowls and supping in silence.

When he'd drained his bowl, MacBain rose. 'No more lazing next to the fire for me – no, you stay there and keep out of my way.'

It felt awkward taking my ease while the barber toiled. For a big man, he worked easily amongst his crocks, deftly reaching for pot after pot, adding powders, leaves and seeds to a hollowed stone mortar and then grinding them. A bitter smell cut through the rosehip and my nose wrinkled.

'What is that foul concoction, MacBain?'

'Only cantharides, nettles and a dab of mandrake.'

'Mandrake? But my goodwife will struggle to get it down and keep it down.'

MacBain grimaced, bad humour shining from his black eyes. 'This isn't for your goodwife. It's for you, man. Sup a big pinch with your evening cup of ale, but only a pinch, or your wife will be set for mourning weeds or the gallows instead of the birthing chair.'

I looked at the door and then at MacBain. 'Do you really think I'd poison myself by my own hand through supping mandrake? And pay you for the dubious pleasure? What if someone found out? Mandrake! We'd both swing.'

'No need for alarm, Sharpe. The only creatures with ears are the rabbits and they can keep a secret. Now get yourself over here and learn how to pinch out the right dose.'

'But it's not me that's lacking, MacBain. The blame lies within my wife.'

'Aye, don't all heirless men have the very same complaint of their goodwives?'

'MacBain, do not take my manhood in vain.'

'Psht, there are plenty of men who've suffered the sheer misfortune to marry two, or sometimes even three, barren wives.'

I dropped my eyes to my bowl, 'This is too much insult.'

'Insults must sometimes be borne to get to the truth of the matter. Now, I've no time to make words fine enough to suit your delicate ears. See sense, Sharpe, and you shall have your child.' MacBain passed a crock under my nose.

My eyes watered. 'Something so foul smelling is sure to finish me off.'

'No man has died at this barber's hand yet. Put it in some strong ale or sweet mead and you'll not notice it. Try to get a pinch like … this … into a cup when your wife's fertile time is near. Keep away from her until then and make sure you go to no cheap women, as men will. Do you understand?'

'Cheap women, indeed. Don't judge me by your own standards, MacBain.' But he gave me a dark look, so I dropped my eyes. 'Yes, I understand.'

'A draught of this five nights in a row at your wife's fertile time should produce a child. Now, show me your silver.'

'It irks me to pay for something that may not work and may yet kill me. Perhaps I should withhold payment until my goodwife has the babe in her arms.'

The barber snatched back his crock. 'You need not pay me, but you'll leave here with hands as empty as your wife's womb. Away with you and don't waste any more of my time.'

'It's too dear.' I pressed the coin on him and willed my tongue to be silent. No doubt, this contrary man would withhold his remedy just for the sport of it.

MacBain tucked the silver coin out of sight. 'It's not too dear if it gives you the child you need. And you're in no danger of starving as long as the forest flourishes. You gnaw your lip like a maid, now what troubles you?'

'I don't mean to show bad faith in your remedy. But what if it doesn't work?'

MacBain pulled his fur jerkin about his body. 'It'll work, Sharpe, you have my word. This compound will fetch a bairn from a stone, if there's one to be got.'

* * *

After watching the moon change, and keeping a close eye on my wife, I'd forced down the foul concoction with my ale. Almost as if she knew what was in my mind, Lucy wore only her shift, despite the frigid night air. When she moved in front of the firelight, her body was visible through the garment. I eyed her, my jaw slack.

'What's this? Naked flesh on show? You're a disgrace, woman, and enough to tempt the devil.'

109

But my eyes devoured her. I crossed the room and grasped her round the waist, pulling up the shift and forcing my hand into her. She pulled away. I wiped my mouth on the back of my hand and grabbed her again. Lucy's face was suffused with firelight and my member was suffused with blood. She looked at me, her eyes wide. Surely, MacBain's compound hadn't taken effect so soon? Quickly, I pressed her down on the table, raised her shift and entered her. With only a few thrusts, I was spent and shoved her away.

'You see what you've done to me? The devil rides in my loins tonight. Now make yourself decent, for you're enough to make a decent man's gorge rise. And get my meal ready. Or are you too busy with your sluttish ways to think of feeding a hard-working farmer?'

I cuffed her as she got up, and she put a hand to her face. In time, she'd thank me for helping to amend her wicked ways. She turned to the fire, pulling her kirtle around her and I looked at her belly, wondering whether a child was taking root inside her at this very moment.

* * *

Three Sundays later, Lucy approached me, looking me right in the eye. I jumped up.

'Aye, what new insolence is this? Quick, now, before I knock it out of you.'

But before I could move, she spoke. 'You'll punish me no more now that I'm with child. From now on, whatever you do to me, you do to him as well.'

'What's got into you? I have my rights.' I lunged at her, but Lucy sidestepped me, somehow filled with new-found courage.

'Lay one more hand on me, John, whether in lust or in rage, and I'll take my own life and that of the bairn.'

'Why, you wee bitch. I'll–' I raised a hand, but she didn't flinch.

'You have my word, John. Keep away from me. Now, give me your word.'

I wondered how to bargain away my pride in the face of a woman's threat. Did she not realise that I only chastised her to keep her from sinning, so that we'd go to our reward in heaven together? She could no sooner kill a child as kill herself. Still, women were strange creatures who became stranger once they were with child. A muscle worked in my jaw, but otherwise, I smiled. Having a child would save my face in the town and with my uncle. I could stay my hand safely for a few months. How much sinning could my wife possibly commit when she was in a state of God-given grace?

'Aye, all right. You have my word, though you've made a bargain worthy of the devil. I'll spare you from chastisement, not because of your vile threat, but because it's God's will. I'll leave your body to its God-given business of cosseting my child towards his birth.'

14

Jane

Ten Moons

I sat in the front pew with Mam, and Tom sat one pew over with Bill. But it was pointless trying to keep us apart and the sermon was nearly over.

Reverend Foster leaned forward. 'Take heed of my warnings ahead of the Beltane celebrations. There is magic in the air and too much licence. The old custom was meant to make the land fertile, but many bairns are born ten moons from Beltane.'

Bill put his head down when the Reverend said this, perhaps because Tom was born on Imbolc.

'Young people especially must take care, because when the smell of hawthorn hangs heavy in the air, when winter is just a faint shadow and the next one not yet thought of, only heat and desire occupy the minds of maids and youths.'

This made me blush and I didn't dare look at Tom. But the Reverend was right – it was hard to concentrate on work. The lads had felled a birch for the maypole while the lasses plaited ribbons and threaded daisy chains to decorate it. Even the little bairns had fashioned masks to disguise themselves as small creatures. It was too hot for sitting in church. I hoped the sermon would soon end so I could escape without further discussion about Beltane behaviour.

* * *

I looked up the hill. Tom was still working, but hopefully he wouldn't be long. The eating, drinking and dancing had already started and I wanted him to see me in my white frock, with a flower garland gracing my dark hair as I twirled around the maypole with a pretty green ribbon in my hand. Finally, he came running down the hill towards me. I left my dancing and skipped over to him.

He grabbed my hands. 'Oh, Jane, they've crowned you the Queen of the May and I wasn't there to see it. How will you ever forgive me?'

'Wicked Tom, you will never be forgiven!'

A wide grin spread across his face. 'Come on, Jane, let's away down the river. There's something we need to do.'

I pushed the garland of hawthorn and daisies back from my face. 'Oh, what's that?' But my face was already flushed. There was only one reason young couples went to the river at Beltane.

Tom towed me along by one hand. 'You know fine well what it is, Jane Chandler. So, are you coming, or not?'

I glanced at Mam, who was busy looking over the village's latest babies. 'Yes. Yes, I'm coming, Tom Verger!'

Hand in hand, we ran through the long grass down to the river, with the scent of May blossom growing stronger in the afternoon sun.

'Everything is so green, Tom, isn't it lovely?'

Tom laughed. 'Aye, if you say so, Jane.'

As we neared the river, Tom slowed down, red in the face. 'I'm boiling. Come on, let's catch our breath.' He took my hands and drew me to him. 'Jane, look at me. This is what you want as well, isn't it?' He put his hands on my face and looked into my eyes.

'Yes, Tom, it is.'

'Well, come on, then. We've caught our breath, so let's not waste any more time.'

We picked our way along the riverbank, ducking low-hanging branches as we went, but Tom still scraped his head more than once.

'Either I'm getting taller, or these trees are so weighed down with leaves and flowers, they're in danger of coming down.'

'Well, you're always getting taller, Tom, but you're right. The boughs are bending. Everything is so much greener than usual. It must mean something, but I can't think what. Meg would know.'

Tom squeezed my hand at this little mention of Meg.

'Aye, she would know. Meg's a big miss, in many ways. But she'd be happy for us, though. I know that much.'

As we approached the flat rocks, the river made a rushing sound as it forced itself through a narrow channel and then gushed out in a great surge of water. I took off my clogs and stood on the rock while Tom sat down to unfasten his boots. The rock was green, but it was warm and dry from the summer sun. I wriggled my toes in the warm moss.

He held out a hand. 'Well, Jane, are you ready to jump the rush with me?'

I nodded and leant down to pull him up. Tom's hand was almost twice the size of mine, and it gave me a warm feeling holding it.

'Right, we'll have to take a bit of a run up, so mind you don't slip.'

'You mind yourself, Tom Verger!'

'On three, then?'

'Yes, Tom, on three.'

We joined hands, counted to three and then ran along the flat rock. Tom leapt a second before me and he sailed through the sky, pulling me behind him. I landed very close to the edge and almost fell backward, but Tom wrapped his arms around me and pulled me close. Now, we were as good as married.

'You're safe, Jane. You're mine and I'm yours. For always.'

I nestled against him. He kissed the top of my head and held me close. My eyes were closed, enjoying the warmth of him, the smell of him and the feel of his racing heart. It was a good day. The best day.

'Come and sit yourself down, Jane. There's something I must do. Hold out your hand.'

I sat on the riverbank. Tom raised my left hand, examined it for a moment and then plucked some buttercups. Quickly, he pierced their thin stems with his thumbnail and fashioned them into a small ring. He knelt before me and slid the buttercups onto my finger.

'Here's gold for you, Jane. I love you and very soon, it'll be real–'

But Tom was interrupted by a stone skimming past his head and skipping across the river. I looked up to see Andrew Driver perched in the fork of the old oak.

'Hey, Tom. Did you two just jump the rush?'

Tom didn't let go of my hand, but he turned his head slightly.

'Aye, and what of it, Driver? Jealous, as usual?'

Andrew Driver jumped down from the tree and came to stand on the riverbank.

'Jealous? Of you two? Hardly. The whole village has known for years that you two would end up wed. So when's it to be? And what will the Reverend say when he hears you two have jumped the rush?'

I frowned. 'It'll be soon, Andrew. And Reverend Foster will be pleased for us.'

'No doubt, Jane. But Verger, you should have asked him first.'

Tom frowned. 'I will ask him. But I wanted to ask Jane first.'

'Well, let's just hope he doesn't turn you down. You being no better than a verger's lad.'

I glared at Andrew. 'The Reverend won't say no to Tom. He loves him like a son. And there's nothing wrong with being a verger. I'll be a Verger myself soon enough, and I'll be proud to bear the name.'

'Only jesting, Jane. No need to be so serious all the time. Now, you'll be heading up for the feast, so I'll walk with you.'

Tom let go of my hand and punched his friend on the arm. 'More goosegogging, Driver? We need to find you a lass of your own. Jane, are there any lasses daft enough to have this lump?'

'Let me think on it, Tom. A name will come if I think hard enough.'

I wished Andrew would go away, or that he'd not been there in the first place. But he was Tom's oldest friend, so I had to make room for him.

Tom looked Andrew up and down. 'Well, you're shorter than me and stouter. Jane has a hard labour on her hands thinking of a lass for you.'

I dug Tom in the ribs. 'Well, May Green has always liked your curling hair, Andrew, so I could do some matchmaking—'

Driver snorted. 'May Green? Not a chance. Let me do my own matchmaking. Anyway, let's get going to the top field, or we'll miss the fire-wheel.'

* * *

It was a long walk to the top field. Even though the sun had fallen, the air held the day's heat and sweat ran down my spine. Small knots of people stood at the top of the hill. The fields were empty of beasts, they being held on the other side of the river for safety. A huge roll of hay sat at the top of the hill, contained within two wooden hoops, with a shaft of wood passed through the middle. I pressed one hand into the hay. It was warm and dry, and it would have been under cover since last year's harvest. The roll was thick and it must sorely grieve the farmer to make this sacrifice in years when his beasts went thin. The farmer and his lads came over bearing torches. I linked Tom's arm and hopped up and down at his side.

'Come on, Jane, we'd better stand well back. There's no telling which way the wheel will roll when it's alight.'

The farmer stood behind the wheel, brandishing his torch, while his eldest sons stood to either side. All at once, they lowered their flaming torches, and with a great crackling, the hay took the flames. The farmer gathered the torches and stepped back while his two sons took the shaft. Bracing themselves, and grunting with the effort, they heaved the burning wheel onto the lip of the hill, where it careered downwards in a flare of sparks and flames. We stood in the dark and watched its fiery progress down the hill. It travelled in a straight line, never once pausing in its flight, leaving trails of small fires in its wake. The speed of the fire-wheel amazed me. All the villagers began to chase it downhill, watching it bounce and trying to dodge the sparks, until it eventually reached the river, where it landed with a huge hiss and a plume of black smoke.

The farmer sent his sons to the hilltops to light the lucky fires. The farmer himself came to the centre of the village to light the main bonfire. When it was well away, his wife and daughters would lead their beasts past the purifying fire. The fire quickly grew bigger and brighter as people fetched out their old floor rushes and bedding in readiness for a new year. The smoke made my eyes water and I rubbed them with my arm. Tom swallowed some mead from Andrew Driver's flask, but he made a face and refused a second pull.

Andrew snorted and swallowed a long draft. 'Hey, Verger, they're bringing out the carline cake. Do you fancy your chances?'

Tom scratched his chin. 'I'm not that fussed about cake, but you get yourself some.'

'Well-spoken by my friend, the coward.'

Andrew jumped forward and jabbed at Tom's arm. But Tom turned quickly and Andrew fell into the night air.

May Green came forward, carrying a platter with a large cake resting on it. She approached friends, family and neighbours, holding the platter out until each man took a small square. As May approached us, Tom grimaced, but reached out for a piece. As he reached out, Andrew jumped to his feet, snatched the piece of cake Tom was about to take and stuffed it into his own mouth. May Green giggled so hard that she almost let go of the platter.

I glared at him. 'Andrew Driver, that was Tom's piece and you know it.'

But Andrew swallowed his portion and grinned at Tom. 'Go on then, your turn, Verger. Unless you're scared of an old superstition?'

Tom shrugged, 'I'm scared of naught, especially not a bit of Beltane daftness. Here, Jane, you hold the platter for me. I'll close my eyes and take my chances.'

May passed the platter. The cake smelt of ginger, cinnamon and cloves. Tom stretched out, groping until his fingers lighted on a piece, which he lifted to his mouth. But I gasped and he opened his eyes. The cake in his hand was blackened.

Andrew Driver punched the air. 'Tom Verger got the carline!

Verger's the Beltane Carline! You're a dead man, Verger, you're dead to us all.'

I looked at Andrew, wondering at his fire-crazed features. 'Ignore him, Tom, it's just a stupid game. Come, throw it on the fire. No harm done.'

But Andrew pushed himself between us. 'No, Jane, it's not a game. There's a price to be paid at Beltane. And Tom's it. Come on, Verger, into the fire with you!'

By now, the village children had surrounded Tom, no doubt full of excitement at the idea of sacrifice, but hiding their eyes behind their hands all the same.

Andrew's father joined the chorus. 'Come on, Verger, over the flames you go. Don't bring us barren fields by dallying like a maid.'

Tom crushed the blackened cake in his hand and winked at me. 'Clear the way, then, I'm coming through.'

He walked twenty paces away from the fire, then turned and sprinted towards the flames. He scattered blackened crumbs behind him as he leapt the bonfire and landed in a heap of long limbs on the other side. A loud cheer erupted. Tom stood up and brushed the ashes from himself. At least he'd not burnt in the fire – plenty had over the years. He looked over his shoulder, trying to catch my eye, but I couldn't look at him. The game must be played. Tom Verger was no more. Tom Verger was dead and gone. Tom Verger would be ignored as a walking wraith. My shoulders slumped. This wasn't how I'd hoped to spend Beltane and now Tom must stay alone for hours, if not days or weeks, depending on the villagers' mood.

* * *

I stood alone in the silent dark, trying to hold my breath until the sun rose. The only light came from glowing fires and from the sliver of old moon left in the sky. Almost dead moon. Tom came to my side and smiled at me. He snaked an arm around my waist and pulled me close, breathing hot air into my ear. I pushed him away.

'Tom Verger, you reek of mead! Are you drunk?'

He guffawed, seeming to find this question very funny. 'A bit, but then I'm a dead man and so I must have some merrymaking. Come on, Jane. Tell me what you think of me. Can you truly see me? For I'm the Beltane Carline and I'm no longer the boy I was.'

I laughed and turned to face him. 'Well, Carline, you're a tall man, red of hair and beard. Or is that just the firelight casting you in its own image?'

He placed his hands on my shoulders and it was all I could do to keep my breathing even.

'Jane Chandler, I'm your red man made of firelight.' He leaned forward and kissed me on the forehead, where my crown of daisies hung low.

'Tom, what are you doing?'

'I wish you to heal my heart, Jane.'

'Heal your heart, Tom Verger? How much mead have you had exactly?' My voice was stern, but I was smiling.

'Well, now we're betrothed, we need only wait two moons until our handfasting. And it's such a clear night, with the bonniest moon hanging in the sky.'

'But it's my fertile time, Tom, I can't lie with you – we'll surely make a bairn.'

I felt the blood rise up my neck and into my face, and Tom grinned at me.

'Jane, divvent blush so! The blood's risen so fast to your face our village might mistake you for a false dawn.'

'Sh, Tom, you'll only make me blush more! But at least you sound more like my Tom and not this strange carline man made of firelight.'

He leant down and murmured warm breath into my hair. 'Anyway, would making a bairn be such a bad thing, my lovely Jane?'

He hardened against me, making my breath catch, and then ran his hand down my back until he reached the small of it and drew me against him.

I stretched up to kiss him, but then stopped and looked at him. 'Tom, your eyes have taken on a strange hue.'

His eyes bored into me and something gave inside. I slipped a hand into his jerkin to cover his heart and he started as my hand met his skin. My fingers pushed through coarse hair. His heartbeat was very strong and deep, and my hand listened to its rhythm. This silent gesture was as good as any handfasting.

Tom put an arm around my shoulder and walked me towards the meadow. I was warmed through sunshine, dancing and mead, and instinct began overtaking good sense. Tom's arms tightened around me, he smiled into my eyes and drew me into a kiss. Then he laid me down gently behind a sheltering knoll. His hands slipped from my shoulders to rest on my hips, pulling me against the length of his body. There came a faint roseate glow from the east, which lit up his dark eyes. As the sun's rays lengthened, he kissed me, still holding me tight. I could feel his heart pounding against my own.

Wordless, Tom took me to him and I breathed him in, my Tom, who smelt only of goodness. He unfastened the ties at the neck of my white dress. I lifted it over my head and I was naked against the earth when he kissed me again. His breath was hard. Tom pushed into me, I bit into his shoulder and there was a small giving way and a bloom of heat as I accepted him. He held me tight to him and I was afraid his weight might crush the breath from me. But I began to shift beneath him, my eyes wide, staring into his, as he moved deeper inside me. Every part of me yearned for him as I rose to meet him, to absorb him, to own him. Then I pressed my face into his shoulder as he pushed himself into me again and again, moving faster and faster, his hip bones grinding against my own, his breath hot in my ear. I clung to him and writhed, and our bodies were both slick with sweat.

Finally spent, he raised his weight from me, then pulled me to him and wrapped his arms around me. My head lay on his chest, my breath coming hoarsely at first and then beginning to slow. Tom's breathing deepened and became steadier, and he held me close, pressed to his heart.

15

John

Flux

I watched as a great cramp wracked my wife's middle and she leant against the table, clutching her stomach, crying out as a warm gush of liquid left her. She took a step back and regarded the splash of blood on the floor. Although I felt quite ill myself, I bundled her onto the settle and covered her with a rug.

She gasped through her pain. 'Please, John, go and fetch Dora Shaw. Something is very … wrong.' She placed her hand between her legs and raised it to me, her fingers covered in thick blood.

I began to pace the room, all the while examining her face and recalling my uncle's words on the subject of midwives.

'I don't want that hag near my child. This bleeding must be a sign of your overly sanguine humour, and your body is just ridding itself of the excess. No doubt the barber-surgeon could staunch the bleeding down there by bleeding you up there, nearer to your heart.' I pressed a finger into the blue vein visible in her neck.

But Lucy cringed away from me. 'For shame, if you bring MacBain and his leeches, there will be no child and no mother … please … fetch Dora.'

'That woman's no better than a common witch! You know how I feel about her. And Uncle James will not tolerate–'

'I implore you, John, or you will lose us both. My heart is thundering, and I'm sure it's drowning out the faint beat of our child's heart.'

She pressed her hands between her legs again. Still the blood left her.

'John, please, I can only imagine our child uncoiling his soft grip on my insides, he must no longer have enough strength to hold fast. Please, fetch Dora ... or, if not Dora, then at least bring Kirstie Slater.'

I scrutinised my wife's face. I felt certain Kirstie Slater would not cross my threshold, and the thought of inviting Dora Shaw across my threshold sickened me. Her dark presence would surely invite disaster. And it would be hard to justify this weakening to my uncle, who must find out. But without assistance of some sort, my child would not see the light of day. I would pray every second a cunning woman was in my house. That would help off-set any malevolent intent. Tight-lipped, I left without another word.

* * *

Dora Shaw and Kirstie Slater followed me through the door, Dora clutching a damp sack. She glanced at Lucy and hurried to her side, quickly grasping her hands and gazing into her palms for some seconds. I stood with my back to the wall, keen to keep as far away from these hags as possible, muttering prayers all the while to protect my child in case of demonic ministrations.

Dora felt Lucy's brow. 'We have cause for thanks, lass, that he didn't bring MacBain to bleed you.'

Lucy opened her mouth, trying to speak.

'No. Lucy, your man has explained all to me, so save your strength. Hold your tongue and save your breath for hanging onto this child.'

Dora rolled up her cloak before pressing it under my wife's hips. Although Lucy looked barely alive, the hag kept up her yammering.

'Keep your hips up. It won't stop the bleeding, but it might slow it. Though your man could have thought of that himself. Now, open your knees for me.'

The old woman took a sharp breath and Lucy struggled to sit up.

'No, lassie, you pay no mind to daft old Dora taking on. These things always look worse than they are. Kirstie, open my sack and take out the two largest crocks.'

Her dark apprentice held up two crocks. 'These ones, Dora?

'Aye, that's them. Dried chaste tree berries and cramp bark. Grind the bark up and boil it hard for a quarter hour in two pints of water. See if you can find any honey to take away the bitterness.'

Lucy's eyes were closed and flickering. Dora pulled a rug over her and tucked her in.

'You should have brought me sooner, John.'

'Don't you go giving me accusing glances, old woman, standing over my wife's prone form as you are.'

Dora took Lucy's hand and stroked it. 'Just lie as quiet as you can, Lucy. That's right, you close your eyes and conserve your strength. The water is nearly boiled.' Dora stayed at Lucy's side, murmuring gently until Kirstie came back.

The younger woman eyed me warily and then held out a crock wrapped in cloths. A dreadful smell of wet wood rose from it.

'There was no honey, so this will taste terrible, Lucy, but it should stop the cramping and the bleeding.'

But Lucy shook her head and found the breath to speak. 'No matter, I'll suffer anything to spare my child.'

Kirstie spooned the first pint of tea into Lucy, who drank it as though it were mead. Finally, she lay back.

Dora stood up. 'Lucy is halfway asleep. John, pull your cloak over your goodwife and do not move her from this inclined position. Keep her warm and keep that fire banked. When she wakes, she must drink the other pint of brew. Later tonight, you will have to grind up some more of this bark. Boil it in a pint of water and persuade the resulting tea down her before nightfall. It will help her to mend while she sleeps. Then boil up the berries for when she wakes. There's a long way to go until she births.'

'What? Would you have me turn witch along with you and your accomplice?'

Dora clicked her tongue. 'Time is the best healer, John, and sleep the best medicine. But my brews will help nature along. After that, whether she holds onto the bairn or not, she needs plenty of warm broth and red wine in her. And if you can get her a lamb's liver, feed her small pieces as often as you can persuade her to eat.'

'A lamb's liver? You must think I'm made of gold.'

'You needn't be made of gold. Just bypass the inn and go to the butcher.'

'Get out, hag, before I smite you. And you need not expect any coin after making such dark implications against my character.'

'Kirstie, gather my belongings, but leave those two crocks. Shame on you, John, you are a disgrace to yourself, your mother and your wife. I don't know where the lovely, kind boy who lived under my roof has gone, but he is certainly not standing in this room. You've turned into your father. No, not another word from you. The bleeding has stopped, but if it starts again, fetch me straight away. Do you hear?'

When the cunning women left, Lucy turned to face me. She seemed better and the sickening cramps looked to have left her body. And the cunning women had filled her with warm liquid to take the place of the blood she'd lost. Already, I imagined the liquid flooding her womb to comfort my child and help him to stay in his place. My wife smiled and placed her hands over her belly. I prayed, willing my child to bide longer, to sleep awhile, so all would be well. God would forgive me the small transgression of employing His enemies to spare my child. And I'd deprived them of any coin, so that would go well for me in God's eyes. But my uncle must not get wind of this. And Dora Shaw would pay for speaking to me as if I were still a small boy under her thrall.

16

Jane

Chasing Cloud Shadows

I'd stood at the door for three nights running, watching the moon grow and thinking of Tom. But finally, we were here. The summer fayre in Newcastle was a cause of excitement for the whole area. Stationed at the Town Moor for the best part of a week, people travelled from all over the north to take part. As well as the mart, with pens filled with snorting beasts and stamping horses, there were lads and lasses seeking work. Milkmaids carrying three-legged crackets flirted with lads carrying scythes. There were lively discussions aplenty and coin changed hands as futures were bartered over, promised and eagerly seized.

But the fayre wasn't all work. In its wake, it brought excitement, danger and gossip from afar. And there were stalls whose sole aim was to separate fools from their money in exchange for a minute's excitement and the chance for lads to show off to lasses. The air was filled with sweat and waste, but these were much amplified, given that there were so many beasts and men at close quarters.

The craftsmen were there to show off their skills and market their wares. Smiths, tanners, dyers, fullers, weavers and tailors galore. And farmers' wives and girls sold their produce. Warm cider, weak ale and spiced mead sloshed from jugs. Hogs roasted over fires, filling the air with savoury smells and the crackle of fat melting onto flame. And above it all was the sweet smell of singing hinnies and gingerbread. But I wanted to see the gypsy carts set at the far side of the moor. They were decorated in bright patterns, with no two alike. Horses grazed under the watchful gaze of a small boy.

'Jane, we shouldn't be here.' Tom raised my basket in the air. 'Let's go and eat our dinner and then I wouldn't mind going to have a look at the heavy horses.'

'Sh, Tom. I want to have my fortune told by a gypsy woman. They can see the future in the palm of your hand.'

'Oh, aye, of course they can. Anyway, even supposing they can, what will your mam say? And what about the Reverend, what will he say?'

'They won't know, will they, Tom, for who will tell them?'

'You will, in a fit of guilt, most likely.' He nudged me. 'Look! There's a gypsy woman looking over.'

I looked around and the woman beckoned to me. But I was suddenly seized by fright, grabbed Tom's free hand and ran.

'She'll curse us for that, Jane. We're done for, and a terrible fate will befall us.'

I bent over to catch my breath. 'We've brought her no harm and taken naught from her, so she can't send a curse our way, or it'll return to her sevenfold.'

Tom frowned. 'Why did you change your mind?'

I shrugged. 'Maybe it's best not knowing what's ahead. Mam says there's a reason we don't know everything at once. Come on, let's go and find somewhere quiet and shady to eat.'

We walked to the top of the rise and sat in front of a crescent of bushes. It was a natural windbreak, warm and private. While I unpacked the food, Tom swatted away clouds of glittering insects.

I smiled at him. 'I've got a surprise for you.'

'A nice surprise, or a nasty surprise?'

'Nice. Definitely nice. Do you want it now, or later?'

He laughed. 'Now, of course. Come on, divvent tease.'

From the basket, I took a soft package and handed it to Tom. He weighed it in his hand. It was an egg, nestling in wool scraps. It was pure white and caught the sun, sending it glaring back to our eyes. At arm's length, it seemed smooth and perfect, impervious,

126

impenetrable. Its secret contents protected inside the immaculate shell, safe and precious. Tom held it up to the light between finger and thumb. The sun shone right through it.

'It's raw ... thank you, Jane.'

I'd nearly boiled it and had even put the pot of water simmering high over the fire so the bubbles were just right – big enough to stop the egg clunking on the bottom of the pot, but not so violent as to smash it against the sides. I couldn't bear the thought of it cracking, the thought of that liquid potential being spoiled, the insides turning into a matt sun suspended in a shiny white sky. So I'd just watched the sands pour through the hour-glass, then lifted the pot off the heat and watched the bubbles subside. I'd polished the egg, more precious than a skull, and tucked it into its tiny bed.

'I know it's raw. You can take it home and have it the morrow.'

He smiled and kissed me before returning the egg to its nest.

We ate a game pie and I watched him bite into it. He was so handsome. Tall and strong, with such red hair. I liked to look at his green eyes, narrowed against the sun. When he'd finished, I passed him some cherries from the garden, and we lay back on my cloak, drinking warm ale.

The sky was freshly scrubbed, pale blue and silver white. The air was full of tiny birds singing, but there was no sign of any big birds. The geese, the grouse, the pheasants and the pigeons. Their honking, clanking noises were missing. There was just the sweet tweet of the tiny birds budding on the branches, hunting for lovers. Sparrows fluttered in the hedge behind us and little dogs barked in the distance. We dozed in the sun until a huge shadow crossed us, stealing all the warmth and making the hairs on my arms stand up.

Tom grabbed my hands and dragged me to my feet. 'Cloud shadows. Come on, let's chase them.'

'Tom, you big bairn!' But I laughed as he pulled me along by the hand.

The low clouds were scudding fast, making dark islands on the high pasture. Tom pulled me along, breathless behind him, until my lungs and legs burnt.

'Slow down, Tom, we'll never catch one, it's impossible.'

'No it's not. Watch, I'll show you.' He pulled me tight against him and traced my eyebrow with his thumb. I smiled and leaned into his chest, hearing his heart thumping.

'Right, Jane, look up at me. Now, close your eyes.' He kissed my eyelids with warm lips. 'Keep them closed. Here it comes.'

The rosy, golden garden inside my eyelids was displaced by cold greys and blacks creeping in. I shivered and Tom pulled me closer. Could he feel the baby there? That swimmy fish, eyes tight shut, floating in sweet soup, asleep and dreaming. I'd need to tell him soon. But not yet, not to spoil this loveliness.

'Open your eyes, Jane.'

'Oh, please don't wake me up yet. It's so lovely here, just let me keep my eyes closed for ever.'

But he blew beery breath on my eyelids and made me open them.

'Let me look in your eyes, Jane. There, I can see right down inside you to the soles of your feet.'

It felt like he was looking into my soul, so I placed his hand over my belly.

His eyes widened. 'You should've told me. How long have you known?'

I remembered lying in his arms at Beltane, certain then that I held his child within me. 'Since Beltane. Since the moment you fell asleep.'

He frowned. 'But how could you know then?'

'Something took hold inside me.'

It made me smile, thinking of Tom's seed lying within me, knowing that it was welcomed so very warmly that it had dwelt there and created life.

'Jane, what are you grinning for? You should be worried sick!'

'Well, Tom, what are you grinning for? Perhaps Beltane induced some kind of madness, but our handfasting is soon enough and no harm can come of it.'

Tom took my hands and peered at me. 'What will we call him?'

'Her. We'll call her Rose. After your mam.'

Tom squeezed my hand and all the different greens came alive in his eyes. 'Bless you. You're certain of a girl?'

'Certain.' So he knew. And he was glad. I leaned my forehead against him.

'Listen, Jane, we'll go now. Get wed. We can do it straight away. It'll be all right if we're quick. If you don't mind the hurry and the wagging tongues.'

'No. There's no need to hurry. The wedding's soon enough.' I stretched up to kiss him on the lips. 'And anyway, ours won't be the only baby born shy of ten moons.'

'You should've told me sooner.' He peered at the sky as the sun started to set. 'Come on, duck egg. Let's go and find something tasty to eat on the walk home.'

'Tom! You've just eaten enough for three men. You can't possibly be hungry again so soon. Still, a hot pie will keep us warm on the way back.'

'You don't need a pie for that when you've got me!' He tickled me, making me laugh. 'Come on, we'd best find the others, or we'll be walking home on our own.'

We found the other villagers at the pie barrow, everyone wanting a hand-warmer for the trip home. It was fifteen miles home, but the night was dry and still warm. The whole village would leave soon since we all stuck together, there being safety in numbers. And there was always banter and singing to pass the time.

In the soft night, under a dark canopy scattered with silver stars, we shared a pork pie. I relished the crunch of the hot pastry, the sweet, melting jelly and the salted pork.

We'd finished eating barely quarter of a mile from the Town Moor. Tom took the basket from me, put his arm around my shoulder and drew me close, and I slipped my arm around his waist. We walked, singing along with the others, happily bumping into each other and trying to match each other's pace by way of me skipping to keep up and Tom shortening his stride.

'Not long until our handfasting, my little wife.'

I giggled. 'Sh, someone might hear, and we must keep silent about the child.'

'No one will hear – they're thirty yards ahead of us. Perhaps we should just dawdle here awhile. After all, what harm can there possibly be–'

Up ahead, the singing stopped and a commotion broke out. There was brawling and fighting, and it was hard to make things out in the dark. We ran to catch the others, but when we reached the women, Tom left the basket with me and peeled away.

'I have to help, Jane. You stay with the women and keep safe.'

He ran off into the knot of brawling men. There were shouts and bangs, and my stomach clenched. I dug my fingernails into my palms until they hurt. The Green bairn was bawling, and May and her mother were trying in vain to quiet him. In the dark, it was impossible to see what was going on. There were cracking sounds, which surely meant broken skulls and broken limbs. But who would do such a thing? The town barrow lads? I huddled with the women and children, straining my ears for Tom's voice and crossing my fingers. The shouts seemed to die down then and there was a scattering sound of men moving away. I sighed when I heard familiar village voices coming back towards us. Mr Green appeared, groaning and clutching a useless arm, followed by others who stumbled about trying to find their sweethearts. But there was no sign of Tom. I ran forward a few yards, thinking Tom must be hanging back. Perhaps he was hurt and lying in a dark ditch. But I couldn't see him anywhere. A cold feeling overtook me, and I ran back to the villagers.

'Where's Tom? Where's Tom?'

But no one replied, and Mr Green just stood there, slack-jawed and not saying anything to me.

I could stand it no more, and I shook Mr Green.

'Why is no one telling me anything? What's going on? Where's my Tom?'

The man looked at me and shook his head. 'Jane, pet, you must be strong. The hot press has taken the lads ahead of us, them from the Tyne and practised keelmen. It looks like they've ganged Tom with them.'

I swallowed a couple of times, turned and retched. When I'd wiped my mouth, I faced Mr Green.

'Tell me what happened.'

'There was too many of them, massive men with cudgels. They cracked our skulls and then it looks like they've carried off the biggest and strongest they could find. They weren't interested in me beyond breaking my arm.'

'But Tom's just a lad, an apprentice too! They can't take him. It's not allowed.'

'It's the hot press, Jane, so no exceptions made. Not for apprentices, not for married men and not even for keelmen carrying protection papers.'

'But my Tom's never been to sea! What will they do with him?' My voice rose.

'They'll make him work for the navy. Maybe they mistook your lad for a seafarer. I don't see what use a country verger will be aboard a warship.'

'A warship?' I swung my head wildly from side to side. 'No, it can't be. But he'll come home, won't he? It's not forever …'

* * *

Reverend Foster, on hearing the news, looked past me and into the distance, as if seeking Tom on the far horizon.

'You can say it, Reverend. Tales of the hot press abound. So many impressed men are never seen again. Lost at sea, lost at war, or stranded on foreign shores. And so close to our handfasting.'

'Jane, you must resign yourself to the fact that Tom may not return for many years. If at all.'

Tears wobbled at the brink of my eyelids 'I'll wait for as long as it takes. He'll come back to me, I know it.'

'Ah, Jane, my girl. I'm sorry, truly, I am.'

I fled from the house and ran to the garden to sit amongst Mam's lemon balm. But not even that could lift my spirits today. Tom was taken from me – for how long and to where, who knew? I buried my face in my arms and sobbed, grieving Tom's absence as if it were his death, sure in my heart I'd never set eyes on him again.

* * *

The dock heaved with activity. Men in wool coats patrolled the quay and bare-chested men carted loads of wares and herds of livestock onto the ship. The air was fresh with brine and full of whistles, shouts and bleats. The ship's masts were festooned with neatly furled sails and cobwebs of rigging, which tiny men scrambled up and down. It made me dizzy to look up and watch them against the blue sky, especially with the sun so bright in my eyes. A pale-blue flag rippled in the mild breeze. On the stern of the ship was her name, *The Durham*, and along the side were holes, through which poked the snouts of a dozen cannon.

'Oh, Mam, it is a warship, after all, and my Tom's being sent to war!' I clutched Mam's arm. 'We must get him back.'

'Jane, Jane, whisht, or you'll make yourself bad.'

'We must speak to someone, Mam. When they know Tom's to be a father, they'll surely set him free.'

I ran towards an armed man, with Mam close behind me. He quickly turned and trained his gun on us. I drew to a halt, with both hands over my belly. He didn't lower his gun, but used it to indicate that I should move away.

'Please, sire, how long? How long will the ship be gone? Where is it bound?'

'Can't say.'

'Please, sire, my child's father has been taken aboard this ship. His name is Tom Verger. He's very tall, with red hair. He must come home, else we can't survive.'

'Plenty more in your boat. He'll be back one day. If he lasts.'

Mam stepped forward 'What do you mean, sire, if he lasts?'

'Young lad overboard this morning and ship not yet under sail. Cracked his head. Dead as a doornail.'

My hands crept up to cover my mouth. 'How young? What was he like?'

The guard shrugged. 'Long, skinny streak. Ginger–'

'His name? What was his name?'

He snorted. 'No name. Not aboard long enough.'

'Oh, but … Tom. That sounds like my Tom!'

'Then your Tom will be buried at sea. Be off, else I must waste precious lead on you.'

Ice-cold, despite the summer heat, I turned to face my mother. 'Oh, Mam. He says Tom is dead. My Tom! Oh, I wish I could fall into the sea and be with him.'

My mother caught my hands. 'Tom can't be dead so soon. He's a big, strong lad. The guard is most likely just trying to get a rise from you. Look! Look! There's your Tom!'

'Tom! Tom!' I turned and made to run at the ship, but the guard held me back with his gun and Mam drew me away. But then a shout came from the ship. Tom waved at me and shouted to catch my attention. I cupped my hands to my ears, straining to hear his words, but the sea breeze took them. It was enough, though. It was enough to see my Tom alive and breathing, even if he was being taken away from me.

'Oh, God, thank you, God.' I hopped up and down trying to get a better glimpse of him. 'Tom, Tom, I'll wait for you. Come back to me!'

A man with a stick hit Tom in the back of the knees and he crumpled before being hauled away out of sight. Tears pricked my eyes.

'Oh, Mam, how can they treat him so cruelly? How will he bear it, my lovely Tom?'

Mam hugged me and pulled me away from the ship. 'He'll bear it because he knows he has you to come home to. Come, the ship is readying to go and Tom with it. You must be strong, for the sake of Tom and your bairn.'

17

John

In God's Hands

Lucy woke me up and I was still thick-tongued with whisky and sleep.

'What's that? What are you yammering on about?'

'John, John! Get Dora, it's time.'

'It can't be. Barely six moons have passed.'

'Six moons or no, he's coming, my birthing pain has started.'

'Go to sleep, there'll be hours yet – the first ones always take their time. So let me rest and cut your greeting.'

'But, John … I'm scared, the birthing pains are … very close together … and that pain in my head is much worse. Please, fetch Dora.'

With a sigh, I sat up, rubbing my eyes. Such a selfish wee bitch. 'Could you not wait until morning?'

I took a draught of whisky from my flask.

'John, please!'

'At least grant me time for some warming whisky since it's not you who must go out in the night.' I wiped my mouth and stared at my wife. She was sweating, the whites of her eyes showed and her colour was very high. 'You can have the barber-surgeon, but that hag isn't coming in my home again.'

Lucy forced herself up on her elbows. Aye, the woman could find wind aplenty when she fancied.

'But, John, MacBain knows nothing of birthing–'

'He's a practised surgeon and he'll more than do for you.'

She clutched her belly, panting like a sick dog, and I looked into her glittering eyes. She sank back onto the pallet, her hands pressed to her head.

'Please … get Dora, there's so little time. It's a woman I need. Please go. There's no more time … for whisky.'

'Time must be made. It's a wet night – not that you'd care – you who gets to stay in your warm pit while I walk three miles there and back to the barber-surgeon.'

I meant to help her back to her senses, but a surge of bloody liquid from between her thighs stayed my hand. She let out a mighty groan that left her unable to speak for a time. Her belly went rigid and then it softened again.

'There's my waters broken. I beg you. Please get Dora. She can be here in no time.'

'Stop your yammering. That woman is not getting her killing hands near my bairn.'

'Something's wrong, John. My heart pounds in my ears and my head throbs in time with it.'

'Ach, away with you, all women suffer the same, as decreed by God.'

'No, John, there are white stars in my eyes.'

I looked at her eyes. 'Your eyes look fine to me. The whites are a bit red, but that's no doubt caused by all your crying. It's just the trials of childbirth.'

'Not these exploding stars in my eyes … and not this headache.'

I looked at her again. She did look in a bad way, but childbirth was something that women bore and surely without all this fuss.

'Please, John, it's as if my heart has moved into my head – my entire body pounds to its beat.'

Was this usual? My uncle never referred to pains in the head. 'But it's the pains in your lower body that will bring out the baby? How are they?'

'Much outweighed by those in my head, which must burst at any time.'

I peered more closely and laid a hand on her. Lucy's forehead was hot. I put a finger into her mouth, where it seemed so dry that

135

it was a wonder her tongue hadn't stuck to the roof of her mouth. I thought of my mother. And Dora Shaw accusing my father of not fetching help in time.

'All right. You shall have your way. Or some of it. If you must have a woman, I'll fetch Kirstie Slater.'

My uncle would surely be less angered at an apprentice than at a full-blown witch.

Her belly turned rigid once more, her purple face deepened its hue and she wailed and clutched at herself, so I took my cloak and left, hunching over against the driving rain. I looked to the wood where Dora's shack was. For a second, I considered fetching her. It would save the soaking walk, if nothing else. The hag might bide with Lucy until I got back with MacBain or Kirstie. But Uncle James had convinced me that there was no way Dora Shaw and her wicked ways could be in the room when my child was born. Her presence alone would contaminate his clean soul at his most vulnerable hour. So I set away, stamping through the night air to fetch Kirstie. She was nearer than MacBain and would have to do. Lucy was making an unnecessary fuss when these things always took hours. Even so, I lengthened my stride.

* * *

I knocked Kirstie out of bed. She threw on her cloak and snatched a satchel from next to the door. I took this load from her to speed the journey. But for all her stoutness and shortness, she was a sturdy maid and fleet of foot. While we huffed our way up the hill, heads down against the rain, Kirstie questioned me.

'How did your wife seem?'

'Like a great sow groaning on her pallet.'

'I see. And her waters, have they broken yet?'

'Aye, she lies in the wetness that fluxed from her.' I thought of the ruined straw, which would need replacing.

'And how is her heat?'

'Sweat runs from her and her mouth is hot and very dry.'

Kirstie nodded. 'Anything else?'

'She's complaining of lights in her eyes and pains in her head. Is that usual?'

The young hag frowned at this. 'No, it's not usual at all. How are your wife's hands and feet?'

I glared at the girl. 'What of it? Her hands and feet looked tight and swollen.'

'Come, John, we must run. I don't like the sound of this. It sounds like Lucy is set for birthing fits. You must fetch Dora quickly. I'll go to your wife and do what I can till she gets there. Quick, go.'

'You stupid wee whore. Call yourself a midwife?'

'This is no time for name calling! Just fetch Dora and I'll go to your wife.'

I ran into the dripping woods, cursing as my feet tripped on roots and my cloak snagged on branches. As I approached Dora's shack, I sent up a prayer to God. Uncle James must surely understand my need in such a dark hour. I hammered on the door with both fists, before bursting in on the old hag in her bed.

'Dora, you must come. Kirstie Slater thinks Lucy is set for birthing fits. You've got your own way, but be quick about it.'

I stayed long enough to make sure the old woman was stirred from her sleep. Then I ran out, leaving the door open in case she had any ideas of returning to sleep. I ran on to my own cottage, but the light was out. Once inside, I was met with cold air, so I started to bank the fire.

Kirstie was feeling my wife's brow. 'Is Dora coming?'

'Aye, I shook her from her bed.'

'I'll do what I can until then. Get me some light and some water.'

I lit the lantern and then passed the pitcher, wishing only to return to the blessed sanctity of the night while the young hag ministered to my wife.

'Come, Lucy, let's try and cool your blood.'

Kirstie pulled muslin strips from her pouch, soaked them in cold water and laid them across Lucy's forehead. Before I could stop her, she lifted up my wife's shift and gaped at the scars on her swollen breasts. Even I was shocked, for the rapid growth of Lucy's breasts had stretched and distorted the bite marks. And the leaping flames of the lantern made them flicker and move. Quietly, Kirstie began laying strips of wet cloth across my naked wife. Then she dripped water into the corner of her mouth.

'Lucy, take some water from the cloth. You're burning hot and your skin is red and shining as if your own blood would cause you to burst. I must keep laying cold cloths on you.'

Kirstie replaced the dried-out strips with newly wetted ones and then turned to glare at me.

'Your wife has a terrible fever and a pounding heart. I'll use hawthorn and mugwort to ease her blood and soothe her. But she may need to be bled before she has apoplexy.'

'You damned slattern, you know nothing. Keep your nasty knives to yourself. And none of that witch poison, for that is what finished my own mother.'

But before she could reply, Dora Shaw entered and came to Lucy's side. She laid her hands on Lucy before speaking.

'You did well to send for me, Kirstie. She's in a bad way, John. We'll do whatever we can. But your wife has the same condition as your mother. Both Lucy and the child are in God's hands. You'd do well to start praying.'

I reared as if to strike one or both women, but the will left me and I knelt by Lucy. I'd pray for my child. That, I could do. I was a godly man. The Lord would show mercy and spare my child. While I prayed, Dora and Kirstie spoke in hushed voices, the older woman asking the younger one what she'd tried so far and nodding at her replies.

'Well done, Kirstie, there's no more I could have done myself. All we have left is to bleed the lass.'

My eyes flew open and I stopped praying 'No, I forbid it, bleeding is the work of the devil and it'll kill the bairn.'

'John, there's no choice. Lucy's blood has boiled to a dangerous head and it'll soon cause apoplexy. That is sure to end her, and with her, the baby.'

'If Lucy dies, you can cut the bairn from her, can you not?'

Dora turned wet eyes on me. 'Aye, John, we can. But there's no certainty that the baby won't already have been killed inside her.'

At that, Lucy's body wracked, her belly tight and her face puce. She fitted for a moment and blood-specked foam appeared at her mouth. Then she fell back, slack-bellied and open-eyed on the bed.

'Don't just stand there, hags, cut my child free. Shift and I'll do it myself.'

Dora held up a hand. 'We'll do it, else you jab the bairn. But I warn you, Lucy's blood was as furious as a furnace and the heat may have killed the child already.'

Kirstie raised her flenching knife. Once Dora confirmed that Lucy was dead, the girl pushed her knife into Lucy's body. Together, the women opened her belly and lifted out my slippery child. Dora rubbed his blue flesh and cleaned his face with muslin. She dandled him by his feet and cracked his backside with the flat of her hand. Then she swaddled him and gave the silent child to Kirstie.

'I'm sorry, John, he's still. They've both gone.'

She drew a sheet up over Lucy's destroyed body.

I looked at her, dry-eyed and silent.

18

Jane

The Brief Candle

I was making syrup from dried violets, which in normal times was my greatest joy, but today the fragrance was overwhelming and made me queasy. Somehow, dried violets had an even more cloying smell than freshly picked flowers. When I was a child, Mam would wave a spoon in the air at me, telling me how the syrup eased pains of the heart and the head. She'd let me lick the spoon, but always warned me to be careful with violets, because once you'd smelt them, you could never smell them again. That certainly wasn't true for me in my present condition, as I could smell violets a mile off. In truth, it would be a blessing not to smell them anymore.

A sound jarred me from my thoughts, and I saw Reverend Foster hurrying towards the house. This was unlike the Reverend, who never hurried a day in his life. When I opened the door, he had a bad look about him.

'What's wrong, Reverend? You don't look quite yourself.'

'Oh, Jane. There's such dreadful news. I might never be myself again. Where's Annie?'

'I'm here. Why, Reverend, what's wrong? You look terrible. Come and sit next to the fire. Jane, bring some wine.'

But he shook his head. 'No, Annie, you fetch the wine and let Jane sit next to the fire.' Reverend Foster pressed me onto the fireside cracket. 'Jane, you need to be ready for a terrible shock. The most terrible of all shocks.'

Lead settled in my belly at these words and I looked up at the Reverend, my face crumpling. 'No, please, no … not my Tom.'

Reverend Foster took my hands between his own. 'Yes, dear Jane, I'm afraid so. I heard it this morning in Newcastle. Tom's ship went down, with all souls lost.'

* * *

There was no spirit in me and I stared woodenly into the hearth.

My mother held me tightly to her. 'Come, we'll boil up chicken-enwort for a warming broth.'

'But it's the height of summer, Mam. What do I want with a warming broth?'

Mam frowned. 'It'll sustain you and prevent you from succumbing to a fever.'

'Oh, I wish I could succumb to a fever, and then I could join Tom.'

'Whisht, Jane, you mustn't say such things.'

'It's true! I can't bear it. For him to be snatched away like that and then to drown in the cold, dark sea, with not a single person known to him.'

Mam pulled me closer. 'Jane, I'm sorry for you, truly. And I know this is a very bad time for you, but you must stop to consider your future.'

I sprang away, my eyes wide. 'Mam! I can't believe you could say such a thing. Tom lying in a watery grave and now you'd wish the same fate on his child. Well, I'll not do it. I'll not. This baby is all that's left of Tom.'

'Sorry, pet. But please don't make your life harder than it needs to be. Come on, we must get going. We must tell Bill these dreadful tidings.'

My mother put her arm around me and drew me back to her. Together, we went to seek Bill Verger and found him walking up the hill from the village. As he drew near, his brow wrinkled.

'What's wrong? Not even a twinkle from either of you.'

I scarce knew how to tell him, and doubted any sensible words would find their way out of me, so I stood back while Mam took Bill's hands and looked him square in the face.

141

'Bill, the Reverend heard terrible news this morning. *The Durham* went down, with all souls lost.'

He pulled away from Mam, sank to the little hillock behind him and put his head in his hands.

'Dear God. Dear God, my own sweet lad taken.'

Mam said nothing, pulled me to her side and we waited for Bill to gather his wits. When he looked up, his face was wet and he struggled to keep his voice even.

'I must arrange my lad's burial. Even though his ... his body isn't here, this was the place of his heart and he must have a cross in memory.' He swallowed noisily. 'It's not decent, a Verger lad being committed to the sea. I'll ask the Reverend if he'll pray for my lost lad. Will he do that, do you think?' He turned rheumy eyes on Mam as he struggled to his feet.

Mam nodded. 'Oh, Bill, of course the Reverend will pray for Tom. He'll give a service, as is usual for men ... men who are lost at sea.'

'I'll put our Tom's cross next to his mother. She'd want him close and safe.'

My chin quivered and I didn't trust myself to speak without crying. It felt wrong for me to mourn, seeing Bill, who'd lost both wife and child.

But Mam spoke. 'Tom would like that. It'll give comfort to mother and son.'

'God bless you, Annie. And you, Jane. Instead of looking forward to a wedding, all we have to look forward to is a funeral, without even the grace of my lad's body to bury.' He shook his head. 'My sweet lad, him that spent his days making sure that the departed were safely delivered into the earth.'

Tears glazed Bill's eyes once more. He'd not even have the comfort of performing that last terrible service for his own son.

* * *

The church was packed and I sat in the front pew, flanked by Bill and Mam. Reverend Foster prayed for Tom's soul and for the souls of all the other men lost on *The Durham*. He also prayed for those still at sea. It gave no comfort to me and tears ran freely down my face. Reverend Foster explained that Tom was in a better place, but it just made me angry, and I was tired of hearing his voice. I laughed bitterly and Mam put a hand on my arm.

After the short service, the villagers came to speak to me and to Bill. Andrew Driver was amongst them, but he hung back to shake hands with Bill and Mam while I took comfort in the arms of May Green. When Andrew approached me, cap between his hands, May untangled herself from me and scurried away.

'Jane, I'm right sorry about Tom. If I could've swapped places with him that night, then I'd have done it gladly. I only wish I'd been there. The hot press might have taken me instead.'

'They might have taken you as well, you mean. And what might that have achieved? Then it would be your mam and dad standing here grieving as well.'

'Aye, I know. But I wouldn't be leaving a sweetheart behind. Or a bairn.'

I baulked at this and hissed at him. 'What? What are you saying?'

Andrew shook his head. 'Settle yourself, Jane. It's not hard to guess for anyone looking close enough. But don't worry, I'm deep as the … at any rate, deep. I'll not breathe a word. But listen, there's no need for you to hide yourself away any more.'

I glared at him. 'There's every need. Someone in my condition can't be seen living under the church's roof, or any roof, for that matter. No one was meant to know. You must promise not to tell another living soul.'

Andrew stuffed his hat into his jerkin and grabbed my hands. 'Jane, marry me. I can look after you and Tom's bairn–'

But I snatched my hands back. 'How could you? How could you? My Tom is barely in his grave. In fact, he's not even in his grave, but lying in the cold sea and you're trying to steal me and his baby. I'd sooner starve than marry a man who would betray his best friend!'

With that, I left Andrew staring and fled to the house.

* * *

143

In the morning, I went out to gather roses to place on Tom's cross. Although he wasn't resting there, it gave me a place to remember him. The spiteful thorns scratched me and the pain was welcome, since this day was too beautiful for a world without Tom in it. I was sucking the blood from my thumb when Bill came towards me. He'd aged, and no wonder, considering the loss he had to bear.

'Morning, hinny. Those for our Tom?' Bill nodded towards the roses climbing up the wall.

'Yes, Tom might like them on his ... on ... well, he always loved roses the best.'

'Aye, he did that. They were his mother's favourite flowers and he always picked them for her when he was little.'

The old man smiled crookedly and I wondered at his pain. The thought of Tom as a motherless boy made my breath catch and my chin quiver. Bill put out his calloused hand and clasped my shoulder.

'Now, Jane, don't go being sorry for me, or for our Tom. He's gone to his reward and he'll be with his mother, God rest her, so you mustn't take on so.'

But it was no use and my tears refused to be held back. 'Tom was such a good person. I just can't bear the thought of his bairn never knowing him.'

'His child will know him through you and me. But he isn't coming back and you need to decide what to do.'

I eyed the old man. 'But what is there to do?'

Bill patted my shoulder. 'You can see sense and do what Tom would have you do. Marry young Driver.'

The basket of roses fell from my hand. 'Bill Verger! You can't mean it? Surely, you of all people wouldn't have this? And what would Tom think?'

'Lass, it would please my lad's heart. The very last thing Tom would want in all the world would be for you and his bairn to suffer because he can't be here to care for you. Young Driver is a kind lad to offer himself.'

'What will people say? I was promised to Tom. Our wedding was in the offing.'

'Tongues will wag as they always have. There's not a law in the land that says a lass can't be married to another in this situation. None need know that the bairn isn't Andrew's, or even that there was a bairn to begin with. Only a few of us know and we'll not tell another living soul.'

'But, it's disloyal to Tom's memory, to you, to the baby. And it's not even fair on Andrew, making him settle for a wife who loves someone else.'

Bill plucked a white rose and passed it to me. 'Come on, we'll place this beauty on Tom's cross. And you can make sure that he's the first person you tell. My lad will give you his blessing and you already have mine. Then go and see young Driver.'

I looked at Bill Verger's shining eyes and wondered how the Vergers came to be such good people. He took my hand and we walked to the plot of earth that he'd marked out for Tom. Kneeling before the little wooden cross, I placed the rose beneath it. There was a lump in my throat that was somehow connected to a new flood of tears pricking at the back of my eyes. There was plenty for me to say, but my voice was certain to come out in a rush of tears and croaks, so I swallowed hard first.

'Oh, Tom. I hardly know how to begin ...' But the one thing I couldn't do was marry Andrew Driver. Just the thought of it gave me a cold feeling in my heart.

19

John

Satanic Kisses

In front of the kirk session, I retold the anguish caused by the two women, Kirstie Slater and Dora Shaw, who'd conspired to kill my wife and child. What I did not tell was the feeling of rage that had overtaken me in all my recent waking hours.

'Aye, the elder witch, Dora Shaw, not content with taking my blessed mother all those years ago, has waited for another chance to cause me yet more agony.'

The moderator peered down his nose at me. 'Very well, Sharpe, explain what took place.'

'Kirstie Slater, the youngest witch, was left alone with my wife while she sent me to fetch her dark mistress, Dora Shaw. When I entered my home, it was to see my wife's swollen body made naked, with her breasts laid bare to the night. But they were covered with the bite marks of the devil's own satanic kisses—'

'That's a plain lie!' Kirstie pointed her finger straight at me. 'You made them marks with your own teeth. You're a cruel man and you were a liar from birth!'

This fire from the young hussy was quite unexpected. Although under oath, I felt certain that God, who saw all, forgave all. Even so, to be safe, I closed my eyes and recited a silent prayer to Him, seeking forgiveness. If the truth needed to be managed to avenge my mother, my wife and my child, then so be it. But it was a relief when the moderator's eye was taken off me for a few moments as a small struggle broke out amongst the rougher elements. The scuffle took two burly sergeants and their clubs to quieten it. The moderator pursed his lips and looked ready to continue only once peace was restored and the injured removed from the premises.

'These are strong words, Kirstie Slater, mayhap with little foundation to them. Mr Sharpe being renowned as a God-fearing man and raised by our own pastor.'

Kirstie opened her mouth, seemed to think better of it and then hung her head.

The moderator made a note. 'Very well, as the maid seems done with her tale, the crowner may give his record.'

The crowner stepped forward and waved his soft hands before his face as if trying to rid himself of flying insects.

'As crowner, it has been my terrible duty to make a searching examination of the late Goodwife Sharpe.' He paused and wrung his hands. 'It's true that her breasts were scarred by bite marks both numerous and demonic in their nature.'

I nodded, glancing around the room, pleased at the stir created by this news. Even the crowner seemed to enjoy the sensation. But the moderator looked less impressed.

'Yes, yes, we shall get to that, crowner. But could these bite marks possibly be the work of John Sharpe. Pray, can you tell us that?'

The crowner rested his eye on me. 'I can certify these bite marks were not the work of John Sharpe. It is my belief that the hag, Dora Shaw, did counsel with Satan, bargaining the souls of Goodwife Sharpe and her child.'

Dora's face became livid and she shouted out. 'Crowner, those marks were old. They'd healed and scarred since they'd been made months ago—'

The sergeant cuffed Dora, who fell down in a heap of bones, nursing her lip.

The moderator frowned. 'Crowner, this seems most unsatis-factory. Is there any possibility that these marks were made by John Sharpe? Think hard on it, man.'

The crowner rubbed his nose and then shook his head so thoroughly that his jowls wobbled.

'Assuredly not, moderator. At my examination, I put callipers to the bite marks and also to Sharpe's jaw.'

The room fell silent as the man produced two pairs of callipers. He adjusted them and held up the first pair, whose points were two inches apart.

'Please note the opening of John Sharpe's jaw. Stretched to its utmost, there's scarce two inches between upper and lower incisors. To whit ...'

He nudged me and I opened my mouth.

The crowner inserted the callipers.

'A perfect fit, you see, perfect.'

A man in the crowd ran forward and pointed at me. 'Look at Sharpe's huge dog teeth! He could take a bite from a horse's backside!'

The ensuing rumble of disgraceful laughter was quickly put down by the moderator and his gavel, along with some encouragement from the sergeants' clubs.

'We will have silence. The crowner must be allowed to continue.'

Consulting his notebook, the crowner took the second pair of callipers and fitted them to a set of marks set out on thin paper.

'I made an ink replica of a bite mark on Goodwife Sharpe's left breast.'

He held up the paper, which showed a meticulously drawn bite mark – albeit a distorted one. Then he held up the second pair of callipers, whose points were four inches apart. Once more, I opened my mouth and the throng hushed as they saw the callipers run wide of my mouth.

The crowner nodded. 'You see, moderator, no man's teeth could make this bite, which is the mark of the devil's jackal. And it cannot be coincidence that he marked the left breast, which is the devil's own side, is it not?' My eyes swept the room as the crowner pointed to the variance in size between the callipers and my open jaw.

Dora appealed to the moderator. 'But sire, a woman's breasts must engorge when she is with child. Oft as not, they'll double in size. Surely, you see that this accounts for the enlarged scar–'

But the crowner interrupted. 'I repeat, as a man of science, that no man's jaw could make this mark. No woman's breast can stretch to two times its original size. I've witnessed naught like this during my time as crowner.'

Kirstie spoke up. 'But, sires, as Dora says, the scars were old. They were pink and silvered, which is the colour of old scars that have healed–'

The crowner butted in. 'That is of no consequence.'

The moderator peered at him. 'Pray, explain why not, crowner.'

'Two reasons, sire. First, the elder hag sent the devil's imps to find suck long before Goodwife Sharpe's milk came in. In their infernal frustration, the imps set to biting her instead.'

I observed a fainting woman being carried out by her reluctant husband. When the crowner gained the room's attention again, he continued.

'Second, it is a known fact that the devil's imps secrete in their saliva a special healing quality. Simply put, they do not want to dry the teat that feeds them – whither of milk or blood. So the marks must seal themselves.'

Oh, the crowner was thorough, very thorough indeed. But I'd help him.

'It's true! It's true!' For weeks, my wife complained of pains and flashing lights in her head. It was impossible for that lady to rest when even her sleep was stolen from her. Thus, the devil's imps were draining her of goodness, taking what belonged to my child before the mite even got a chance to draw breath.'

I wiped tears from my eyes and pointed at the two cowering women.

'The blame lies in the wicked hands and black hearts of the old witch and her accomplice. Between them, they've stolen my sweet mother, my goodly wife and my child. All died unshriven, my babe not even baptised and therefore condemned to limbo evermore.'

My own words moved me so that tears flowed down my face, which moved some of the ladies in the room to dab at their own eyes with dainty kerchiefs. Hopefully, the moderator was also swayed by this spectacle and the mighty surge of feeling in the room. I watched closely as the moderator spoke again.

149

'These women stand accused of stealing the lives of innocents, but also of stealing their eternal souls, thus damning them to an eternity deprived of heaven. But first, we must be certain that these women are witches and not just bunglers. So they must be pricked, which will determine the manner of their deaths and the destination of their eternal souls. George Campbell will assist us.'

At this, the moderator nodded to the sergeants, who dragged forth Dora. A tall man, carrying an elegant cane and shod in soft leather boots, took the centre of the floor. He had to be well paid, judging by his finery. No doubt, the throng was similarly impressed as a low rumble of conversation grew until the moderator spoke again.

'Silence, George Campbell must be allowed to concentrate.'

The pricker clenched Dora's shift and ripped it so that it hung either side of her body, showing her spindly frame and slack breasts. With the tip of his cane, he lifted her left breast, indicating a discolouration on its underside.

'It's here! The devil's teat. Though I must prick it for certainty.'

His voice rang around the room and I envied its resonance.

Dora was quaking and a trickle of urine ran down her legs, pooling at her feet. Campbell stepped away, no doubt fearing for his boot leather. From his belt, he removed a silver implement. It resembled a giant's bodkin, ten inches long, with a handle making up more than half of its length.

Upon brandishing this instrument, Campbell turned to the crone, lifted her breast and pricked her in the centre of the ragged-looking brown mark. He pressed his pricker ever deeper until the hilt met her skin. Dora uttered no sound and only blinked.

'The hag bleeds not and feels no pain. So witch she certainly is, on both counts.'

A feverish chant rose around the room. 'Kill the witch! Kill the witch!', accompanied by a great stamping of feet, which made my heart leap. Finally, I was to be avenged. When the room quietened, the moderator turned to Dora.

'George Campbell has found your devil's mark. We have seen with our own eyes that the mark lets no blood and feels no pain.

Therefore, this kirk session must find you as a witch. What words have you, witch, before you meet your end?'

Dora ran to the moderator and threw herself at his feet. 'But I felt nothing at all when Mr Campbell pricked me. Sire, there's trickery afoot. I beseech you, please don't take this man's word. I'm no witch. I've never harmed a soul.'

It was impossible to hold my tongue any longer. 'Sire, the old woman is nothing if not convincing. But she must not live. She must suffer for what she's done to my family. She must be destroyed as they were destroyed.'

The moderator raised his hand. 'Silence, John Sharpe. We understand your agony, but we will determine this woman's guilt, not you. Pricker, bring the instrument so I might determine its veracity.'

With a flourish, Campbell presented the implement on his flat right palm.

The moderator took the proffered device and examined it. He beckoned the crowner. 'A moment of your scientific time, crowner.'

The crowner walked towards the moderator.

'Hold out your hand, wise and reasonable crowner.'

The crowner did as bidden, and the moderator plunged the pricker into his fleshy palm. The crowner bled copiously and then sucked at his wound, looking most aggrieved at this turn of events.

'Thank you, crowner, please be seated. I am satisfied there is no trickery afoot. Apologies to the crowner and pricker, both. Dora Shaw, you are to be taken to a place of execution, strangled to death and then burnt. Your immortal soul will trouble men no further, so that their goodwives and children will be safe once more.'

Dora Shaw screamed as she was dragged out and Kirstie Slater wept.

The moderator banged his gavel. 'Bring the sister witch.'

While a sergeant pinioned Kirstie, the pricker ripped her shift and her solid flesh trembled in fear. I gaped at her nakedness. It was impossible not to and there were bawdy offers of assistance from the lower men. The moderator banged his gavel three times for quiet and only succeeded in bringing this about by threatening to clear the floor.

Campbell was no blunderer and didn't go jabbing in any old place. Not for him the bony, skinny planes of the shoulder. For him, the softest, most succulent parts of Kirstie's body. He stroked the delicate skin inside the wrist, the creamy vellum of the inner thigh, the heavy under-moon of the breast. He'd no sense of constraint, the big arseworm. I could see by the curve of the man's hands that he was fair itching to weigh Kirstie Slater's tender orbs as he ran his hands to the north and south of them, seeking supernumerary teats. It filled me with envy, watching Campbell fingering the girl's breasts, heavy yet pert, teasing rosy teats to terrified peaks. After a thorough examination of her plush hide, he announced that there were no marks.

'However, there are two hiding places that remain to be searched.'

Campbell nodded to the sergeant and the room fell silent. The sergeant forced the wailing girl over a table and then the pricker rammed two long fingers into her rectum, making her howl.

He withdrew his fingers. 'No mark of the devil, but hold her down, sergeant.'

The sergeant pinioned the struggling Kirstie once more and Campbell forced his dirty fingers into her vagina. Kirstie kicked and screamed until he finally withdrew his fingers and held them up – bloody.

'A virgin maid, a virgin maid, a virgin maid!' cried an excitable man from the rabble. 'The dark saint has not yet ridden her with his chilly prong. She is a maid, or was!'

The justice shut him up immediately. 'Quiet! Or I will have the room cleared! Her blood makes her innocent, does it not, Campbell?'

'It does not, sire.' Campbell sniffed. 'This is only womb blood. She's no maid, for she has a child – a bastard – already. Sire, it's unlikely this one is a witch since she does not bear his mark. Yet, for certainty, prick her I will.'

A nervous laugh ran round the room. I rubbed my forehead, feeling too hot. Campbell pushed the blade no more than half an inch into the girl's flank, but she yelped and blood flowed down her leg. She collapsed, clutching her naked body.

The moderator held up one hand. 'Thank you, George Campbell, that will be all. Kirstie Slater, we have found that you did not give suck to the devil and you have not lain with him. However, you have willingly – if unknowingly – consorted with one of the devil's own bitches, thereby resulting in the death of innocents. Yet, you are innocent of witchcraft and so this session will show mercy.'

Kirstie gazed at the moderator. 'Oh, bless you, sire. God bless and keep you.'

My spirits plunged. Was the witch to escape justice before my very eyes a second time?

The moderator continued, 'Kirstie Slater, you will be taken to a place of execution and there hanged by the neck until dead. You will have benefit of clergy and your mortal remains will be buried in the kirkyard. Take her away.'

Kirstie screeched and kicked, and needed to be restrained by the sergeant's club.

'Try not to kill the girl yet, sergeant, else she escape her just punishment.'

The moderator paused until Kirstie was taken away, and then he turned to face me.

'John Sharpe, thanks to the services of George Campbell, a certain hag and her unwitting accomplice will be banished from this world. This act cannot restore your mother, your goodwife, or your child, but I hope justice being done will bring your soul some much-deserved Christian peace.'

20

Jane

Thirty Shillings

I laid some roses next to Tom's cross and then looked up at the sky. It was fine today and a soft breeze wound itself around the graves, giving lie to the same wind that howled around the dead in the middle of winter. It made me wonder what winds must have wrapped themselves around *The Durham* and what terrors my Tom had endured before dying in that cold, dark sea. It was unbearable to think of him at the bottom of the sea, his resting place unknown and unmarked. Swallowing back tears, I looked over at the part of the graveyard unmarked by stones and pondered the layers of ordinary people buried, quickly and anonymously, without their resting place even being marked.

The ground was uncommonly warm from the gaze of the sun, so I lay flat on my back, arms and legs flung wide to the elements. Weather-beaten gravestones towered over me and I felt myself sinking into the warm grass, as if being pulled down into the welcoming earth. But it didn't feel right, lying here enjoying the sunshine when Tom's life was over. If only Tom were back here, standing on the firm earth of home. This was our home, this hill, this land, all the way to the bottom of hell and all the way up to the top of heaven.

At this thought, joy bolted through my body and – hoping I might be spirited away to join Tom – I shut my eyes, clenched handfuls of grass to either side and pressed my toes into the warm earth, imagining digging down through the soil until reaching bone. It felt strangely comforting, as if all those people sleeping underground were watching me, encouraging me down and down to join them. But then a shadow slowly crossed me. I wiped my eyes before sitting up.

'Andrew Driver! What are you doing creeping up on me like that?'

He shrugged. 'I've just come to see how you fare.'

I wrapped my arms around myself and hunched forward. 'I fare as well as can be imagined with Tom being sent to a watery grave. So now you know, you can be on your way.'

But Andrew grabbed my hands and dragged me to my feet, holding me very close to him. I arched away from him and twisted my wrists free of his hands.

'So, you want me to be on my way, do you, Jane?'

'Yes. You've no business being here. Tom wouldn't like it.'

He laughed and blew his hair out of his eyes. 'Only, Tom's not here, is he?'

'No, but his da is, and Bill Verger will soon see you off.'

'What, that old bag of bones will see me off? Well, I'll not stay where I'm not wanted. But I'll come back. In fact, I'll come back every day and you'll change your mind, Jane, you wait and see.'

* * *

As good as his word, Andrew Driver came to the house every day. And every day, he went away again without a word from me. After today's visit, he'd finally just left after standing outside the door, being ignored as usual, but I could still see him dawdling on his way home. All I had to do was bide my time and stay inside the house. My belly was showing, but with care, no one need know. And it would be easy to pass off the baby as a foundling, as babies were left on church steps all the time. The Reverend and Mam would move heaven and earth to protect me and the bairn.

The sound of an approaching horse interrupted my thoughts and I moved towards the door. Then, looking at my belly, I thought better of it and stayed at the window. It looked like a messenger, but what business would he have here? Maybe it was the official news of Tom. The rider pulled up next to Andrew Driver and they exchanged words. The messenger gave something to him, which he put in his pouch. What could it be? Why would the messenger come near the church and give something to Andrew? I wanted to run out and demand to know what was going on, but it wouldn't be wise to reveal my belly to this stranger. As soon as the horseman turned tail, I opened the door and ran to Andrew.

'Who was that man? What did he have? Was it for me?'

Andrew nodded. 'Aye, it was. The messenger stopped to check that this was where Jane Chandler lived. I thought you'd not want to be seen, so I told him there was fever in the house and that he could rely on me to pass the message on.'

'Oh, sorry. Thank you. That was kind. But what's the message?'

Andrew held out a pouch. 'It's from the navy. For Tom's loss.'

I took the pouch and emptied it into my hand. There were three golden coins.

Andrew plucked one from me and held it to the light. 'Angels, Jane. Golden Angels. See, a galley on one side and the archangel Michael slaying a dragon on the other. There's thirty shillings' worth there.'

'Thirty shillings? Is that what my Tom's life is worth to the navy? For snatching him away and letting him drown? Was there no note?'

Andrew shook his head. 'No, just this pouch and the message. That was all. The messenger said to pass on the message and the pouch, and that was all. No note.'

'Well, this is blood money and I'll not have it.' I flung the pouch into the garden and ran back inside. From the window, I watched Andrew retrieve the pouch and walk to Bill's shack. The coins would be better given to Bill now that he had no son to look after him in his old age.

21

John

God's Work

Dreams of Kirstie Slater tortured me. The remembrance of George Campbell fingering her breasts and orifices stirred me somewhat, but the terror on her face roused my blood. Memories of him pricking her with his implement, her shriek, her blood and the bloom of fear on her face caused my loins to erupt, leaving me breathless, damp and grateful for my concealing cloak.

The spectacle moved me so greatly that I considered it at length, with myself as pricker. At first, my consideration took an innocent path, with me doing God's work by seeking super-numerary teats. But soon, my thoughts took a darker turn, as I pictured myself ramming my own fingers into Kirstie and prick-ing her endlessly. I imagined her udders dangling over my face so I might bite them at my leisure. But after abusing myself, I was drenched in a wash of guilt. Perhaps I'd mortify my flesh in the hope of bleeding out the impure dreams that had haunted me of late. It also occurred to me to take my woes to Uncle James, but in truth, I feared his bad opinion of my transgressions. Quickly, I knelt on the cold, hard floor, closed my eyes and clasped my hands, all the while begging God's forgiveness.

'Almighty God, please forgive me these transgressions.' I decided not to point out that they had only happened because He'd taken my wife before I'd fully enjoyed my conjugal rights. 'In return for your forgiveness, it will be my lifelong mission to prevent other men from losing their mothers, wives and bairns at the hands of these satanic slaves. Forgive me, Lord. So be it.'

I stood up and rubbed my knees. Kirstie Slater had slipped through my hands the first time I'd tried to prove her a witch, and she'd escaped justice, despite being guilty of the most heinous acts of witchcraft. And yet the justice explained away the maid's actions as if she were as mild as mother's milk. There must be a better way to make sure that God's will was carried out. Had I succeeded the first time, she might not have lived to kill my wife and child. But George Campbell, that blessed man, had succeeded where I failed and brought her to justice.

It struck me then that it wasn't enough to report these women to the authorities and leave someone else to determine their guilt. Justices were too easily swayed. And in truth, while Campbell had ended Kirstie's life, her eternal soul was still safe. I imagined myself in Campbell's place. That was where the power lay. The pricker could influence the judgment for good or ill. That would be my way. I had to become a witch-pricker. I'd attend more trials until I understood this art of witch-pricking, for art it surely was. Once I'd apprenticed myself, I'd free Scotland of this dread scourge. In this way, I'd avenge the death of my mother, my wife and my son, that innocent lamb who never once drew breath.

* * *

I followed George Campbell, who was kept so busy testing witches that it was a wonder he found time to sleep. After witnessing his work, it seemed that the involvement of lawmen and juries only made it harder for the witch-pricker to prove the accused guilty. In particular, it seemed impossible to achieve a guilty verdict when the assizes sat. Many more women were found guilty at the kirk sessions, where perhaps those overseeing the cases enjoyed more success due to their being fuelled by godly fervour. But the hastily arranged lay sessions achieved the best results. These were run by local men. Because these laymen owned close knowledge of the accused, it seemed easier for them to get a witch confirmed.

These hearings then, which meted out almost instant justice, these were where I'd offer my services – where the people knew the sinners in their midst and where a little religious zeal never went amiss. God would find His channel in me. And there was no need to wait for the legal system to grind into action. Instead, I'd go into the villages and offer my services, rounding up the witches myself, if necessary. I'd travel from village to village, following news of strange happenings and make the necessary interventions.

In the event of there being no strange happenings, it was the work of a moment to uncover some. It struck me that people were not so very observant and their memories often required some encouragement. By telling them of the queer goings on in nearby villages, I'd dislodge memories of similar behaviour in their midst. In this way, I'd intercede on behalf of God. It would take time and money, this itinerant life, but if I was to serve in poverty, then so be it. And if I succeeded and God saw fit to reward me, then so be it. I was in His hands, to be used as He saw fit.

* * *

In the tavern, I could feel George Campbell's eyes on me. The big man drained his tankard, crossed the room and indicated with his chin that the serving wench should follow. When he sat opposite me, the stool creaked under his great weight.

He placed his tankard on the board between us and the wench appeared. 'Leave the jug, Popsy, my new friend here is feeling generous.'

I flushed, but nodded at the plump doxy. She put down the jug and I passed some coin to her. 'And two tots of your best whisky.' It never hurt to oil a reluctant man's tongue.

The big man took a draught of his ale. 'What fetches you to my corner of the world, friend? I've seen you at the trials. What presses you? Guilt? Or are you one of those men who thrills his horn from hurting maids?'

I spluttered and almost choked on my ale. 'Neither! I'm simply a man of God, who has lately pledged his life to becoming a pricker to help eradicate this dread scourge of witches.'

He raised his newly arrived tot. 'Then, here's to you who would be a pricker.'

159

I raised my whisky and drank. The pricker emptied the remains of the ale jug into his tankard and took a draught before wiping his mouth on the back of his hand.

'Admittedly, it's well-paid work and fondling the queans is a harmless enough boon. But why would I encourage another onto my patch to halve my income?'

I smiled. 'You've no choice, Campbell. You must furnish me with a pricking implement because I've taken the time to discover your dark secret. If you prove unwilling to assist me, then I need only drop a word in the crowner's ear.'

The pricker paled beneath his elegant beard and then recovered, leaning forward so his mouth was within kissing distance of my face.

'You dirty weasel, I ought to tear the slanderous tongue from your head. You'll see no crowner until you're flat on his table, when it'll be too late to tell your tales.'

My face twisted into a humourless smile. 'You've no cause to threaten me, Campbell. And should any harm befall me, word's been left behind and the sergeants will know where to come knocking. What say you to setting our differences aside and coming to terms? There's surely enough trade to serve us both, eh?'

While the big man pondered, my heart raced as I wondered whether he'd been fooled by my ploy. Finally, the pricker conceded and handed a blade to me.

'Take this one, you conniving wee thief. I can soon fashion another. But this will be the last you get from me, sergeants and crowners, or none. Now, be gone and leave me to my cups.'

22

Jane

A Fallen Woman

'Bill, is that a sergeant trudging up our hill?' I put Gyb down and he wound his way through my legs. 'What could he possibly want here with a stout stick and a coil of rope?'

Bill put down his spade and dusted his hands. 'It's hard to say, but he looks like trouble.'

The air was very still in the morning heat and sweat pricked my oxters. As the man drew near, I smoothed my pinny.

'I'm Sergeant Bell from Durham. Jane Chandler? Is that your name? It'll go better, maid, if you own it straight away.'

I looked to Bill, but saw only fear in his eyes. 'Yes. That's me, Jane Chandler.'

The sergeant looked me up and down. 'And is it true that you're a fallen woman?'

Bill answered in my place. 'What do you mean by that, sergeant?'

'Simply that. Jane Chandler is a fallen woman. Her condition is clear to any man with half an eye in his head. The maid has loosened her bodice, she's not wed and has a bellyful of bastard.'

The blood drained from Bill's face and his hands clenched into fists. I stepped forward, placing my hand on his arm.

'It's true that I have a bellyful. My child's father was pressed by the navy and taken aboard *The Durham*.'

'A convenient arrangement, certainly. You'll find there are many foolish maids in the same condition where you're destined.'

The sergeant was a man who liked his drink, judging by his red face, veined nose and bloodshot eyes.

'Me and Tom were to be married, but he was press-ganged and then his ship …' the words wouldn't come out.

Bill patted my shoulder. 'Aye, sergeant, that's true. My son and the lass were betrothed.'

The sergeant spat at Gyb and grinned at me. 'For a maid in such a parlous condition, your faith is touching. Not much to rush back from sea for, though. A mousy maid and one with low morals to boot.'

'Look here, sergeant. Jane was set to wed my son, but his ship went down. He won't be coming back. And that can hardly be blamed on him, or the girl.'

The sergeant sized Bill up. Bill was a gentle man. But who could tell what any man might be capable of if subjected to enough provocation?

'Sergeant, it's true. My Tom was spirited to sea just before our wedding. Plenty of babies are christened less than ten moons from the wedding day, so my condition isn't unusual. A promise of marriage is the same as marriage, is it not, in the eyes of the law?'

'A clever little slattern, aren't you, Chandler? But it's not me you've to convince. I have my orders from the Justice of the Peace. And since Tom Verger lies at the bottom of the sea, he's hardly able to make an honest woman of you, is he? So there's no choice in the matter.'

The child moved within me then and my hand flew to my belly to rest over her. The quickening. Nothing more than a fluttering of tiny limbs, a heart no bigger than an onion seed beating inside me. Joy raced through me. Tom's child was alive and well. But the sergeant interrupted my joy by reaching forward and gripping me by the upper arm, all the while grinning lewdly at my belly.

'Jane Chandler, maid of Mutton Clog near Shotley Bridge, I'm charged to punish this lewd behaviour by taking you to Elvet.'

Bill turned from me to look at the sergeant. 'You mean to take Jane to Elvet? I don't understand.'

'It's very simple, old man, she'll go to Durham's house of correction at Elvet.'

Bill frowned. 'But it can't be, the house of correction is for cutpurses and nightwalkers … jades and sturdy beggars.'

'Aye, that's right. And lewds like young Chandler here.'

'Bill, please find Mam and Reverend Foster.' I turned to the sergeant. 'Please unhand me, as there's been a mistake. You can't take me to Elvet. I was to be wed. I'm as good as wed. I had a promise.'

The sergeant leered at me. 'Well, maid, let's see whether this promise holds water from beyond the grave. The justice will be the judge of it, not you. Come.'

He pulled my arms in front of me, slipped the coil of rope from his shoulder and lashed my wrists together.

Bill turned to the sergeant. 'You intend to lead the lass? Like a beast?'

'Aye, for fear the slippery maid should escape her righteous justice.'

'Have pity, man, look at her. And in this heat.'

The rope was already biting into my wrists. When I moved them to gain a measure of comfort, the flesh of one wrist tore at the other, so tightly were they lashed. Tears stung my eyes. The thought of walking to Durham in this heat was bad enough. But it was worse to think beyond the walk to what might happen at the house of correction. Who could have informed the sergeants? The only person outside the family who knew was Andrew Driver, and he would have no reason to report me. I looked at the sergeant, hoping to appeal to his better nature.

'Please let me walk unbound, Sergeant Bell, you have my word that I'll not try to escape.'

The sergeant sneered. 'I'd be a rich man and a poor sergeant if I had a groat for every prisoner who promised me that. Come, enough of this whingeing.'

Bill held up his right hand. 'Wait. You can't lead a girl in her condition, she'll lose her child.'

'Then that will be an end to her trials, won't it? You, maid, get moving, unless you want to travel by dark.'

The sergeant aimed his foot at my right ankle and a searing pain shot up to my knee, causing me to buckle. Gyb hissed at him and sprang onto a ledge out of harm's way.

'Don't fall, maid. I'll drag you to Durham, if necessary.'

The man looked as though he meant it, so I righted myself, taking the weight on my left foot. When we started walking, Bill looked to be praying. *Oh, Bill, save your breath, for praying will not help me.*

The sergeant had long legs and he didn't shorten his stride, so I had to trot to keep up. At least the sergeant hadn't paraded me through the village, but we'd no doubt travel through the hamlets outlying Durham on our way. During the long climb to Berry Edge, my thighs burnt and the speed of the sergeant's walking gave me a stitch.

'Please, sergeant, please stop! The pain in my middle is bad and my child must be suffering.' I panted the words out, my throat already parched.

The red-faced sergeant stopped and glowered at me. 'Five minutes only.'

Sweat haled from the man's brow. So we hadn't stopped for my sake, but for the sergeant's, as he panted more than me, even though I had a great belly and a sore ankle. Down in the valley, the heat haze shimmered across the pale pastures and the dark woods. There was too much sweat running in my eyes to blink away, so I raised my bound hands to my face to wipe it away. The rope reeked of horse. Any horse would surely be better treated and at least allowed to stand in a cool beck and drink his fill. The thought of drinking cool water crazed my parched throat. Hopefully, the sergeant had a flask, or we might stop at a well soon.

'Come, Chandler, no dallying. We must press on. Our next stop will be Lanchester.'

My heart sank. It was five miles to Lanchester.

* * *

My body yearned for water. The sun had reached the crown of the sky and there was little shade on the long path, which was straight and unforgiving. To either side was woodland, cool

164

and inviting. I closed my eyes and imagined myself there. No longer were my feet pounding this hot track; instead, they were immersed in the cool mud, my head shaded by a canopy of oak trees. There were many small burns in the woods and it would be heavenly to scoop up cold water with free hands, pour it into my dry mouth and splash my dirty face so the salt was cleansed from my skin.

'Please, sire, can we stop? My throat is as dry as dust and my belly is heavy.'

The sergeant shook his head, tightening his grip on the rope over his shoulder. 'Keep walking, maid.'

'Well, might we at least walk in the woods for a while?'

'And be troubled by footpads and cutpurses? Keep walking. And no more of your brassy lip, maid, unless you want to feel the back of my hand.'

With that, he yanked the rope, which caused me to pitch forward and forced me to stagger to stay upright.

I hung my head and tried to think only of putting one foot in front of the other and not of the heavy weight in my belly, the dryness of my mouth and the throbbing pain in my ankle.

We stopped for water and a brief rest at Lanchester and again at Witton Gilbert. The humid heat made walking hard. As we approached Elvet, the sky blackened, casting the vast cathedral and castle into shadow. Fat drops of rain began falling and I turned my face to the heavens. The sergeant held me tightly until a door was answered by a woman whose face was the size, shape and colour of a side of beef.

'Evening, Mistress Avice. Here's a new one needs correcting. Let me take back my rope and she's all yours.'

'Another hour, sergeant, and my doors would have been shut to you.'

'Aye, well, it's kind of you to keep them open for me.'

The sergeant untied the rope. Because my wrists had swollen with the heat, the binding and the chafing, they were red and bloody. As soon as the rope was off, the feeling flooded to my wrists and hands, sickening me with the sudden pain. I wanted to lick my wounds, but had no moisture in my mouth to spare. I closed my eyes instead.

'Thank you, sergeant. You, girl, never mind standing there asleep on your feet, unless you want to be punished for idleness as well. Follow me.'

The woman ambled through the wooden door, with her hips swaying and her grubby grey gown sweeping the floor as she went. I stumbled as my eyes tried to adjust to the darkness. There was a smell of damp earth, which must come from the river.

'I'm the keeper of the house of correction. You'll call me mistress. Name?'

'Jane. Jane Chandler.'

'From?'

'Mutton Clog near Shotley Bridge.'

'Transgression?'

I closed my hands over my middle and said nothing.

'As if I need ask. I can see your condition. One that might be described as delicate, but not by me. You'll find no favour here, and you'll work just as hard as the other girls brought low by similar means.'

There was not a single sign of kindness in this woman's face.

'You'll work for your keep, Chandler. Providing you work hard, you should be able to earn enough to keep your belly lined decently, if not tastily. Your dietary allowance being a quarter loaf per day and as much of Adam's ale as you can draw. That will cost you a shilling a week.'

'I'm not a great eater, mistress, but if I might just have some water, as it has been such a hot day and a long walk.'

The woman put her hands into the clefts above her hips and gave a barking laugh. 'Water, she asks, as if this were a gentry inn. You'll draw your own water in the morning. You've missed the day's meal, so you must make do until the morrow.'

The inside of my mouth was rough with dryness. I hardly dared rest my tongue on the floor or the roof of my mouth lest it stick there.

'There are several works for girls like you. What are your skills?'

'The usual sort of skills for a midwife. Keeping house and garden, growing and mixing herbs, helping the sick and attending birthing mothers.'

The woman sneered. 'Always an amazement to me, that these girls who need no assistance whatsoever to get the baby into them, make such a creation getting it out of them. Well, there's plenty here in your condition, so you'll be kept busy. But that will be an offering to the greater good that you'll perform on top of your normal duties. You'll start by beating hemp for ten hours each day. The rest of the day should be spent on prayer and exercise in the airing yard. But the airing yard is too pleasant and the walls not high enough, so all exercise is taken inside the house. You'll need to make ready for an early knock. But before that, give me your clothes. All of them.'

'But, mistress, the clothes I stand in are all I have.'

'Don't back-answer me, girl. Strip. Your rags are fit only for the fire.'

The keeper looked towards the flames. 'Look lively, Chandler, you've nothing new under God's sun.'

I turned my back. First, I loosened the bindings of my bodice and pulled my frock over my head. Underneath was a thin chemise, and when this was off, I was standing naked. Beneath the keeper's gaze, it felt as though my tight, round belly had grown to occupy the whole room.

'You do right to look ashamed, Chandler. Sit on that cracket and remove your coif while I attend to your hair.'

As I unwound the soiled coif, my hair hung down my back. 'My hair?'

'Aye, your hair. Can't let a mane like that loose in here – we're jumping with lice as it is.'

'But, mistress, I don't have lice. I'm clean.'

I sat down anyway. It was too hard to argue without even the paltry armour of a chemise to protect me.

The keeper reached into her pinny and fetched out shears. I folded my arms across my breasts and hunched my shoulders. The keeper took a shank of hair in one hand, close to my skull, and yanked hard. Little pains shot through my nape, down my shoulders and back, making my eyes water.

I screwed my eyes shut and vowed not to cry, not even when the heavy shears started hacking so close that the cold iron was against my skull. My hair fell in long tresses to the ground. The keeper stepped in front of me to admire her handiwork. Then she replaced the shears in her pinny pocket and produced a pair of tongs. With these, she picked up my clothing, carried it to the fire and threw it in.

My frock. What would Mam say when she found out? The wool made a terrible stink when it burnt and the black smoke stung my eyes, finally releasing the tears I'd vowed not to cry. The keeper scraped my hair into a pile with her clogged foot and then she grabbed it with the tongs and fed it to the fire.

'Nearly done. Though at this time of night, a body shouldn't have to be bothered with these tasks. Stand there, with your back to me.'

I stood up and faced the smoking fire. The keeper raked around behind me; there was a clanking of metal against wood and then my whole head and body were drenched in icy water that smelt of the river. Even though parched, I was careful not to take any water into my mouth. I'd heard enough tales of the River Wear to know better. All the short hairs on my body stood on end. My scalp and skin felt as though they were shrinking and becoming too tight to fit my skull and skeleton. The baby fluttered, perhaps woken from a sweet sleep. I put one hand to my belly. *Please don't let my child be hurt. Please protect my child.*

'Wave your arms till you dry. Then put on your new frock.'

There was an off-white linen in the keeper's hands.

'Thank you, mistress. I'm dry.' I pulled the frock over my head. It would fit a woman twice as tall and half as wide, and it pulled taut across my belly. 'But might I exchange it for something more fitting?'

'More fitting?' The keeper laughed, her sour breath blasting me in the face. 'What could be more fitting in a house of correction than being reminded constantly of why you're here?' She shook her head, as if to remark her disbelief. 'Quite the jester, you are, Chandler. Follow me and let's see if we can rid you of the sanguine humour.'

The keeper beckoned me through an arched door and removed an iron key from her pinny.

'Go on. Get yourself in there, Chandler. It's dark, but secure. No one is coming in. No one is going out. And the river rats are not too bad at this time of year, since they're too busy weaning their young to bother with the likes of you.'

I remembered the day Meg brought Gyb and told us about rats carrying the plague. *Oh, Gyb, what would I give to have you here with me?*

* * *

I'd pressed myself against the corner nearest to the door, and had barely managed to close my eyes when the door to my cell opened.

'Get up, you lazy slattern. You're needed.'

My eyes opened to see Mistress Avice's big face looming over me. The night had not improved her breath, and I turned my face from its foulness.

'Up. Now. Peggy Greaves has started her travails early.'

I checked a sigh and climbed up off the floor. The keeper scowled at my belly and then left my cell. I hurried after her into the room where I'd been stripped and sheared. Lying on the floor was a girl, perhaps younger than me. Her face was purple, she was drenched in her own sweat and she clutched at her stomach.

I turned to the keeper. 'How long has she been this way?'

The woman shrugged. 'Not long. She started while I was busy seeing to you and that mane of yours.'

I knelt at Peggy's side and felt her brow. She was burning and her breathing was very shallow. 'Mistress Avice, this girl needs a proper midwife. I've never delivered a child without my mother's assistance.'

But the keeper was unmoved. 'No need to waste money on the likes of Peggy Greaves while you're here. You've seen plenty of births. You know what to do. Now get on with it.'

The girl's belly was rigid and then it went slack. I closed my eyes and counted, but it was barely a count of a hundred before her belly went rigid again.

'Peggy, I need to check inside you and see what's happening.'

But the poor girl was beyond hearing me and only whimpered at the contraction wracking her body. The keeper held the candle nearby so I could make my examination. Peggy's body was ready

169

to give birth, but something was wrong. I prayed it wasn't a foo-tling breech, otherwise neither the girl nor the baby would sur-vive the night.

'Mistress, there's something wrong. This is not something I can do on my own. We need someone with more experience – like my mother – or another midwife.'

The keeper frowned. 'There's no time now. You'll have to manage as best you can.'

The floor beneath Peggy was soiled, and I put my hand into the warm wetness between her legs, then lifted it to the candle light. There was blood in the water. Peggy's belly tightened, and she clenched her teeth as the pain went through her. The pains were coming one on top of the other now and she cried out, her face contorted with pain.

'There, there, Peggy. Your labour has started in earnest. Mis-tress Avice, do you have a birthing chair?'

The keeper snorted at me. 'Birthing chair, for the likes of Greaves? She no doubt got the child like a beast in the field, so she can birth it the same way.'

I waited for the pain to subside while Peggy came back to nor-mality. 'Peggy. Peggy. I need you to get on your knees. It will help the baby to come out. Can you do that?'

She nodded, and I tried to support her as she turned her body. But she was heavy, and we were both tired. She made it onto her knees and braced herself against the wall. I bent between her thighs and pressed a hand into her birth canal. The girl stiffened until I withdrew my hand.

'Peggy, you must be strong, so very strong. The baby's head is coming now, and you will want to push hard, but you must not. So try to hold back. Can you do that?'

By way of reply, the girl grunted. But I could feel her body straining to bear down and push out the child.

'Good. Now, I must work quickly, Peggy.'

She moaned deeply, then howled, as the head crowned. I supported the baby as Mam had taught me. Finally, and with a great gush, the child was free. Peggy screamed with pain. When she turned to face me, I was smiling and rubbing the baby vigorously.

'You have a little boy, Peggy. Here, hold him tightly while I cut the cord and deliver this placenta. Mistress Avice, your shears please.'

The keeper handed them over reluctantly. Once I'd cut the cord, I pushed one hand into Peggy, and pressed her abdomen with the other. 'Oh, you're badly mangled, Peggy. I fear there will be no further issue from you.'

Mistress Avice looked up at the ceiling. 'Then that will be a blessing for all concerned. You, Chandler, if your work is done, get back to your sleep.'

I opened my mouth to object, but Mistress Avice did not let me speak. 'You'd better obey me since you won't be excused your shift in the morning.'

With a glance at the new mother and her child, Mistress Avice walked me back through the dark passages to my cell. I had never felt so tired in all of my life. Without Tom to save me, my child must rely on the mercy of Mistress Avice, who had none.

* * *

Four days had passed, and each night, I was so tired and hungry that I barely noticed or cared about the rats that shared my cell. There had been no word from my mother or the Reverend. I had never felt so alone.

Mistress Avice came to dole out our bread. I looked past the other girls and women on the bench next to me. Peggy Greaves tucked her baby beneath her shawl and nursed him, tears coursing down her face.

'Mistress, the suckling is sore and the pains are moving the length and breadth of me body.'

The keeper stood over the nursing girl, arms akimbo. 'Well, Greaves, the feeding pains might take your mind off your hunger pains.'

'But, mistress, I'm famished all the time. There wasn't enough to eat before the bairn came and now there's no filling me. Please, can I have some more bread?'

The keeper grimaced. 'Only if you can earn more. And I doubt you're in a position to do that.'

171

Peggy blinked back her tears. 'I try so hard not to resent him, for he's such a small bundle. But the flesh is falling away from me every day. Since the bairn was born, me insides feel as though they're clagging together. And it's not even as if he's taking anything from me. He must be starving.'

How could that woman have no sympathy for the weeping girl and her grey infant? The child looked as though he wouldn't see the week out. When Mistress Avice turned her back, I'd share my meagre ration with Peggy, and I'd try to work a little longer each day to make it up. By the looks of Peggy, she'd never had any flesh on her. At least I'd never known hunger before coming here. But I'd have to feed my own child very soon and where would it all end?

* * *

Yesterday, Peggy's child died. He hadn't been named, and he hadn't been christened. Peggy wept during the whole working day and all of the girls with her. But not Mistress Avice, whose only aim was to see that we met our daily hemp-beating requirements. I had not slept all night, gripped with fear. And my child had not moved once during the night. I wondered at its stillness. For a second, I felt a fleeting joy. My child would be spared birth in this hellish place. But the strange feeling of joy was quickly extinguished by guilt. It was wrong to wish a child dead, for I'd seen many children born still. I clutched my still belly and wondered whether I'd wished away my child. Tom's child. What would he think of me? I'd been in the house of correction for less than a week, and already I was exhausted. And no doubt worse was yet to come.

My cell door opened. It was Mistress Avice, with a smirk on her face. 'You've a visitor. It confounds me how the sergeants have allowed it, but they have, so be quick about it and do not be late for your shift.'

My lip trembled. It must be Mam and the Reverend. It was barely light, so they must have walked through the night. I knew they wouldn't leave me here. I tried not to smile as I followed the keeper out of my cell. They would find a way to set me free. My child would be spared the fate of Peggy Greaves' child.

In the shearing room stood Andrew Driver. My heart sank at the sight of him. His eyes widened, and he took a step back.

'Andrew? Where's Mam and the Reverend?'

'They're outside. They're not allowed in. The sergeants said only me.'

'Oh!' I had to put my hand to my mouth to stop myself crying out their names. It was unbearable to think they stood only a few feet away, and yet I couldn't see them or speak to them.

'We're all agreed, though, this is the best way, Jane.'

'What? What's the best way? What do you mean, Andrew?' But I knew what he meant. And I knew now why he was here.

He looked down at his feet for a second and moved his hat from one hand to the other. 'Jane, you know fine well why I'm here. To save you. Say yes to me, and the sergeants say I can take you with me now. With your mam and the Reverend. We can all be on our way. Your child will have a father. You will have a husband. And you will be free from this prison.'

My eyes glazed with tears. 'But I don't love you, Andrew, and I don't think I ever could.' Something about him made me not trust him. 'And how can I betray Tom's memory?'

His eyes darkened for a second, and then he shook his head firmly. 'You're betraying no one. Would Tom really want you to risk his child's life in this place?'

I thought of Tom's dear face. His lovely green eyes and his kind smile. And then I thought of Peggy Greaves and her little boy. His grey little face and her weeping all day yesterday. And no doubt all day today, and for many more days to come.

23

John

Purge

Although it had taken me a good week to return home, I was still hot-blooded from the ease of my victory – fancy a big, clever man like George Campbell being so easy to take in. My feet flew the last few miles and fetched me home at speed. Although dark, I couldn't wait until morning to examine the pricker at leisure. All night, I manhandled the novel device and practised flourishing it and presenting it as Campbell had done. Carefully, I pressed its point to my own flesh, judging how much pressure was required to blanch the skin and send my terrified blood fleeing from the point of the bodkin. How much pressure was necessary to create a glistening blister of blood? How much to cause a great gout?

I pressed myself all through the night, mining those parts of the body apt to give up their blood at the slightest prick and those that refused to let one drop even under great provocation. Satisfied with this progress, I recited my prayers, promising to seek justice for my mother, my wife and my son, and to save others suffering at the hands of malevolent midwives. Then I put my wounded and bleeding body to bed. I was sore all over, but savoured the pain as an investment in the future. Although my father's fearsome temper had finally found its nest in my heart, I'd transmute its energy and vent it on the hunting, pricking and execution of witches.

When the midday sun woke me, my head pulsed and my tongue was thick and dry. Sweat haled from me, yet I was freezing cold. It mystified me why I was still lying in bed when good Christians had been about their business for hours. Still, it might serve me well to keep the witches' dark hours. My cuts bothered me and I was still sore all over. The queer excitement that had occupied me in the night had gone, but it left me feeling unclean. God would help me, so I got onto my knees and began to pray for His intervention and mercy.

But although I prayed until my knees ached, I did not feel any better. And now it was possible that I'd placed myself beyond God's help. Worry flowed through me and I wondered at my own simplicity. How innocent I was of witches' magic. I'd pierced my hide with a blade designed to root out evil by plunging into the insensate flesh of the devil's own coven. In the same way a knife drawn across a beast's throat retained the stain and stench of the slaughter, this blade would surely be tainted with the stain and stench of devilment. Damn that pricker! He was not so green after all. What foul succubus had I introduced into my pure body? Why had I not the sense to practise on a beast – a swine would have sufficed? In my fever, I fancied a fiendish revolt rising within. I must be purged of this evil. My uncle would know what to do.

* * *

Uncle James was hardly satisfactory, eyeing me silently while I explained how I'd become possessed. The man seemed reluctant to touch me – his own flesh and blood.

'John, are you quite well? Inside your head, I mean? You seem … well, I hardly know what name to give it. Perhaps the grief of your recent loss has taken hold of you. We should pray together. Come, it will help you.'

He touched my arm and looked at me, his eyes searching my face. As if I'd let him pray over me like he had over the convulsing Cummins woman all those years ago. But I wouldn't be unkind, as he'd treated me gently over the years and he meant well.

175

'No, Uncle, this isn't grief. I've been awash with grief for so long, it's like a friend to me. This is far greater than grief.'

'Then you must seek help from the barber-surgeon. He might know what to do in a strange case like this. Only, say your prayers before and after you go to him. I'm certain he carries a taint of something quite unholy of late.'

Disgruntled, I left him and took myself to see MacBain.

* * *

The barber's face darkened and he listened to my tale of woe with considerably less interest than had my uncle. After a cursory examination of my lacerated carcass, he tugged his beard and mused.

'It's a bleed of sixty-five ounces you'll need, Sharpe. And a purge – a mercury clyster is what I'd recommend.'

'Sixty-five ounces? I want curing, not killing, MacBain!'

'Aye, it's always a risk with large lettings, but I could put you to the leech instead if you prefer. It'll take longer and you'll need to bide here for some time. And the sorry buggers must be burnt after – they being full of your ungodly blood – so it'll cost more. Then there's the mercury. And I'll need to put slippery elm on you – that's from the New World, so that won't come cheap.'

'All right, MacBain, whatever you deem necessary.' The thought of leeching filled me with horror, but it must be safer than bloodletting. 'How long will it take?'

The barber eyed me up and down. 'Say two days by the time I catch them and put them on you. Then you'll need to sleep off the fever.'

'Two days!' Clearly, the man thought I'd nothing better to do with my time. Still, he wasn't to know that I was on God's errand.

MacBain shrugged. 'It gives me no cause to rejoice either, as you'll be breathing my air and festering the place with your unholy wastes. Maybe your uncle–'

'No! I'll stay.' Sweat haled from my brow and ran into my eyes. This big bastard was going to leech me in more ways than one, but there was no alternative. I watched him prepare the cure. The clyster had a very long spout.

'It's ready, Sharpe. Go and find a tree to brace against and then bend over.'

Outside, I looked about in case of an audience, then I dropped my breeches and bent over. My eyes watered as the barber inserted the clyster spout into my rectum.

'Clench, man, and hold the mercury inside as long as you might.'

But my innards writhed and cramped – the mercury and the evil succubus doing battle – and my flesh was too weak to hold back the vile conflagration.

The barber stepped back just in time to avoid being sprayed with the noxious contents of my bowels. After this purging, the barber threw a bucket of pond water over my head and then I was wrapped in a rug and taken back inside. I rested on a pallet while MacBain cooked a paste from powdered bark, which he then painted onto each incision. The paste was too hot to bear, but it brought a strange comfort.

'Listen, Sharpe, these poultices of slippery elm will draw out any badness that might be festering within. I must leave you awhile and go fishing for leeches, since I can't bear to put my own to the fire.'

Lying on the pallet, covered in fiery paste, I imagined the barber removing his breeks and wading thigh-deep in the pond, waiting for the slithering creatures to clamp their jaws to his blood-rich veins. The man was so big and sanguine, I fretted in case the leeches drank their fill before they ever kissed my own flesh. Before long, I fell asleep, dreaming that the cuts pinching my legs were leeches clamping onto me.

The barber woke me when he came striding back in, his white legs spotted with dozens of shining brown worms. Through half-closed eyes, I watched as the barber sighed, perched on a stool and began the laborious process of removing the leeches from his legs, dropping each into a jug of pond water. As he peeled each sucker from his skin, the man's blood ran freely.

My eyes widened. 'Good God, man. You'll bleed to death in front of me! What are you doing?'

The barber laughed, took a crock from his shelves and began dabbing the wounds with thin, brown liquid.

'Acorn tea will soon stop the bleeding. You're very womanish in your ways, aren't you, Sharpe?'

The barber donned his breeks and brandished the pitcher of leeches. 'I'll set these little beauties on you and let them feed. Although it might be a task to find enough clear skin for them all, as you've left yourself like a pincushion.'

'Just get on with it, MacBain, I don't have all week.'

The barber scooped a slithery leech from the jug with a long-handled spoon and nudged it into position on my bare flesh, near to the visible veins. I cringed as each creature latched on and began suckling.

'Don't overreact, man, their bite has a numbing quality, so you shouldn't feel their efforts after the first bite.'

'I feel faint at the thought of the hideous creatures and can't bear to look at them swelling their vile bellies on my blood.' I shuddered, but hated myself for it.

'It would be a mercy if you did faint, Sharpe and then I might be spared your womanish whittering for a time.'

Finally, my torso and limbs were populated by glistening purple creatures, bulging and replete. Once sated, each fell from my body. The barber harvested the fallen fruits one by one and tossed them into the heart of the fire. Each gave off a monstrous stench as it burst in the flames, filling the room with an acrid miasma of burnt mud and metal. I felt thin and pale.

'I'll cover you in rugs and leave you to sweat in the warmth of a purifying fire made with dried yarrow flowers. Soft-headed bugger, fancy wounding yourself with a dirty knife, never mind being infested with the blood of witches.'

In the heat, I thrashed about as my fever reached its crisis, trembling and sweating as the barber tossed lavender into the fire. It banished the stench that had settled, pall-like, in the shack, soothing me and bringing peaceful sleep.

* * *

Two days later, recovered, but weak, I accepted some broth. The barber gave me a bottle of tonic, a crock of ointment and a lavender plant.

'Plunge the blade into the earth around the plant and leave it there when it's not in use. The lavender will keep it clean. Plant it in a sunny spot. Clean things need plenty of light. And strop that blade properly before you use it on yourself again. There's nothing as bad as a mucky knifeman, or one with a blunt prick.'

I eyed the barber to determine whether he was trying to get a rise from me. Then I paid the extortionate bill and scurried away, considerably lighter in purse, flesh and spirit.

Once home, I was determined to rest while my humours regathered. But my mattress was spotted with black blood and my stomach lurched at the sight. It was a dreadful extravagance, but I'd have to burn the straw and its coverings. This would attract comment from the nosy hag in the next cottage, but I couldn't risk poisoning my body or spirit again with this witch-infested blood. When I set the fire away, it gave off black smoke and tears streamed down my face. While it did its purifying work, I dug a hole to plant the lavender in readiness for the cleansing of the blade.

* * *

Now that my body, my home and the blade were cleansed of their unholy taint, I considered the nature of pricking. I'd almost killed myself in my enthusiastic self-cutting. Instead, I should have uncovered the bodkin's secret, for secret there surely was. After resting, I'd take some time to understand its workings.

When the bodkin finally gave up its secret, I shook my head at the simplicity of the trick. To the willing eye, a hollowed cylinder of metal has exactly the same appearance as a solid one. Once George Campbell had found the devil's stain, it was the work of a second to slide the catch and let the pricking needle retract. Oh, Campbell was pressing hard enough and the blade looked as though it was plunged into the accursed one's flesh down to the bone, but did the witch wince or emit one drop of blood? She did not. And that was how he proved the witch's guilt.

And this blunt instrument made quite a pleasing impression, blanching the skin so the blood fled to other parts, sped on its way by none other than Satan. I realised that Campbell had taken the time to find those special places on the body where pain can't find its way in and blood can't find its way out.

Still, Campbell was a man blessed with an inventive turn of mind. In turn, he'd blessed me with this witch-finding device. And a device that found witches so easily must save more innocent souls in the long run. That would be to the benefit of my neighbours. But I was a mere man, and I could not undertake this great task unaided. I took to my knees and cast down my eyes to pray to God for His guidance.

'Dear God, there is such a moot of witches in this neck of the woods. Without your help, the dark ones will have their way with the soul of every newborn in Scotland. And so I pledge my life to your holy service. If you will only guide my heart and my hands, I swear to root out this terrible evil in our midst. So be it.'

24

Jane

A Taste of Poppy Milk

The day I became Jane Driver was a subdued occasion and it was a relief when the day's end came so I could climb into bed and escape the curious stares.

'It's so good to be away from everyone, Andrew, I felt your mother's eyes were on me all day. She must wonder about Tom ...'

'I'm sure you're just imagining it, Jane.'

'But how much of the truth does she know?'

'Jane, I'm a man and you're my wife. That's all my mother needs to know. And the sooner we stop talking about Tom Verger, the sooner everyone will forget him. You're my wife now, and that's all that matters. You're mine.'

The last thing I wanted to do was to forget about Tom, but Andrew's face reddened every time his name came up, so I decided to just try being grateful. There would be plenty of time to remember Tom once Andrew went to sleep. But there was something that had to be borne before then.

'I can never thank you enough for saving me from the house of correction. You're kind, Andrew, very kind.'

He took my hands and smiled. 'That I am, Jane. But you know that I don't expect you to lie with me. Not until the baby's born at any rate. And in the meantime, promise to forget Tom Verger. I'm a patient man, but you're mine now.'

'Thank you, Andrew. But they'll expect to see the bloody linen on the morrow.'

'Well, had you married Tom, there would be no bloody linen. Your growing belly is all they need to know on the matter. Get some sleep, for the cattle wait for no man.'

Andrew turned from me in the bed and was soon breathing heavily. I looked at the rafters. Andrew was being fair and he'd always been Tom's friend. But he wasn't Tom. I cradled my belly and a tear ran from the side of my eye.

* * *

Over the years, I'd delivered enough women to know that birth was one of the most dangerous moments in the life of the mother and the baby. But Mam was by my side and there was no better midwife in the county.

She straightened up. 'Well, Jane, I'd say this baby will be here within the hour.'

'Ah, Mam, half of me wishes the baby would come late.'

'Oh, why's that, Jane?'

'Well, it's just that there's so much gossiping, and everyone keeps saying the bairn's Tom's.'

'Well, the bairn is Tom's. And Andrew knows that as well as any.'

'It's just … well … it's not fair to burden Andrew with any more humiliation than he's borne already.'

Mam clicked her tongue. 'Humiliation? The lad went into this with his eyes open. That mother of his is putting words in your mouth, I'll wager. Bett Driver and her proud ways.'

'No, Mam, I don't think it is Bett. It's just, well, he gets very jealous and angry. I daren't mention Tom to him at all. It's hard to believe they were ever friends the way he scowls if I so much as even mention Bill Verger.'

'He hasn't struck you, or anything?'

'No, no. Of course not. I'd have told you sooner, it's just his words sometimes …'

'Then, don't trouble yourself just now, Jane. Let's get this baby delivered safely, and then we can think what to do about Andrew and his words.'

I clutched myself as the pain welled. Mam rested one hand on my rigid belly, eyes closed and counting, until the pain passed.

She winked and heaved me to my feet. 'Jane, can you walk awhile? Link my arm and let's see if we can get this baby moving before Goodwife Driver returns from the market to assist us.'

* * *

When Bett Driver arrived back from the market, she was red-cheeked and soaked through.

She frowned. 'So your time has come, Jane. Has anyone told my son yet?'

I bent over, blew out a long breath and shook my head. Mam held my hands, nodding and counting slowly. When I finally straightened up, Mam spoke.

'Not so far, Bett. Jane has a way to go and there's no sense hurrying Andrew back from his work just yet.'

Bett smoothed her skirts. 'Well, a man needs to know when his wife starts her birthing pains. I'll send a lad to him, dreadful though the weather is. There's quite a storm brewing out there today.'

Mam steered me back to the birthing chair and pushed the hair off my face before turning to address Andrew's mother.

'It's not a man's place to be here for the birth. Let him come home in his own sweet time once Jane is safely delivered.'

Bett wouldn't take kindly to being told what to do in her own home.

But she seemed to make her mind up and took off her wet cloak. 'Your Jane's very narrow-hipped, of course.'

There was a note of criticism in this comment, but Mam was as calm as ever.

'She'll do just fine, Bett. Jane knows what she's about. And plenty of narrow-hipped lasses ease out fine babies.'

I was wracked by another pain and this one took me down inside myself, so that the conversation between the grandmothers became no more than an annoying buzz.

'A terrible shame the baby has decided to arrive early, as it'll make it all the harder to pass off the child as a Driver.'

Mam snorted at this. 'Aye, Bett, but it might mean the child is easier to birth. Had the baby gone over, Jane might have struggled, what with her being so narrow-hipped.'

I wiped sweat from my brow and looked out of the window. A storm had begun to rage and the ice-ridden wind battered the windows. It howled down the chimney, blowing soot into the room and threatening to put out the fire.

Bett looked around the room. 'It doesn't bode well for a baby being born with this storm and the wind trying to break into the house. It's as if God Himself is angered ...'

Mam gave Bett a hard stare. 'It's nothing of the sort. Just the usual winter squalls. At least we're on dry land. Pity help those at sea–' She grimaced and glanced over at me, a clear apology in her eyes, but a new pain was peaking and I was too busy panting to acknowledge the gesture. The sweat was running down my back and a fresh wave of pain convulsed me.

'Look, the pains are getting closer together. Bett, give Jane your hand. Mop her brow to keep the sweat from stinging her eyes and I'll help the baby out. Jane, don't push until I tell you.'

There was an overwhelming pressure low down in my belly, accompanied by a sickening pain, and I clenched my teeth and began bearing down.

'Jane, Jane, the baby's head is starting to crown. Try not to push hard, or the baby will come too fast.'

I tried not to push, but my body was in charge and continued to bear down. As the baby's head emerged, I let out a shrill scream. Mam supported the baby's head, turning it to ease out the shoulder. But this baby was in a hurry and slid out quickly.

Mam laughed. 'Oh! Such a tiny soul, with flaming red hair! Jane, pet, you have a beautiful little girl.'

Rose. I smiled to myself and sent up a prayer for Tom. Mam pressed the baby to my breast and I smiled at the scrap of humanity until tears welled in my eyes.

'Come on, baby, try to feed.' Already, my breasts were aching. Although the child's eyes were still closed, she snuffled and moved her tiny lips until she found my teat and began to suckle. A pain like a knife shot through my breast, causing me to wince.

'Come, Jane, let's see. This child isn't properly latched. Hook your smallest finger into her mouth to break the seal.'

I did as Mam told me and the baby began to mewl.

'Patience, my hungry girl.' Mam adjusted the baby's position and nudged her back towards my teat.

'There, try that.'

This time, the baby latched on, but the pain was much less and my daughter suckled easily. More than anything, I wished Tom could be here to see his bairn. But I mustn't cry in front of Andrew's mother. I hugged Tom's child and gazed down on her.

'Jane, you keep nursing the child while I deliver the placenta. Bett, it's usually straightforward, but be ready to take the baby, if necessary.'

Bett's eyes fixed on my child. 'Oh, this little one will have to wear a bonnet. There's none in my family with red hair such as this. And what will our Andrew say?'

Mam clicked her tongue. 'I'm sure your Andrew will just be relieved that Jane and the child are both safe. And he'll be delighted that this little girl takes after Jane's grandmother. My late mother, God rest her, was graced with the same bright hair.'

I looked up from my nursing baby, wondering whether God would forgive a lie of such magnitude, but there was none here to prove otherwise. I smiled and touched my baby's red curls. Mam's lie would allow Bett Driver to be a proud grandmother and it would ease Andrew's life somewhat. It was for me to decide what to tell my child. The convulsions began again, so I tried not to clutch the baby too tightly and closed my eyes against this new, but milder pain.

'Jane, your placenta has come away in one piece.' Mam held up the strange organ. 'This has sustained your little girl. It's not so big, though, and perhaps this is why you've delivered early. Do you see, Bett? Most often, I see a placenta greater than this, even from girls as young and narrow-hipped as Jane.'

Bett nodded. 'Aye, I see. Well no wonder the little mite has turned up so early.'

'Jane, you need some stitches. Bett, please take the baby as the pain will be sharp and Jane may flinch.'

'Aye, Annie, of course I will. And then I'll send a lad to find our Andrew and tell him the glad tidings.'

Bett swaddled the baby in a piece of clean linen and snuggled my mewling daughter close to her. Mam was very clever. Underneath everything, Goodwife Driver had a kind heart and she'd not be able to resist such a pretty child. Especially knowing that she took so much after my grandmother and that she was bound to be born early because of an under-developed placenta.

* * *

Andrew burst into the room, his face wreathed in smiles, and he chastely kissed me and the baby.

'Ah, Jane, what a relief that you're both well. Such a bonny little girl. And the image of your own granny by all accounts.'

Reverend Foster followed him in and exchanged glances with Mam, but he also smiled. 'God bless you, Jane and Andrew, and your little girl. Have you a name for her?'

Andrew nodded. 'We're going to call her Rose.'

It was decent of Andrew to honour my wish. Bett wouldn't be happy, but she'd learn to live with it. And it was important to keep the promise I'd made to Tom that day we'd chased cloud shadows on the Town Moor.

Finally, Bett Driver took charge of her own home once again. 'Come, Reverend Foster and Annie, it's time to leave Jane and my grandchild in peace. They've had a tiring day and they must rest. Andrew will go with you to make the baptism arrangements.'

Mam kissed Rose and felt my brow. 'You're too hot. I'll come and check on you before nightfall to make sure all is well with you and the little one.'

Bett Driver closed the door, sighed and began to bank the fire. 'You do look hot, my girl. You've not got the fever on you, I hope? Maybe you should go back to your mother for a few days. I'll get the supper going today, but you can take care of your own work from the morrow. No lying in like a fine lady around here.'

186

'Thank you, Goodwife Driver, you're most kind.'

I hugged Rose and traced a finger round her face. *Oh, Tom. Tom Verger, we have such a beautiful baby girl and she looks so much like you. I hope you somehow know that Rose is here. And when she's old enough, she'll know all about you, I promise.*

With that, I kissed my baby's downy head and blinked back tears. Tom belonged to the past, God rest him, and I should be more thankful that Andrew had saved us from the house of correction and that we'd been spared the fate of tragic Peggy Greaves and her grey infant. I'd promised myself to Andrew in the eyes of God and had to be faithful to him in mind as well as deed.

* * *

I could only hear the sounds of my own body and could only see what was painted on the inside of my eyelids. But then I became aware of the presence of many people. They crushed and they pressed, their smells and noise taking up all the room around me. It added to the pressure in my head. They sucked the air out of the place with their constant gabbling.

It was impossible to follow them with my ears, to separate their voices, but the gruff tones and the high squeaks forced themselves together into a horrible fog of noise. It squeezed itself into my ears, muffling everything until I was pulled down into the darkness again. Then came a terrible clattering in my ears. It filled my whole skull and shook my thoughts ever looser. Then it was gone, just a tiny fly buzzing away, getting smaller in the distance.

'Sorry, Annie, let me pick these sticks up.'

'Don't worry, lad, just be glad your mother's taken Rose for an airing, or she'd have howled the place down. Jane will be glad of the fire. You're frozen, aren't you, Jane? Andrew, it might be as well to split some more wood for the night ahead.'

The door opened and closed, much more softly than it ever would normally. No foundation-trembling slam. No window-panes clinging to their frames for dear life. No crocks jumping in surprise from dusty shelves. A certain heaviness had left the room, leaving just me and Mam.

'Oh, Jane, what's happened? You were doing so well. You're such a strong lass and never ailed a day in your life. Though I don't know why I'm asking you, it's not as if you're going to answer me, are you?'

I counted the seconds in my head until the door crashed open.

'Oh, Andrew. You're back. Thank goodness, Jane's breathing sounds bad.'

'It does sound very bad. Here, Annie, let me put this wood down and bank the fire up.'

'Jane, I'm going to give you something for your pain. You must be in a lot of pain, pet. The least I can do is take that from you. Poppy milk, Jane. It's all I can do for you now – take away your pain, keep you warm and just pray. Come, pet, take a drop or two for me.'

Something trickled from the corner of my mouth while Mam dabbed with the end of her shawl. Then there was cool liquid in the other side of my mouth, where it ran backward. It clogged my dry throat and I spluttered.

'There, Jane. It'll bring comfort and take away your pain. See how peaceful you look.'

But there was a catch in Mam's voice and there was pressure on my hand as she squeezed hard. My brain told my hand to squeeze back, but nothing moved. The toxic broth crept through my veins and sucked its way through the dark pathways of my body until it exploded in my brain. Then I plunged into the swirling black again.

* * *

Everything sounded muffled and very far off. It was exhausting for me to listen.

'It can't be very long, Andrew. You can leave the fire.'

'Then one of us must fetch the Reverend, Jane mustn't pass unblessed.' There was panic in Andrew's voice.

Mam tried to comfort him. 'There's no time, Andrew. Besides, she's been blessed on most of the days of her life …'

Then Andrew again. 'Don't cry, Annie. It comes to us all. I just wish she didn't have to suffer like this. It must be frightening, lying there waiting to die, especially knowing you're unblessed. Can't you say something? You know the words. And you're a midwife – you're allowed to do it for mothers and bairns – go on.'

'It's not words that matter at a time like this. All I can do is hold Jane's hand and pray that her onward path is a kind one. I'm just glad she has someone with her. Sorry, Jane, we shouldn't talk about you as if you're not here. I think you can still hear us, can't you, Jane? Look at you, my own, sweet girl.'

From afar, I felt Mam's tears running down my hot face.

⊪ ⊪ ⊀

It was still windy because the window rattled. It must be late afternoon, because it was light outside my eyelids, so the sun must be very bright. It was lovely to feel the sun on my face again. My eyelids were light pink, but every so often, a black shadow crossed for a little while. It must be the clouds scudding. Then a big cloud crossed the sky and its dark twin slid over the earth, bringing shivery cold and darkness to everything it touched. Turning light green to grey, turning dark green to grey. Stripping colour in seconds. But these shadows wouldn't stay long. I could chase them away, these ghostly butterflies.

Everything felt slower, thicker. It was harder to pull my thoughts together; they were bleeding out of me, somehow. Everything was hot and dry. I could hear the jagged edges of my own breath and feel the jagged edges of my body, which felt like it had been ripped in two. My hands were being held. My right was in a soft hand. I could smell fennel. Mam. My left hand was in a hard hand. Tom. It must be Tom.

'Jane, wake up, come back. Look, Annie, she was nearly back.'

'Tom.' I gargled for breath. 'Tom.' But nothing came out. There was a cold waft of air as the door opened and then slammed shut.

'Oh, Jane, please don't go, the baby needs you so much!' Mam's voice. 'And Andrew needs you too.'

Andrew. Not Tom. Tom was dead. I could go to Tom. My old colours were leaving me, the ones that I'd worn all my life, the pinks, yellows, purples and reds. And now the new ones,

189

the blues and greens, were pushing them aside, getting me ready for a new place, with Tom. But what about the baby? Rose. I'd promised Tom. Under the darkening sky, the big shadow of night seeped into me, blackening my blood. The saliva gathered in my mouth – saltpetre.

Part Three

25

John

Infestation

After my dealings with George Campbell and the barber-surgeon, I'd felt well equipped to carry out God's work more effectively. Armed with my holy instrument, it was hard even for the most learned magistrate to argue with the evidence before his eyes. Once I'd pricked a witch and she'd failed to bleed, there was no explaining it away, no matter how many clever words were used.

At first, I'd worked in those areas too far out of the way for George Campbell to take himself. In this way, I quickly earned a reputation, with word spreading fast from village to village. And because I always tried to make myself available, the suddenly arranged lay sessions could be accommodated. What really set me apart was that I didn't wait to be summonsed to a village to deal with witches already found. I could go to any village in the land and pick out the witches. My eye was keen and I became renowned for detecting witches in villages that were ignorant of their problem until I arrived and helped them realise it. Once I'd unlocked the secret knowledge of George Campbell and his ilk, it was possible to undertake God's work to greater effect. Within only a few short months, I'd ridded His earth of many sullied souls. With God's grace, I'd have years and strength enough to continue this work.

* * *

I opened my door to an English sergeant, who was richly dressed, considering his lowly position and the heat.

'John Sharpe, sire? I am Sergeant Nicholson. Following a petition from the men of Newcastle demanding the destruction of an unholy presence in our town, I have been sent to Scotland to seek you.'

My heart soared at this news. Soon, I'd be let loose to restore purity to another country. Finally, my moment had come. I would be the man to cross the border to rid the English of their diabolical scourge.

The sergeant handed me a scroll, which carried the town seal of Newcastle. It made my heart swell that my name had become known in England, but I immediately castigated myself for this misplaced pride. It was God's hand that guided me. Any grace accorded me belonged to God, and it was important not to fill myself with vain pomp, but to remember that my mission was in God's name and for His salvation, not mine.

I nodded to the man. 'I'll come at once, Sergeant Nicholson. The fair town of Newcastle must have lost its moral centre if it has to send so far afield for a witch-finder to rid itself of a hellish infestation.'

The sergeant took back the scroll. 'Well, I'll need a fresh horse, as I've fair ridden the legs off this one.'

I shook my head. 'You must put up somewhere for the night. I can make my own way to Newcastle. I'm on God's errand and He'll light my path for me.'

The sergeant glowered, but didn't speak again and just led his horse in the direction indicated by me. There was no time to pray – plenty of time for that once I arrived in Newcastle – and I selected only what was necessary for the journey. My favoured bodkins and my Bible – to keep me focused and clear-eyed in my work. These were the only tools necessary, along with my finest clothes, which were needed because God's work should be carried out by a man worthy of a town's respect. I took my best boots, my thick cloak and a strong sack to carry everything in. Then I rode out, certain that my destiny awaited me in England.

Even so, I was surprised to be chosen by the men of Newcastle. Clearly, news of my work along the border had travelled that far south. It was a perilous journey to Newcastle, but I was keen to make it. If so many witches could bide in the God-fearing hamlets of Scotland, how many more could be hidden away in the sinful towns and cities of England? It was my duty to take this journey. And any silver gained could be invested to protect poorer villages who couldn't afford to offer a bounty.

Perhaps, once the witches were cleared from Newcastle, my reputation might proceed to York and then to London. That hotbed of wickedness must surely bear the greatest infestation of witches in all of England, if not the known world.

Now that my reputation as witch-finder had grown fearsome and I was properly equipped with the tools to serve God, I'd make sure no witch slithered through the fingers of justice. These women were anointed in the loathsome juices of Satan and it sickened me when I thought of what I'd lost at their hands. But it was vital not to let bitterness grow in me. I worked hard to ensure that my loathing was driven into the hunting down and destruction of evil.

Now, there was this invitation from Englishmen, praying me to visit their town and rid the place of accursed witches. This was enticement enough for me to cross the border. But I was neither naïve, nor complacent, knowing that in certain quarters, witch-finders were held to be little better than the women they tried. But I was different, being lit from within by the flame of righteousness. The flame purified me and made me fit for my station. Since swearing my oath to free Scotland of this dread scourge, I'd kept myself chaste in thought and word and deed. I'd lain with no woman, had swallowed no strong drink and had abstained from bloody meat. The flesh fell from me until my bones glowed through my tautening skin.

That my sparseness made my resemblance to my father more obvious was somewhat troubling. But since enough time had passed, it was possible to see that my father was surely a man more sinned against than sinning. After all, he had lost his wife through dark forces, and so had I. His mistreatment of me was surely misguided. The man had blamed me for killing my mother in childbirth and had taken out his sorrow on me. I still bore scars from his hands and feet, but now, I could see that he was also a victim of these vile witches. And it was still in my mind that Dora Shaw had contributed to his death. In truth, I should add him to my list of lost souls who must be avenged.

* * *

During my first meeting with the Newcastle aldermen, I asked them to pray with me. It gave me a feeling of honour and respect. Now secure in their confidence in me, I set out my plans and they confirmed their price. Indeed, so keen were the aldermen to be rid of their scourge, that they agreed to pay twenty shillings per witch, with no limit as to numbers. So I'd round up as many witches as possible before good sense – or good accounting – set in. Their coffers must be bulging, for Newcastle was a town with money, that much was clear.

I set out my needs. Along with two horses and a cart, ropes, chains and a hand bell, I'd take two sergeants. Eight more sergeants would be sent to interrogate the guards at the town gates to see what suspicious women might be at large and where they were headed. Using this system, I intended to traverse the town, ringing my bell and inviting people to identify the witches in their midst. This wouldn't be a hard job since the people of Newcastle had gone to the trouble of petitioning the common council. They would no doubt send out their witches in droves.

Once the contract was sealed, I sought an inn and dined sparely on bread, cheese and weak ale before taking to my bed. In the morning, there was to be a public meeting with the magistrate. He'd introduce me to the townspeople, to show that he'd responded to their petition. I was keen to take to the streets, but I supposed it wouldn't harm my cause to have a room full of fired-up men on my side. It was in my mind to round up a score of women for a score of shillings apiece. This would make a fine start to the proceedings, and the joiners had already been sent to hew the wood for the gallows. I'd grant the people of Newcastle freedom from evil, but I'd also give them a spectacle and make a name for myself in England.

* * *

The cart set off, drawn by two horses. I began tolling the bell to capture the attention of passers-by. We passed an ornate church, which I disdained. There was no need for ornament when it came to praising God. Honest and plain fare sufficed for the Lord. It was actions that pleased Him more than fancy tributes. I watched a woman walk by, fastened into a scold's bridle – the metal contraption known as the branks. A well-deserved punishment for a gossiping woman. She would be a sensible place to start. If not a witch herself, her busy tongue might be persuaded to incriminate practising witches. I nodded to the sergeant in the cart, who then stepped down to speak to the man leading the scold. After showing the council's writ, the man handed his charge to the sergeant.

There was relief on the woman's face as she was freed from her captor. A relief that would be short-lived, depending on the outcome of my talks with her. It didn't take much to persuade these women to talk. I preferred not to have recourse to contraptions, as I'd heard terrible tales and their use seemed against God. I allowed myself only one instrument – the pricking device – beyond that, I relied purely upon nature and my own resources.

The body was frail, after all, and women's bodies more so, except when possessed by demons, which often lent women hellish strength. I preferred walking them and waking them, resorting only to swimming them when absolutely essential. Walking the witches rarely failed. Something in the rhythm of walking could move a body to talk. The monotony of step after step after step built a drumming in the head that somehow opened the mouths of these women. Finally, their secrets would spill, because the act of walking, walking, walking on God's earth loosened the grip of the evil one long enough for confession to spill forth.

Likewise, with waking. Often, witches slept deeply, which was when the devil occupied their soul most fully. While asleep, their bodies gained strength and vigour, fed by the demonic possession of their souls. By breaking a witch's sleep, it was possible to weaken her body and also the devil's grip on her soul. Waking and walking combined achieved the best effect. So I rarely resorted to swimming them as this only killed the innocent women, which struck me as unjust. I prided myself in my fair approach.

Fairness in all things was my watchword. It was vital that no foul witch should escape her eternal justice. But neither did I want to send innocent women to untimely deaths without the benefit of clergy.

Sometimes, I had to supplement my waking and walking technique with other forms of persuasion, but these instances were few and far between, and only deemed necessary for the most stubborn of cases. It grieved me to cause pain to a virtuous woman, but I knew from long experience that women whose souls were occupied by God were lent strength by Him through the power of prayer. This strength shone from them, and at the pinnacle of their suffering, I was able to see into these upright women's souls.

Often, these women of virtue were proven innocent during the trial by nature of their bleeding once they'd been pricked. Aye, it was testing work, but God had chosen me for it. In spite of my sleepless nights, caused by the fear of making an innocent woman suffer, I had the satisfaction of freeing God's lambs from the devil's grip. It was my life's work, and now I was here to share this gift with the English. I put my hand into my pouch and turned over the milk teeth there. The memory of losing my mother, my dog, my wife, my boy and even my much-wronged father renewed my resolve. Every time I put one of these witches to death, it brought me closer to my loved ones, lost though they may be.

26

Jane

Elder Linctus

Whether I was sowing, harvesting or preserving, the earth offered up her seasonal gifts at just the right time of year. So the elder tree offered her dark berries to make a glistening linctus that would prevent the ailments brought by the autumn mists and winter frosts. The purple syrup would barely have a chance to settle in the bottles before the damp weather started stealing in, bringing stiff bones, high fevers and wheezy chests.

Mam often tried to persuade the village women to set by a store, but they seemed reluctant to tinker with what they didn't know. Elder was treated with great suspicion – the dark berries much more so than the heady white flowers. But I loved elderberries and a snug feeling stole over me whenever we put a new batch of linctus away, knowing there was enough goodness to loosen chests and comfort folk all through the white months.

There was a glut of early berries this year and I'd left Rose with Granny Driver so I could help Mam fill some bottles to exchange at the apothecary. The hardest part was getting the water, which meant going down to the hally well. There was clear water in our own well, but the hally well was renowned for its special properties and people came from near and far to take the waters. Really, it was no hardship going there, as it was situated on a long run of pretty riverbank and I had to resist the urge to while away the morning sitting on a flat rock, trailing my feet in the sparkling water of the Derwent.

The afternoon before full moon was the best time to pick berries for healing, so I took my flat basket and the stout stick from the pantry. I needed to venture beyond home as elder wasn't allowed in the garden because it throttled the daylight out of anything nearby. Superstitious folk said elder gave off a dangerous miasma, but perhaps she had to suck in so much goodness to produce her dark berries that there was just nothing left for anything else to grow.

Down by the river, there was a large clearing, bordered on three sides by wooded banks and on the fourth by the river. In the middle were three hawthorn trees, sparkling with red berries, but they would have to wait a few more days. The best elders were those fringing the riverbank, which meant getting clarty, but the dense clumps of berries made it worthwhile. Carefully flattening the nettles and prickles with my stick, I gathered my skirts and squelched through mud to a thicket of berry-decked elders. I whispered my request for permission from Mother Elder and waited silently. Then, reaching for a branch festooned with berries, I worked quickly, plucking sprigs, but never too many from the same tree, always paying heed to Meg's warning: 'You may make two or three passes of the trees, but don't stand picking away at one tree for any amount of time, for the elder has her own breath and who knows the toll she might take.' So I kept moving, pausing to seek permission at each new tree. Soon, my fingers and wrists ran with purple juice, my arms ached and the basket creaked.

'That's enough. Thank you, ladies.'

Satisfied that there were more than enough berries for my needs and plenty left for the insects, birds and gods of the forest, I picked my way back to the drier part of the meadow and set off up the hill.

Mam was waiting for me. 'Thanks for coming to help, Jane. Four hands are quicker than two. Here, let me take that basket from you while you catch your breath.'

We stripped the berries from their stalks, removing every precious bead of goodness. The scarlet sprigs, which Meg had always assured me looked like the insides of lungs, I carried beyond the garden boundary and buried.

'Jane, can you get the honey ready, please? There's enough for a half-pint to a quart of water, so it will be very sweet and keep well.'

I nodded. 'And what about warming spice, Mam? How much have you got?'

'A stick of cinnamon and a thumb of ginger to each pint of honey. That should be enough fire to warm everyone's chests this winter.'

I nodded. 'More than enough, Mam. If you can manage to get all the berries into the cauldron, I'll go and fetch the Reverend's middling hour-glass.'

I ran to the Reverend's desk to fetch it, as boiling the berries for more than quarter of an hour would leave a worthless syrup fit only for its flavour. I set the hour-glass on the table and Mam hefted the cauldron onto the hook over the fire.

'Jane, keep an eye on it for me so the linctus doesn't boil over into the flames and go to waste. I'll get the cheesecloth ready for straining.' She smiled at me. 'Now tell me, how much does an ailing body need to take?'

I laughed. This remedy had been lodged in my head since childhood. 'Oh, that's easy. A spoonful on winter mornings as a preventer for those with weak lungs or too much yellow bile. If a cough, sore throat or fever has already set in, a spoonful or two in hot water before retiring. Then, swaddle and prepare to sweat.'

'Jane, you know these words better than I do myself!'

'Your lessons are etched on my mind, Mam! Before long, they'll be etched on Rose's mind as well.'

She smiled at me, but she had a faraway look in her eye. 'You know, it barely seems a moment since I was learning these lessons from my own mother.'

At this, we both turned our eyes to the sands running through the narrow neck of the hour-glass. The grains moved slowly. The smell of the berries, honey and spice was suddenly cloying and I was grateful for the acrid smoke from the fire. Finally, the last few grains of sand ran through the glass, so I placed a sheet of clean muslin over a pail and Mam lowered the boiling cauldron onto the hearthstone.

'I'll ladle it out, Jane. The cauldron's far too heavy to tip without scalding one of us. But I'd best be quick, as that hot cauldron is still cooking the berries and they'll spoil.'

She began ladling the linctus into the pail. Once it was all transferred, I gathered up the corners of the muslin and lifted it clear of the sweet liquid, squeezing hard to get the last of the syrup out. Then I opened the door and flung the contents of the muslin outside. The birds would make short work of the waste. Mam raised a ladleful and poured the glossy syrup into brown bottles. These, I sealed.

'There's only another hundred bottles to go. Keep it up, pet, keep it up.'

Bending over was making my back ache, so I straightened up just in time to see Reverend Foster pass the door.

'Annie, whatever that delicious smell is coming from, may we have some on buttered crumpets for tea?'

'Sorry, Reverend, it's all for bottling. Enough cough linctus to see the village through until spring. And we're selling the rest to the apothecary in Newcastle.'

'Very well. But I'll keep a bottle, if I may? The old throat has a tickle that's bound to cause mischief during my sermon.'

Mam plucked a hot bottle and passed it to him. 'You may, Reverend. Only because it's you. But don't even think about mixing it with that bottle of liquid fire you keep in your secret cupboard.'

The Reverend smiled benignly, 'Thank you, Annie, and I'll take my hour-glass while I'm here, now that I have your newly sealed magic warming my palm.'

Mam fished in a pouch at her belt and pulled out a bobbin of red thread. 'Here, Jane, cut lengths of this scarlet and I'll knot them round the bottle necks to keep the elder spirit in her proper place.'

I put my head down to stop myself from laughing.

Mam caught my eye. 'Aye, well might you grin, Jane Driver. But Meg wouldn't rest at the thought of elder not being held back by a knot of red thread.'

'I'm sorry, Mam, I know.'

Mam gave a watery smile. 'I remember when Meg half-killed Tom and Andrew when they were just bairns. She caught them hacking and sawing at an old elder tree. Innocent they were, but intent on getting a couple of sticks.'

I turned, alert to Tom's name and wanting to hear a tale of him that was new to me. 'What happened, Mam?'

'Let's just say it was a lesson well learnt. Meg told them never to harm the elder, as Mother Elder would remember them for it all her life. Then she sent them away to find a friendly willow for their sticks.' Mam frowned. 'Although Andrew took it badly. He ran off, shouting "witch, witch", but only when he was beyond chasing distance.' She shook her head. 'Yes, Meg said we must respect the elder, always. She gives us so much of what we need, but she's not very forgiving.'

* * *

We set off at dawn for the walk to the apothecary in Newcastle. Rose was at home with Granny Driver while we went to barter our elderberry linctus in exchange for spices. Weighed down with heavy bottles, it was a long walk, being at least fifteen miles, but not unpleasant.

'Jane, are you well? You seem out of humour and you left your cheese this morning.'

Under Mam's steady gaze, I looked down, colour rising up my neck.

'You're with child again? Are you certain?'

Although I shrugged, tears threatened, and Mam put an arm around me.

'Oh, don't weep. A new baby will be a joy to you both and it'll be the making of your little family, you'll see. But before you start making plans, we'll need to make sure.'

I forced a smile, but pulled away to pick at the clover blossoms growing nearby, plucking the tiny pink petals and sucking their sweetness. 'I'm sure, Mam. It just feels like a betrayal of Tom, that's all. It was one thing marrying Andrew to escape the house of correction. But now I feel as though I've let down his memory.' I put my head down.

'Ah, pet, if you've fallen in love with Andrew and you have a proper marriage, then there's no shame in that. And once this new child is born, Andrew's troubling jealousy about Tom might wane. You know full well that Tom would want you to be happy. You have to be a bit kinder to yourself.'

I wiped my eyes. 'Easier said than done, Mam. Tom's still in my heart, but I know it's time to let him go, for the sake of this coming child, as well as for Rose. Andrew tries to be kind.'

'Perhaps he could try harder. How far gone are you?'

'Two moons, nearly three. It's hard to be certain.'

'Nearly three moons and your own mother not realising! What kind of midwife am I? I noted you were a little rounder in the face, but I put it down to your being contented. Why did you not say?'

'Sorry, Mam. I couldn't find the words and it's so shaming. And yet it wasn't shaming at all when I was carrying Rose, even in the house of correction.'

Mam shook her head. 'Don't be so daft. Is Andrew pleased?'

'Yes. He adores Rose, but I know he yearns for a lad.'

'You should've said something, Jane. I could've gone to the apothecary myself.'

'Thanks, Mam, but I'm two moons gone, not ten. Besides, I'd never let you set foot in Newcastle by yourself. All these tales lately. They say it's no longer safe for a woman alone.'

'You're a thoughtful lass, but let's slow down a little; we've made good time so far.'

We continued following the River Derwent along its course until it widened into the Tyne at Gateshead. The stench from the Tyne turned my stomach, and I wondered at the hundreds of gulls swooping over the ships being loaded. My chin quivered at the sight of the vessels, still pained by the thought that Tom had been stolen away to a cold and lonely death at sea. Carts heaped with shining coals trundled to the quayside. Great coils of rope were piled high and there was a general commotion from horses and men as they laboured under the hot sun. The rope made me recoil and I was grateful that the stench from the Tyne drowned out the smell of the hemp from the ropes. The merest scent might throw me straight back to those dark days in the house of correction. I closed my eyes briefly, grateful that Andrew had saved me. There was much to be grateful for and it would serve me well to remember it.

We followed the Tyne until we reached the bridge, crossing our fingers as we set foot on it, and followed the line of people slowly crossing the stinking river. At the blue stone marking the boundary between Durham and Newcastle, the line slowed as people moved through the gate into the town, which was protected by a great wall of golden stone.

'Oh, Mam, imagine how much swifter our journey if not for the town wall.'

'Oh, Jane, imagine how much swifter the Scots' journey if not for the town wall. Although they've had quite a go at taking it down by the looks of things. Still not properly fixed, I see.'

In spite of my misgivings about Newcastle, I laughed at my mother's proprietary air. 'Mam you talk as though you own the wall yourself.'

But she did not return my smile and slowly shook her head instead. 'Jane, curb your amusement and straighten your face until we pass through the gate. Look at the keen edge on the guards' halberds and that should sober you nicely.'

The first guard towered over us and there was no pleasantry from him when he spoke.

'State your names, place of habitation, business and destination.'

My mouth dried at the sight of the guards and their sharp blades, and I couldn't speak.

Mam answered him. 'Annie Chandler and Jane Driver from Mutton Clog near Shotley Bridge. We're here to trade with the apothecary – just off Amen Corner.'

But the guard held us back. 'Open your sacks.'

Mam untied the sacks and opened them out for inspection.

The guard poked through the sacks. 'Explain the contents.'

'Well, there are bottles of elder cough linctus made by my daughter and myself only yesterday, and some dried lavender flowers.'

Although I'd done nothing wrong and wasn't planning any wrongdoing, guilt washed through me and my hands shook.

'Then move through, cunning women. But be certain you're back outside the walls and on your way home before dusk.'

While I tied the sacks, Mam passed two coins to the guard, who moved aside and admitted us to Newcastle. Already, a clump of people had built up behind us and tempers were rising in the heat. Why had we been singled out for a search and such an interrogation? What on earth did the guard think we were planning? I followed Mam through the stone tunnel and almost laughed when I emerged into daylight at the other side. We walked in silence for some time, but I had the troubling sensation that someone was at our back, listening.

'Mam, let's catch our breath for a few minutes and look at St Nicholas's church.' The hill was steep in this heat and it was a relief to stop and stare up at the high tower, with its intricate crown and spires.

'It's so beautiful. You know, I like this church much better than Durham's cathedral.'

'Well that's no surprise, Jane. I imagine you never want to set foot in Durham again. Come on, if you've caught your breath, let's go and look in the goldsmith's window for a minute or two.'

We spent so long savouring the glowing metal that the goldsmith's wife chased us with her broom, accusing us of wearing away the sheen of the gold with our greedy eyes. Still laughing at the woman's wrath, we reached the street that led to the apothecary. There, a great din arose and we turned to see what was going on. A silent woman was being led along on the end of a rope. The woman wore a hood of metal, which forced a metal prong into her mouth. Children skipped along beside this spectacle, jeering and tossing stones.

Mam paled. 'Dear God, not this barbaric practice again. Jane, avert your eyes at once.'

A bystander leaned over and spoke to me. 'Aye, lass, listen to your mother. It's the Puritans. They do just as they please, taking no note of the law. I hoped never to clap eyes on the branks again, but it's become a daily spectacle of late.'

'Mam, what's this ... branks?'

'It's a scold's bridle and it's used to humiliate women.'

'Why? What's she done?'

Mam lowered her voice and spoke softly into my ear. 'Probably nothing, but she'll have been accused of idle talk.'

'But, Mam, surely it's no sin to talk?'

'Sometimes, pet, it's sin enough to be a woman. We mustn't tarry here, a pair of women gossiping in the street. Come on, hurry.'

My eyes remained fixed on the woman, who was bleeding from the mouth. It was hard to believe we were laughing only moments ago and now the world had become a darker place. The visit to the apothecary had lost its shine. Finally, I tore my eyes from the suffering scold and turned towards the apothecary's shop.

It was a pretty building, which was fronted by glass divided into tiny frames. When we opened the door, all the heat and the noise from the streets of Newcastle vanished. We entered a quiet room that was light at the front, and darker and cooler at the back. It was just possible to make out the apothecary, his wife and their son at the back of the shop. Goodwife Keen said something to her menfolk, who vanished down the back stairs without hailing us, and then she turned towards us.

'Annie Chandler! And Jane! Well, I've been hoping to see you both … I hear there's an early glut of elder berries this year.'

'Hello, Goodwife Keen. It's good of you to welcome us so warmly. And yes, quite a glut of elder for the back end of August.'

'Now, come this way, and we'll carry out our exchange first.'

I smiled my greeting and watched as my mother turned out the sacks. In return, she was given five small vials of dark glass, which she tucked into her shawl. It didn't seem such a fair exchange. But Mam must know what was in those vials, and so she must know their value and properties, even if she wouldn't share the knowledge with me. I sighed and turned back to studying the shop, wondering where the apothecary and his son had gone. It wasn't like them to leave the shop in the middle of the day. The stairs at the back of the room led down to the cellar where barrels of wine, oil and honey were kept, so perhaps they had deliveries to deal with. From the stairs came the muffled sound of men's voices, hasty footsteps and then a door slamming. The apothecary's son running a message, no doubt. I turned my attention back to the shop. On such a hot day, the smells were heavy on my senses. Many were so familiar that I barely noted them, but others were strange to me and these perfumes invaded my nose. I tried to be still, to take everything in and remember it, but knew it an impossible task.

'Ah, Jane, still trying to inhale my whole shop in one lungful?'

'Don't mind my lass, Goodwife Keen, a trip to the town is always overwhelming for us country folk.'

The apothecary's wife laughed and beckoned us deeper into the shop. 'You'll take some ale, both of you and then show me your wares?'

Mam paused before replying. 'Aye, that we will, most gratefully. It's been a hot road.'

'Aye, I don't doubt it, Annie.' Goodwife Keen smoothed down her pinny. 'And did you get across the bridge into the town all right?'

'Mostly, only there was a little trouble with the guards at the gate.'

The apothecary's wife nodded. 'It's no surprise to me. They're coming down heavily on cunning women of late. All women, in fact. Here, take some ale.'

'Thank you most kindly. Jane, you may take your ale and go wandering, if Goodwife Keen permits?'

She nodded assent, and I took my ale and wandered over to examine the shelves. Mam drank her ale because she was thirsty, but she would have preferred a light tisane of lemon balm, or failing that, camomile.

'You'll have seen the lass pinned inside the branks as you came by, Annie?'

'Aye, we did. And what a dreadful sight it was.'

Goodwife Keen topped up Mam's cup. 'Mind, the gossiping biddies bring it on themselves, I dare say. The sergeants are ever vigilant of late. And they're always round here asking questions.'

At this, Mam leaned nearer to the apothecary's wife. 'Oh? What sort of questions?'

Inside the apothecary's shop was one of my favourite places to be, so while Mam exchanged tittle-tattle, I admired the wares.

Three of the walls were shelved from floor to ceiling. The shelves contained hundreds of crocks, jars and bottles with powders, unguents, oils and tinctures from all over the world. Beneath the window was a wide chest with dozens of drawers. In the middle of the room stood a long table, which was covered with scales, measuring spoons, and several mortars and pestles. From the ceiling hung wooden racks loaded with enormous bouquets of drying herbs. My fingers itched to let down these racks so that I could examine the mysterious plants. In the shop window were many curiosities. There was a human skull from a hanged man, the shell of a turtle from the South Seas and the shrivelled organ of an Indian tiger.

So entranced was I by the medicinal cornucopia that I'd stopped listening to the conversation. Feeling guilty, I turned back to see Goodwife Keen refilling the cups with ale, even though Mam's cheeks were already pink. Sharing information was an important part of our trade, but it was also possibly dangerous. If the men of Newcastle would fasten a woman inside the scold's bridle just for idle gossip, what might they make of my mother's chatter? I thought back to the guards at the gate, warning us to leave before sunset. And then I wondered about the sergeants who'd been coming around to ask questions. It made me worry about what Mam might be giving away.

Before I could signal to Mam, the apothecary's wife haled me. 'Jane, I was just asking your mother whether God minds her carrying out the dark arts under His roof. What do you say?'

Goodwife Keen's query made me feel awkward. Unaccustomed to ale, Mam's eyes were glassy and it was a struggle to read what was written there, so I chose to be careful in my reply.

'Well, nature grows everything we need to make us better. It's all there for the picking.' I did not add that it was all there for the picking, whether it be apple or pennyroyal.

She narrowed her eyes at me. 'And have you no fear of thunderbolts striking you down?'

It was an odd question, and I wasn't sure how to answer it. I supposed God must not mind our work so very much. Yet my stomach churned for reasons that were not only to do with the child inside me. The apothecary's wife waited for my answer with a sly look in her eye, and I found myself not liking her much today.

My pondering was interrupted by a great crash from the cellar, and I turned to see what was going on. Heavy footsteps pounded up the cellar steps and two sergeants burst through the door. My mother's ale cup smashed on the floor and I ran to her side.

27

John

The Dry Wound

Finally, my hour had come. It seemed all of Newcastle had come to see me try their witches. Ranged along the high bench at the back of the courtroom were the magistrate and the common council. They were flanked on one side by the clergy and on the other by the respectable professions, who were crammed shoulder to shoulder in the polished pews. In a side gallery sat the women who must be their wives. Standing down in the main hall were the tradesmen, and behind them, anyone who'd managed to press his way in. Opposite the high bench stood three rows of ten people. Many of them held hands. To my mind, each of these witches wore the same face as Dora Shaw – that very same hag who'd stolen my father, my mother, my wife and my son. She'd paid the price for her devilry and now so would these damned souls.

The magistrate looked around the courtroom before standing to address us.

'Thanks to our witch-finder, John Sharpe, fetched down from Scotland under petition to the council, thirty people have been rounded up and fetched here for trial in a manner that is most unusual, which gives me some cause for caution.'

Loud jeers rose from the standing crowd and there was a great deal of foot stamping. The magistrate stood his ground until the jeers died out before continuing.

'In summary, these people stand accused of consorting with the devil. But I must consider whether they were just too near the source of misfortune. Crops may fail, beasts die, cows turn dry, men ail and wombs let loose of still children. Can these not just be the result of providence? Must they be given some vessel of blame? I must take care not to send citizens to their deaths for being too red of hair or green of eye, for being old or needy, crippled or soft-headed, or for being otherwise burdensome. For cannot milk turn sour, beasts fall lame and children change their minds about entering such a world? I promise a full and searching investigation before reaching any verdict of witchcraft.'

I walked towards the bench to address the magistrate.

'Thank you, sire, for your wise words of caution. But please be assured that you can rely upon me and my tested methods for uncovering witches. No innocent citizen will be sent to the gallows by my hand.' Then I turned neatly to address the crowd. 'And no corrupt witch or defiled consorter of the devil will escape my most thorough testing.' I cast my gaze along the gallery, causing several women to look to the floor.

I took my place in the centre of the room. When visiting my prisoners in gaol, I'd dressed simply, but today I was in my full regalia of knee boots with polished silver buckles, a thick cape of black, a pure white linen shirt and hose, with dark-red breeches and jerkin. Before me stood a wooden contraption, which was simple, but solid. A raised platform of no more than a foot high and a few feet square. In the centre of the platform rose a wooden stake of seven feet. To my eye, it seemed hastily constructed. The wood was not planed and spelks stood ready to insult the accused. The tang of green oak cut through the fog of sweat and ale that suffused the room. Briefly, I wondered why the council would use oak instead of cheap pine. Money to squander, no doubt.

From my tooled leather belt, I produced a tarnished silver implement of about eight inches long. This one had a sharp point at one end and a filigreed handle at the other. This pricker would prove witchcraft here today. When I brandished the pricker, no light reflected from its viscid blade. A hush swept the room as all eyes fell upon the pricker, and it pleased me to see the accused blanch in fear.

'This is the tool for my witch-proving: the pricker! Be sure to note the congealed blood on the blade, ladies and gentlemen. This isn't dirty blood. What you see coating the pricker is the blood of innocents unstained by the devil. The imp-infested witches do not bleed. The dry wound is certain proof of a witch. Before I begin pricking, do any doubters wish to test the efficacy of my blessed implement?'

A brief buzz of chatter arose and I allowed it to swell. But when my eyes swept the room, the chatter died as people looked to their feet.

'Anyone here present is welcome to test its solidity, its weight and its pricking abilities for themselves … Is any Christian present willing to put this device to the test by inviting a prick to their own thumb?'

The room was entirely silent. There were never any takers when I made this invitation.

'Nevertheless, I shall demonstrate what happens when this bodkin pierces the flesh of an innocent.'

I held out my left thumb in front of me, turning so that all sides of the room could examine that godly digit. Then I plunged the bodkin into my thumb, causing a gash to open and blood to run from it. This caused a rumble of muttering from the floor and I nodded.

'I trust that we are satisfied?'

The magistrate glared at me. 'Good God, get on with it, man. There is no need to prolong the misery. Imp-infested or no, remember that the accused are not yet proven guilty.'

He continued to stare until, somewhat abashed, I addressed the two burly sergeants. 'Bring down the first accused, sergeants.'

The sergeants plucked a wailing woman from the back row, marched her forward and flung her onto the wooden platform, where she cowered. They dragged her to her feet, facing the stake, and lashed her wrists in front of her. The woman had room to move about the platform, but the height of the stake prevented her from going anywhere. She was barefoot, filthy and attired only in a threadbare shift. I withdrew a knife from my belt and cut the woman's shift open. The woman sobbed as her breasts and private parts became visible. She closed her eyes and turned her reddened face to one side.

The magistrate peered at the accused. 'State your name, age and habitation.'

'Margaret Taylor, two-and-fifty years, Spital Tongues.'

The magistrate consulted his scroll. 'Very well, Margaret Taylor, you stand accused of engaging in the gross sin of sortilege to envisage a husband for an ageing maid.'

With a sneer, I turned to the floor to translate for the common herd. 'Sortilege being the old Roman sin of casting lots to determine the future – a right, mark you, that belongs only to the Almighty.'

The magistrate frowned at me and then turned to the prisoner. 'How plead you, Margaret Taylor? Guilty or not? Speak up, woman. Have you no tongue?'

I grabbed the woman's chin, pulled her face towards the bench, shoved my hand into her mouth and pulled out her tongue. 'The hag does have a tongue; she just chooses not to use it.'

An alderman, seeming to enjoy the entertainment, guffawed. The magistrate narrowed his eyes at the man, who ceased his merrymaking on the instant. The woman began to gag and I let go her tongue, allowing her to speak.

'Louder, hag, so the magistrate can hear you.'

'Innocent, sire. Innocent as a newborn babe.'

I shook her. 'Silence, hag. I'll be the judge of that. But first, I'll examine this witch for signs that she has given suck to the devil and his imps.'

At that, I pulled back the linen remnants hanging on the woman's spare frame and scrutinised her body, lifting each breast in turn to examine its underside. I was thorough and twisted each teat, extracting a pleasing wince from the woman. Next, I had the sergeants untie her from the stake, grabbed her by the stubble on her head and bent her over while the sergeants tied her wrists to her ankles. This fetched a shriek of pain from the woman. I proceeded to examine her orifices, thrusting my fingers in deeply, eliciting further cries.

'This hag is as dry as a stick, which is to be expected … '

I paused to allow a cackle of dirty laughter to run through the standing rabble.

A man on the floor leaned forward to catch my eye. 'Turn her round, man, so us lot can get an eyeful.'

214

The magistrate held up his hand before I could oblige, a pained expression on his face. 'Sharpe, pray continue as expediently as possible. We're here to determine guilt and not to provide some form of low spectacle. Must Margaret Taylor remain in that position?'

Disappointment flashed across the faces of the aldermen and the rabble in equal measure. I ran my filthy fingers beneath my nose and threw the crowd a lascivious leer. This seemed to satisfy them momentarily, as a small cheer arose. Margaret Taylor was purple-faced and trembling, and urine ran down her dirty legs, leaving clean tracks.

I ordered the sergeants to untie her wrists from her ankles. She stood up, staggering slightly, the blood already draining from her face. I waited until she was steady and the blood had returned to her body, then I brandished the bodkin before plunging it into her left haunch. She let out a screech that didn't subside, even as the bodkin was withdrawn. Its exit was followed by a gush of blood, which ran down the woman's leg and mingled with her urine on the floor. The room immediately blazed into excited exclamation until the voice of the magistrate boomed across it.

'This woman is no witch. Free her forthwith. Margaret Taylor, you are proven innocent and free to leave. Yet, cover yourself, for you are a filthy specimen and hardly fit for decent people to witness.'

The hag tried to tug the remains of her shift together and hurried from the room, not pausing to look at those prisoners remaining.

When the room had quieted, I nodded to the sergeants once more. Next, they brought the man, Matthew Bulmer. He shifted his feet, reluctant to stand in the waste of his predecessor. The sergeant slashed Bulmer's clothing, bent him over and lashed his wrists to his ankles.

The magistrate spoke. 'Matthew Bulmer, you stand accused that on the full moon, you did summon a black dog from the very bowels of hell, in the full and knowing company of your coven.'

I stepped forward to examine the man. Upon examining him, I cleared my throat and waited for silence.

'There's a hidden teat upon this man in the darkest and most unholy recess. It isn't possible to see it with the eye, so it must be felt manually. If anyone wishes to examine the devil's teat for himself, please step forward.'

The magistrate held up his hand. 'We accept your word, John Sharpe. That is why we employed you. Prick him and be done.'

As ordered, I thrust the bodkin up to its hilt into Bulmer's haunch. Although the man started and roared mightily, there was not a single drop of blood when I stood clear, brandishing the bodkin. Women in the room covered their faces with their aprons and even the men seemed to shrink back.

The magistrate locked eyes with the guilty man and pointed straight at him. 'Matthew Bulmer, as possessor of the devil's own teat and impervious to the pricker, you are hereby found guilty of consorting with the devil and of summoning a diabolical black dog from hell. You are a proven witch and will be put to death on the morrow in a manner concordant with your sin.' The magistrate turned to the sergeants and nodded towards the condemned man. 'Take him down.'

The man's howls could be heard over the noise of the crowd as the sergeants removed him from the room.

* * *

I continued in this vein, working my way through the ranks of the accused. So far, the bodkin had uncovered fifteen guilty women and one man. The magistrate stood up and ruffled his robes.

'The court will try one more prisoner, with the rest to be recalled on Monday.'

Groans and calls came from the crowd and the magistrate held up his hand to hush them.

'Those found guilty today will be executed on the morrow, as planned. But we simply can't be expected to sit here all day and all night in this heat without food or comfort. Sergeants, bring the final prisoner.'

The sergeants seized a young girl by her thin arms. But an older woman forced her body between the girl and the sergeants, shaking her head firmly at the girl's imploring eyes.

'Take me, please. I beseech you.'

The elder sergeant shrugged. 'All the same to me, you daft bitch.'

The sergeants walked her to the filth-ridden platform. The voids of bowels and bladders mingled with blood and there was no part clean or dry.

'Woman, state your name, age and habitation.'

'Annie Chandler, six-and-thirty years, Mutton Clog near Shotley Bridge.'

The magistrate consulted his papers for a short time before drawing himself up and levelling his gaze at the woman. 'Ann Chandler, perhaps the most heinous witch of all, you are hereby accused that in the last twelvemonth you did cause stillbirth in Goodwife Wright, made Goodwife Brown barren and destroyed a dozen babies while they slumbered in their mothers' wombs. How plead you? Witch or no?'

The woman looked at the girl, who I supposed was her daughter. Something passed between them in that look. What was it? An apology? More likely a spell. But whatever it was, the younger witch refused to accept it as she shook her head and closed her eyes, perhaps in prayer. Well, prayer wouldn't save these witches.

The sergeant held up the knife to me, but I brushed him away, reached forward and grasped Chandler's shift at the neck. I braced myself then ripped the garment from neck to knee with an ease that belied my frame. The woman flinched and pressed her face against her shoulder to hide her shame. A hubbub erupted in the crowd and I let it continue, allowing catcalls from lechers in the front of the crowd.

'Oho, it's a pretty wench the pricker has kept himself until last.'

'Turn her, witch-finder, that we might all have an eyeful of the tasty wench and those pert titties.'

'No wonder he was up all night waking this one.'

'SILENCE!' thundered the magistrate. 'Proceed, Sharpe, and do not make a meal of it.'

First, I scoured Annie Chandler's body with my eyes. Then, in the newly hushed room, I began to run my hands over her, beginning with her wrists and working my way up to her shoulders, then from her ankles up to her thighs. I cupped her breasts although they were still high and there was no need to lift them to examine the undersides. Even so, I gave each breast a hard wrench, causing the witch's face to twist in on itself. I looked at the witch's daughter, who buried her face in her hands, no doubt shamed by her mother's misplaced bravery.

Quickly, I bent the witch over, and once the sergeants had lashed her wrists to her ankles, I began my probing, pushing my hand deep into the recesses of her body, forcing her to cringe and her eyes to bulge in silent agony.

'There's nothing in the rectum.' I plunged my hand into her vagina. 'And there's nothing in the vagina.'

She wobbled and would have fallen over had the sergeants not steadied her with hands both large and willing. I took out my bodkin and pressed it up to the hilt in the woman's thigh. She remained silent, and it must have appeared to those present that she'd somehow turned insensate.

'Witness, all of you, how the devil's bitch felt not a thing.' With a flourish, I removed the bodkin. Chandler's flesh was dry and bare of blood. Very real fear troubled her daughter's eyes.

'I give you the witch!' I flung my arms wide to ringing cheers from the floor.

As the cheers subsided, the magistrate cleared his throat and peered at the accused. 'Stand up, woman, and make yourself decent.'

The sergeants dragged her upright and the magistrate consulted his scrolls before speaking again.

'Ann Chandler, proven witch, most diabolical, you are hereby sentenced to death by hanging, with no benefit of clergy. Your execution will take place on the morrow at the Town Moor. Take her down.'

The daughter wailed and sank to her knees as her silent mother was taken from the room.

28

Jane

A Welcome Weight

The first daylight I'd seen since being snatched from the apothecary on Thursday caused me to squint, and the fresh air dizzied me. My feet were raw from the walking I'd endured in the town gaol during the night. With every new step, it felt as though my bones scratched the hard cobbles. Newcastle's streets jostled with folk, no doubt fresh-souled after cleansing themselves at morning prayer. Out of the crowd, a red-faced man lurched forward until he was so close that it was possible to smell his rancid breath.

'Youse divvil's bitches, you're fit for naught but the gallows!'

A gobbet of hot phlegm hit my face, but I'd not the list to scrape it off. My gaze returned to the ground and I thought only of my child. Of Tom's child. What would become of Rose? How would she fare once I was dead? Once Mam was dead. The screeching of cartwheels and the hollow sound of heavy hooves roused me. The sun was already hot and the smell of horses surrounded me. The whip was being used and the crack made me turn my head. But it was the horses being whipped. A caravan of carts followed behind, each carrying a chained prisoner. Someone screamed as they fell from a cart. I shut my eyes and prayed that it was my mother. With luck, she might crack her skull.

The faces of the men, women and children lining the streets merged into a blur of hatred, which had no discernible features, but merely contorted with disgust. The sun beat down on my uncovered head, burning my neck and scalp. It pushed through my shift, its warmth not welcome, but intrusive. My stomach was shrunken with hunger, my parched tongue stuck to the roof of my mouth and my head pounded in the heat.

The Town Moor was thronged and its carnival mood sickened me. The crackle of fire and the sizzle of flesh haunted the air. What base desires led people to have an appetite at such a time? I had to be here, to say goodbye to my mother in this life, to witness men's justice being meted out, to see the fate that awaited me in the coming days. But why were these others here? Too cheerful to be the kin of the condemned, these gawkers pressed in on all sides. Most had come to jeer and give thanks that the town was to be cleansed of its witches. No doubt amongst them, the treacherous apothecary and his sly-tongued wife. But there were some heads bowed, perhaps to acknowledge that there was something badly wrong in England today.

As the procession slowed before a line of wooden gallows, rage swelled in my chest. I bit hard on the insides of my cheeks and only the pain and the taste of blood stopped me from screaming. Each gallows had a noose, which swayed gently in the summer breeze. Joiners' lads scampered up and down long ladders and perched on top of the newly hewn gallows. The smell of freshly sawn wood hung in the air, its sweet sap a terrible scent on such a day.

So many people to be murdered. It was unbearable looking at the terrifying contraptions, one of which would be used to force my mother from this world. Great shame washed through me for allowing Mam to take my place at the trial. In the hour of her greatest need, I'd give anything to change places. Instead, all I could do was hold up my aching head so that I might be the last sight Mam saw: someone who loved her and who would pray for her soul. Word would have spread to Reverend Foster and he must be here somewhere, praying for Mam.

Having done its scorching work on the long walk through Newcastle, the sun had now taken its leave and dark clouds moved across the moor. The sky pressed down, flat and heavy, its dull pewter filled with the promise of rain. It was an ominous portent. I prayed that the executioner would be merciful. Even so, I was mindful not to move my lips, lest anyone accuse me of making a charm against them.

A bell began to sound, followed by distant drums and horses' hooves. Behind the cart bearing the bell ringer and the drummer trailed over a dozen carts, each bearing one shorn and chained prisoner. On the final cart was my mother. These wretched people were being borne towards their end. At the sight of the gallows, they began sobbing, shrinking away from their chains and upsetting the horses, causing them to whinny and show the whites of their eyes, until the horses were rewarded with further whippings.

My mother looked insensible with fear. I stared, willing her to look up. But she seemed locked inside herself, unaware of what was going on and barely able to remain upright. Each cart was driven beneath a gallows and I looked at the dreadful row. Seventeen nooses. Seventeen carts. Seventeen prisoners. One of them my mother. She had the same hollow-eyed look as a beast to the slaughter, except Mam knew her fate and saw no point in scrambling for freedom or pawing at her restraints. My insides contracted as I realised that there was no hope of intervention. Nothing could save her. This would also be my fate and Rose would grow up motherless.

The drummer took up a solemn beat while the aldermen took their places close to the gallows so they could witness the hangings at close quarters. Once they were seated, a Puritan minister passed along the gallows, careful to keep his back to the condemned, almost stumbling in his haste. So my innocent mother would suffer for all eternity, unblessed and unshriven. The minister paused to deliver a short blessing on the executioner, a large man hidden by a hood, with only slashes for eyes. I quickly sent up a prayer for my mother, hoping it would travel on the back of the minister's prayer and stand more chance of being heard that way.

Once the blessing was done, the drumming palled and the magistrate stood up and consulted his scroll, ready to make his terrible pronouncement. A light of hope flared in my heart. Perhaps there was some mistake, or there could be some intervention. Perhaps my mother, who was filled only with goodness and kindness, would be spared and her name wouldn't be read out. I forced myself to attend to the magistrate's words, holding my breath, crossing my fingers and closing my eyes, all in the hope that God would intercede.

But when I heard my mother's name float away on the slight breeze, I opened my eyes. Mam was still here and so God hadn't seen fit to spirit her away to safety. The only sounds came from the whickering horses and from the weeping condemned. I willed Mam to look up, but her head stayed bowed. She was so thin and her neck looked too weak to hold the weight of her head. May God forgive me, but I hoped her neck would snap and bring a quick release. I'd heard of too many strong-necked men and light women swinging until they choked to death. A neck broken swiftly was a mercy.

The newly blessed executioner climbed onto the first cart, drew the noose over the trembling woman's head and then removed her chains. He took a few seconds to adjust the knot to her neck, and then placed his hands on her shoulders and whispered a few words into her ear. His whispered words and the placing of his hands seemed to quieten the woman and bring her peace. This, no doubt, was the hangman's promise. He'd been to see us in the gaol and told us our end would be as swift as he could make it. But I knew the end was rarely swift for women as slender as these. In this way, the hangman continued along the row of carts, checking each noose and whispering his secret words to quiet the wailing prisoners.

Finally, the executioner mounted the last cart. I swallowed, forcing myself to watch as he placed the noose over my mother's head. Mam was so tiny and she was shaking. He fitted the noose to her neck and knotted it tightly. Mam stayed silent, looking up at the sky. She looked so afraid and eternity was such a long time. My entire body shook and it was all I could do to stay upright. To be there for my mother. To bear witness. To pray for her soul.

The executioner stepped down from my mother's cart and took his place before the gallows. The magistrate and the aldermen hung their heads, choosing not to watch what they'd wrought. But the cart drivers all had their eyes on the executioner. When he gave them a deep nod, they raised their whips to their horses.

The shocked animals lit across the moor, their drivers struggling to keep them from careering into one another. A loud roar came from the moor as the seventeen prisoners dropped on the short journey to their deaths.

I could only stare as the cart went from under Mam. Her feet thrashed desperately, trying to gain a foothold and I willed God to take her quickly, hardly able to watch the purpling of her face as the rope began to bite. Mam's neck was thin, but so was her body, and her weight wasn't enough to snap her neck. So she dangled, feet twitching, with her hands clutching at the rope that bit into her. But as soon as the horses were clear of the gallows, hooded men began running towards the condemned, throwing themselves at their legs. A tall man shot towards the gallows, hurled himself at my mother's legs and clung to her until his weight snapped her neck and her feet were finally still. I closed my eyes and silently thanked him, whoever he was.

But now, a great fire raged through my chest. Mam's soul had left this earth, going unshriven to the next world, to spend all eternity in hell. I screamed a silent scream to the black sky, which opened and let loose its rain, cleansing and blessing Mam's remains. My feet pressed into the soft grass, with the earth giving slightly beneath it. My body was so light, I feared it might float away if I didn't keep pushing my feet down. If I could only summon the strength to press harder and sink into the cool and protecting earth, to feel its mouth close above my head and keep me safe amongst the blind roots and the sightless, burrowing creatures.

* * *

Once again, I was in the town hall, but this time without my mother. The courtroom was vast, but so filled was it with people that it appeared no bigger to me than the dank cell where we'd been held. The walls and ceiling were dark wood, which brought them closer, leaving scarcely enough air for all the busy lungs that required it. My ribs brushed against my filthy shift and felt as if they might cut through the flimsy fabric, so sharp were they. Heat coursed through my body. This heat came not from the sun, but was an inner heat created by the poppy milk that Reverend Foster had smuggled into gaol for me. Perhaps it was intended for my hanging, but there was nowhere to hide the vial, for Sharpe would find it, no matter how privately hidden.

I peered down on myself. My eyes shone, bright amber, with no darkness at their centres. I gave out my own radiance and took in little light from the room. Filled with an inner fire, I breathed very slowly, feeling the walls and ceiling of the room breathing in and out with me, alternately pressing in on me and then moving away into a dizzying void. Through the darkness, the crowd was a writhing mass, adorned with hundreds of glittering eyes, snatching hands and devouring mouths.

From around the room came the burr of voices, distant echoes of the same words that had condemned my mother on Friday, a day that belonged to another life. I was beyond tears and the warm numbness swaddled me from my own terrible fate. The voices continued to rise and fall. These voices belonged to men. They were deep and it was hard to hear them. Occasionally, they were run through with sobs and prayers. These voices belonged to women. They were high and it was easy to hear them. These unlucky souls had no poppy milk to help them.

I'd not look at Sharpe, nor watch what he was doing to the woman before him. I'd not hear his proclamations. But the pleading woman's voice found its way into my ears anyway. When my turn came, I'd not speak, plead or whimper, because I didn't have enough breath. My heart was so slow, and my breathing so heavy, that I might simply stop breathing. Maybe I'd do just that. Stop breathing.

Rough hands seized my upper arms and my feet rose from the floor as I floated to where Sharpe waited. My head drooped and the witch-finder grabbed my chin, but I refused to see him for he was just a dark outline to me. His angry voice boomed at me, but I'd admit none of his words entry.

Cool air touched me as my shift was ripped down the front, but I was still warm inside. I didn't shiver. I didn't hear. I didn't see. Sharpe grabbed the short stubble on my head, wrenching me down while the sergeants lashed my wrists to my ankles. The motion almost overbalanced me, but the sergeants held me steady by pushing a stick under my ribs and holding it at each end.

My head became hotter and felt fuller, as if my skull had grown because of the blood pooling there. I closed my eyes, concentrating on the blood pounding in my ears, letting it drown the sound from the room. Now was the time to stop breathing. My sharp ribs would cut through the stick that held me. I'd fall forward and sink into the waiting earth, where it was soft and welcoming. I'd sleep there, floating inside a warm, dark dream. Coiled once more inside my mother's womb.

The witch-finder moved behind me and I felt his cruel fingers inside me. When he withdrew his fingers, I prepared myself for the pricker used on my mother. Sharpe plunged it into my haunch. I made no sound and my body didn't react. The witch-finder ran his hand down my thigh. The blood continued to roar in my ears, blocking out all sound, filling my mind with blessed blackness. But still I could hear men's voices swirling around my head, sometimes entering my ears, sometimes not.

'The witch does not cry out, flinch, or bleed. See how she faints away to escape her accuser! This is proof that she's a consorter of Satan, the devil's own child and–'

But Sharpe's words were cut off by a familiar voice shouting. It was Reverend Foster. 'She's no consorter! Sire, I beg you, Jane is no child of the devil. There's no harm in her–'

The sergeants ran from me and there was a scuffle. Poor Reverend Foster. He wasn't present for Mam's trial, so why was he here now?

The magistrate raised his voice. 'Sergeants, hold your weapons. We will not tolerate the beating of a holy man. Reverend, this girl has been proven guilty. One more word and I'll have you seized. Jane Driver, you are hereby sentenced–'

But Reverend Foster interrupted again. 'Sire, in the name of God, I beg you halt, for there's something most irregular in these proceedings.'

The magistrate paused, perhaps at the mention of God from a holy man's mouth. 'Reverend! There's something most irregular in your continual interruption of these proceedings.'

'If it pleases you, sire, let me put something to you, upon my word.'

The magistrate sighed loudly. 'Since you're a man of God, I'll grant you audience. Continue, Reverend.'

'Thank you, sire. Sharpe, untie Goodwife Driver and let her stand up for a while. Then when she has quite recovered, prick her on another part of her body. This time, I'll bear witness from close quarters.'

Sharpe's voice was alive with outrage. 'This is preposterous. Her corrupted flesh alone should be enough to condemn her–'

But the magistrate shouted over Sharpe. 'Silence! I will have silence. Stand her up straight, then prick her again. Proceed, with the Reverend in close attendance.'

The sergeants unfastened my wrists from my ankles and stepped away from me. I slowly straightened up. My face was on fire and I saw the world through eyes made of flat glass. I swayed slightly as the blood began to leave my head, but my naked body was still on display. The witch-finder bristled and his eyes flickered at the aldermen, but their stares were indifferent.

The magistrate spoke again. 'Do as commanded, Sharpe. Refrain from dallying.'

Sharpe produced the bodkin without ceremony and plunged it no more than an inch into my leg. I shrieked and blood oozed from the shallow wound.

'She bleeds!' roared Reverend Foster, turning towards the magistrate. 'Sire, there's trickery afoot. Jane Driver is no witch. She's bled freely in front of my own eyes. I beg you, sire, set her free and let her cover her modesty.'

The magistrate looked from my bleeding leg to Sharpe's outraged face. He waved Reverend Foster away.

'Return to your place, Reverend, this matter requires further investigation. Sergeants, give the girl cover.'

'Cover her, he said.' Reverend Foster slipped forward and wrapped his cloak around me.

The Reverend held me and passed a small vial of hartshorn under my nose. An acrid smell rushed up my nostrils and burnt its way into my chest until I began coughing and spluttering. I sucked in a huge breath and choked on it. Reverend Foster pulled his cloak more tightly around me. I was parched and much relieved when he held a flask of water to my mouth.

I licked my lips and blinked. The room still felt very small and close, and it was filled with roaring and buzzing voices, which were too loud and too many to take in. Exhausted, I slumped against Reverend Foster.

'Reverend, where have I been?'

'To a dark place, Jane.'

I furrowed my brow, trying to remember, but nothing would come from the blackness. Then a memory surged up and tears filled my darkening eyes.

'When am I to be hanged, Reverend? The morrow?'

He shook his head and pulled me closer. 'No, not the morrow. Not ever. You're safe, Jane.'

29

John

It Is a Tricky Implement

Oh, what fiendish imps were at work in this courtroom? One
minute I was revered as God's own messenger, and the next I was
a lowly criminal. The assembly had collapsed into arguing and
shouting. How easily these people's blood ran to excitement. Too
sanguine by half. Nothing that a proper bloodletting wouldn't
resolve. But this was only false bravery, and in reality, my heart
was pounding and my fingertips were slick with sweat. I held my
hands stiffly, else I give in to the impulse to wipe them on my
breeks.

The magistrate wasn't fit for office and had lost control. The
fool flapped his hands at the sergeants, who were using their
clubs on the unfortunates near the front of the standing crowd.
But where the clubs found their targets, the crowd quietened and
the magistrate's words began to gain ground.

'Not one more word from this room, else it be cleared.'

The magistrate looked each rough man in the eye until the
other dropped his gaze and quiet seized the room. The magistrate sat back in his seat, still eyeing the culprits. But then his gaze
swung round and fastened itself on me, and I quailed inside.

'John Sharpe. Sixteen women and one man were hanged from
the gallows only two days past on the say-so of your pricking
technique. And now it's been called into question by a man of
God.'

I didn't reply, but my Adam's apple bobbed, which must surely reveal my fear to all.

'Tell me, man, in the first instance of your pricking Jane Driver, how might a four-inch bodkin sink into the haunch of such a slender girl?'

The magistrate waved a hand in the direction of the bitch. I looked at her while trying to form my thoughts into acceptable shapes. Despite my trembling hands, I stroked my beard to a point as I'd seen many men of high office do. It conveyed the appearance of wisdom, even when none lodged there.

'The bodkin pierces the flesh and carries on down to the bone, sire, where it then continues through to the infernal marrow of the witch. You've borne witness to this phenomenon here today.'

The magistrate raised his eyebrows. 'As the bodkin forces its way into the marrow, why does the woman not shriek? I'm sure seasoned soldiers might make some sound following such a wound.'

'Sire, witches feel no pain because they're not made as men of God are made.'

The magistrate nodded. 'So then, in the second instance of pricking, how is it that the blade barely pierced an inch on the girl's right haunch, yet she bled profusely and shrieked high enough to curl teeth?'

Oh, this magistrate was tricksy. He kept his cleverness hidden, bringing it into the light only now. I blew out a breath, eyes flicking left and right before replying. 'On occasion, with younger witches, the flesh has not had time to become fully corrupted. This young witch is a perfect specimen. With this girl, the sinister side has been fully corrupted.' I pointed to the witch, indicating her left leg. 'See, all down her left side, she feels no pain, nor does she shed blood.'

I paused, allowing the magistrate to consider this. But he frowned, which wasn't a helpful sign. No doubt, it signalled the unleashing of more cleverness. I raised my voice and spoke quickly.

'Whereas here, on her right, sire, which all God-fearing men accept as the holy side, the devil's corruption has not yet fully spread–'

'Silence, man!'

The magistrate held up a hand to stop me and then turned to the town clerk, a man who looked far too well fed for his station.

'Clerk, how much has the common council paid for this man's venomous services?'

The clerk consulted his scrolls. 'Some twenty shillings per witch, sire.'

There came a low whistle from the crowd, which attracted the magistrate's ire. He pointed his gavel at a young fellow with his long fingers hooked into his mouth.

'Silence, whistler, or you'll feel the sergeant's club. Though granted, you've a right to whistle at the sum of twenty shillings. Thank you, clerk.' The magistrate turned to me. 'And how many witches have you found for us, John Pricker?'

I wiped my mouth on my sleeve, muttering and counting on my fingers, my mind whirring. It was hard to recall the numbers. Try as I might, I couldn't put my mind on the number, and the names and faces seemed suddenly slippery. They all looked as one. Each bore the grinning leer of Dora Shaw, the old hag who'd killed my mother, then my father, and then came back to finish my wife and child. I had to remind myself of my true purpose. I was on God's errand. There would always be naysayers. All that was needed was to keep my head. Thirteen was it, or fourteen? Fifteen. No, sixteen.

'Why sire, the sixteen found guilty on Friday and however many we find today.'

'Seventeen, man, seventeen! Are you forgetting Ann Chandler, this girl's own mother? Have you cleansed her memory so swiftly from your mind?'

I swallowed, my mind flailing. 'Sire, upon my word, it has been a busy time for me, with not much time for sleeping or eating, and it is hard to remember numbers at will.'

The magistrate narrowed his eyes. 'Seventeen so far and twice as many to come, no doubt.' He turned to the aldermen. 'Gentlemen, are we not encouraging this man to find more witches by paying him as we pay the town rat catcher – per head?'

My blood boiled at being compared to a common rat catcher. I considered objecting and pointing out that this was God's errand, clearing the town of a more demonic infestation. I opened my mouth, but the magistrate spoke over me.

'After all, a rat is always a rat, of that there is no question. A man has only to use his eyes and common sense to determine a rat. But to prove a woman is a witch requires more than eyes and common sense. It also requires that infernal blade.'

The magistrate nodded to a sergeant, who plucked the blade from my hand. My hands were so slippery, the pricker just slid from me. My guts plunged and sweat broke on my brow. I must not mop it, lest it draw attention.

'Sire, that blade has been doing God's work and is contaminated. Let me give you a clean bodkin to spare your gloves.'

'Stop your wheedling, Sharpe. This one will suffice. Since witches do not bleed, I dare say my gloves will survive the ordeal of innocent blood.'

The magistrate examined the instrument, eyeing its length while I looked on, trying hard not to appear agitated. The whole room was silent, waiting for the magistrate to speak again. Their eyes were on me, sizing me up. I was used to looks of reverence, but these people had jeering eyes.

The magistrate leapt to his feet. 'Sergeants, seize him. And open his jerkin.'

At this instruction, my heart almost seized. 'But sire, I come only to do God's work. This isn't right. It goes against God—'

One of the sergeants began unfastening my clothing.

The magistrate pointed to my jerkin. 'Tear it, sergeant, we don't have all day!'

Obediently, the sergeant ripped my jerkin to the navel, and I mourned its loss. Such a shameful waste was against God. I'd need to work harder to make up for the loss. Perhaps increase my price. The news of my breaking the Newcastle coven would perhaps precede me and increase my worth.

'John Sharpe, confirm your name, birthplace and occupation.'

I spoke, dry-lipped. 'John Sharpe, from Scotland, come lately to Newcastle to find witches at the behest of this council.'

'Good. Now, you say that confirmation of witching relies upon this sharpened bodkin?'

'Yes, sire.' I wished the magistrate would stop handling the device, and I fought the urge to snatch it back and run from the room. No one could understand what I faced when doing God's work. God's will wasn't always enough against the strength of the devil and his brood of bitches. Sometimes, God needed help – a willing channel to perform His will.

The magistrate stepped down from his bench to the floor, where he faced me. 'John Sharpe of Scotland, I put it to you that are you a witch.'

'I am no witch, sire!'

The magistrate's eyes bulged. 'Sergeants, seize him!'

The stinking sergeants gripped me and their breath was as rotting meat. The magistrate stood so close I could count the red veins in his eyes. A sure symptom of depravity. Perhaps another indication that the magistrate wasn't fit for office.

'Since you're not a witch, John Sharpe, when I plunge this bodkin into your liver, your blood will issue forth?'

I blinked twice and then nodded. Surely to God, this man couldn't be allowed to get away with this. Feverishly, I tried to recall what state the bodkin was in when the sergeant snatched it from me. Dear God, I was to be slain, without fair trial, in front of this mob. And my blood would be contaminated with the taint of the devil's child. After all my hard work, I'd be stained and unfit for my reward. I braced myself for the pain that I knew was coming.

The magistrate plunged the pricker under my ribs. My flesh remained clear and whole, but this was no cause for celebration.

The crowd began hissing and stamping. Cries of 'Witch! Witch!' issued from all corners of the room. The magistrate returned to his seat at the bench.

'This room will be silent!' The volume of the magistrate's voice quietened the room immediately. 'Now, I'll explain my queer demonstration. This man is no witch.'

My heart sank.

'This man before you, John Sharpe, is something worse. He is a trickster and no better than a common murderer.'

One of the aldermen cleared his throat. 'Sire, this is quite an accusation to address at a man employed by the council. Pray, might you explain yourself?'

The magistrate turned to the alderman. 'It is a tricky implement. Watch.' He held the bodkin upright and pressed upon the point with one finger. 'Observe, gentlemen, that the bodkin cleverly recedes into its own handle. It gives the appearance of plunging as deep as the bone's marrow. But it's only a sly illusion.'

Doubt crossed the alderman's face. 'But, sire, some people have bled. I've seen it with my own eyes.'

The magistrate smiled grimly. 'There's a sneck. When it's clicked into place, it prevents the blade retracting and so the victim bleeds.' The magistrate slipped the catch and plunged my bodkin into the wooden bench. 'And when the same sneck is clicked back, there's nothing to prevent the blade sliding back.' He removed the pricker from the bench, freed its catch and pushed the bodkin blade backward and forward against his gloved hand.

The crowd's eyes flicked back and forth. First staring at the bodkin and then at myself. It seemed that some members of the mob weren't able to grasp the concept of God's helper and whispered explanations passed along the rows.

'Sharpe, with his trickster bodkin, has been deciding the innocence or guilt of those accused of being witches. Clerk, how many has he sent to the gallows or the stake? We know of seventeen in this town and its surrounds, but what of elsewhere?'

The clerk scrambled through his scrolls, running his finger along tiny columns and making notes.

'Sire, in Scotland, one-hundred-and-twenty-eight people, some eight of them men and twenty-three of them juveniles. Some hanged, but many burnt.'

At this, I drew myself upright. 'Aye, sire, one-hundred-and-twenty-eight witches who can no longer cast their evil upon innocent and God-fearing folk.'

Jeers rose from the ungrateful wretches in the crowd.

'Sire, do you not know what you've been spared from? The demonic ways of these conniving bitches that will bring you to your knees? Is this my thanks?'

233

The sergeants shoved me and looked set to use their clubs, so I fell silent. The magistrate handed the pricker to the clerk. He eyed the aldermen, white-faced to a man, and then stood up.

'Gentlefolk, John Sharpe has murdered seventeen of our citizens. And we've not only paid him, but also encouraged him with the lure of more silver.' He paused and looked to me. 'Good God, man – seventeen were sent to their doom only two days past. Oh, what have you wrought here? What have you wrought? A dreadful misdeed has been committed by John Sharpe. It would seem that he's sent innocent people to their deaths, depriving them not only of their lives, but also of their afterlives – their being executed without benefit of clergy. We can't bring those unfortunates back, but we can save these women here today from that same fate. Sergeants, free the prisoners and take him down.'

The sergeants looked at the magistrate, confusion on their stupid faces.

The magistrate's eyes blazed at his sergeants. 'Sharpe, take Sharpe down.'

I opened my mouth to speak, but the magistrate raised his hand. 'Your time to speak will come when it's your turn to be tried, for tried you will be, Sharpe. You've grievously taken in the men of this town. After all, we are only men. You will be tried, and if found guilty, executed. There's nothing more to say today. I declare this assembly closed.'

The sergeants took an arm apiece, not caring that they jarred my bones, and they hauled me roughly down some dark steps. The smell of the river rose sharply in my nostrils as they pressed me ever downwards. Bile flooded my system, making a bitter taste in my mouth. Was I to be thrown in a common riverside dungeon, where the water might seep into my bones? There must be a way out. There must.

'Sergeants. Silver. I have silver and plenty of it. I can pay you to let me go. It would go well in the eyes of God. You'd be serving Him if you let me go. Let me go to continue my great works. Think on it, sires, think on it hard. Let me go back into the world as God's servant, there to do His holy works.'

I sighed. This work was without end. It would never be done.

30

Jane

A Message

We returned from St Andrew's in Newcastle. Mam and the others who were executed with her had been given a Christian burial in the churchyard there. It was the least the magistrates could do, after killing innocent people on no more than the say-so of an evil trickster – one who had now escaped justice. And it would pain me all my days that they'd been sent to their deaths without so much as a prayer to bless their departing souls. That they had now been taken into the church gave me a very small measure of comfort. They were laid to rest in an unmarked grave, so any forgiveness was still grudging. But at least I knew where my mother lay. Perhaps it was right that when I visited her, I would also visit the people killed alongside her.

These thoughts thrashed around my mind so much that they communicated themselves to Rose and she wriggled in my arms. The Reverend held out his arms for her and I busied myself over the fire, setting water to boil, while he amused her with his smallest hour-glass.

Finally, I could put it off no more and went to my mother's pantry. I drew in a large breath as I crossed the threshold, and all the familiar smells and tastes rushed inside me. Everything was in its place. The drying rack hung from the ceiling, stocked with fennel, rosemary, comfrey, lemon balm, mugwort and lavender. There was Mam's satchel, packed with implements and her favourite remedies. I opened it carefully. Inside were tiny vials and crocks. I removed the top from each crock and sniffed the contents. I knew each by sight, smell and taste. The dried hawthorn berries, the powdered mugwort, the fennel seeds. Next, I examined the vials. Again, I knew them all. Tincture of camomile, decoction of shepherd's purse, infusion of motherwort, and milk of poppy. Tucked in a dark corner of the satchel was a vial I did not know. I removed it and held it up to the light.

The vial was made of dark glass, so it told me nothing, other than that it was only half full. But I recognised it as being the same dark glass my mother had tucked in her shawl at the market all those years ago. It was the same dark glass I'd seen Meg pass to my mother by the fire all those times when they thought I wasn't watching. It was the same dark glass I'd seen passed to my mother by the apothecary's wife during our fateful last visit. This dark vial, in its many guises, had passed into my mother's hands on countless occasions all though my life. Carefully, I opened it. Immediately, my senses were seized by mint. I frowned, thinking of my first Gyb, dead and rotting in the mint garden with all her kits inside her. It must be pennyroyal. My eyes watered at the smell beneath it – bitter rue. And beneath that, sage and something camphoraceous like rosemary, perhaps tansy. The longer I inhaled, the more scents assailed my senses and turned me queasy.

For the contents of this vial, and what they could do, my mother had died. The executioner had put her to death, the magistrate had found her guilty, the fraudulent pricker had made her appear guilty. But I was certain now that the sly-tongued Goodwife Keen – the very same woman who'd sold my mother the makings of this toxic concoction – had sat in judgement of her. I weighed the vial in my hand and thought of my mother's work, and how much of it she'd kept from me. I thought of May Green and the Greens' baby. And I thought of Peggy Greaves and her baby. I closed the vial and stowed it back in the satchel.

Standing in my mother's pantry, the dreadful realisation finally struck me. I would never see her face, or hear her voice again in this world. She had given up her life for me, without a second's thought. How could I have let her do it? This question would haunt me all my days. I sat on the floor and hugged her satchel to me, letting my tears flow. My only mother gone from the world, and to save me, her wretched daughter.

Only a sharp cry from Rose stopped me, and I smiled through my tears. I knew then why my mother had taken my place. She had done it to spare me. But also to spare Rose. And I knew I would do exactly the same for my own daughter. The realisation brought no comfort with it.

I placed her satchel on the shelf, where it would be ready when needed. Then I returned to Rose and the Reverend, carrying a sheaf of seventeen long stems bearing heart-shaped leaves with the tiniest of white flowers. I placed them on the table and scooped up Rose. Looking at my daughter, feeling her warmth against me and seeing her trusting green eyes made me see that my mother had sacrificed herself for me, and I must not wash my life away in tears. I would carry on her work.

The Reverend looked at my eyes, but he said nothing. His own eyes were often red enough of late. And though I'd never been able to ask the question about my mother and him, his constantly rheumy eyes, his lack of appetite and his pallor told me what I needed to know. He had loved her, and she had loved him. I supposed the church would never sanction his marriage to my mother and so she'd had to remain his hearth woman. How could he ever forgive me for being alive when she was not?

When Rose was soothed, I laid her down on the settle next to the Reverend and put a cushion nearby to stop her rolling off. Then I set about making a tisane. I poured hot water into two bowls, picked up the long stems from the table, stripped their leaves and flowers into the hot water and stirred the contents with a bare stem.

'Here, Father, lemon balm. It'll help strengthen our spirits. It was Mam's favourite.'

He nodded. 'I know, Jane. I know. We'll drink it, and we'll remember her, and then we'll go to the church and pray for her soul.'

Even the smell of the scented brew turned my stomach, so I made to pour it away, but a movement outside caught my eye. My hand went to my mouth, but failed to stifle my gasp.

'Jane, what ails you?'

'I think it's a messenger outside, Reverend.' I didn't need to remind him that the last time a messenger came here, he'd delivered coins to pay for Tom's life.

He put down his bowl and stood up. 'You stay here, and I'll go.'

While he walked down the path, I peered at Rose and glanced at my wedding ring. Soon, we'd have to go home. Since I'd returned from the trial, Andrew didn't like me to be away from his mother's house, or his ever-watchful eye. He said it was for my own protection, but I sometimes wondered.

The door opened, and the Reverend stood there, not moving. He held up a purse. It looked very much like the purse that the golden angels had arrived in. I closed my eyes. Surely the navy couldn't be so cruel as to send more blood money.

I waved it away. 'Please take it to Bill. He has more need of it.'

But the Reverend shook his head and held out the purse. 'You must take it. There's a message this time. I've read it. Dear God, Jane. Dear God.'

There was a quaver in his voice, and my stomach turned at the thought of what the note might contain. With trembling fingers, I took it.

My lovely Jane,

My heart is broken that you've not replied to my last note. But you might not have received it, and so you wouldn't know where to write. Or, you might have replied and your letter's gone missing at sea. So many do. If you didn't receive my last note and the advance on my ship's pay, then you may suppose me still aboard *The Durham*, and lost with all the other poor souls when she went down. But before she went down, I was moved to another ship as a volunteer, along with the physician who has written this note for me.

Anyway, sweet Jane, our child must be born by now, and I have sent you some more money to keep you and little Rose. Soon, I'll be home to see you both. And we'll be wed at last. I've missed you so much, and can't wait to be with you once again.

With all my love always, your Tom.

Afterword

This novel was inspired by the Newcastle witch trials in 1650 when either fifteen or sixteen people were executed on the same day. There is a discrepancy in the number executed. The parish burial records for St Andrew's Church in Newcastle list fifteen women and one man buried as witches in the graveyard. However, according to John Wheeler's deposition in Ralph Gardiner's book, *England's Grievance Discovered in Relation to the Coal-Trade* (1655), fourteen women and one man were executed for witchcraft; this list does not include the name of Jane Martin. I have erred on the side of caution and included her name in the list of those executed.

This particular witch trial took place after a Scottish witch-finder rounded up people from the streets of Newcastle. According to John Wheeler, the witch-finder was revealed as a fraud and one girl was set free. However, the others were still executed and the witch-finder escaped. There are no details about the freed girl or the witch-finder. So *Widdershins* is my imagined story of the girl who escaped the hangman's noose. This book and its characters are a work of fiction. However, the witch trials were real, and I hope the people killed will forgive my addition of Annie Chandler to their number. Below are the names of those executed.

Elizabeth Anderson
Elizabeth Brown
Margaret Brown
Matthew Bulmer
Jane Copeland
Katherine Coulter
Elizabeth Dobson
Elianor Henderson
Alice Hume
Jane Hunter
Margaret Maddison
Jane Martin
Margaret Muffet
Mary Pots
Elianor Rogerson
Ann Watson

About the author

Helen Steadman lives in the foothills of the North Pennines with her family and her dogs. She is particularly interested in writing historical novels about the north east of England. Helen wrote this novel for her master's degree in creative writing at Manchester Metropolitan University. She is currently working on a new historical novel for her PhD in English at the University of Aberdeen. For more information about her writing, please visit helensteadman.com.